# Dividing Worlds

# Dividing Worlds

# Jan Ögren

www.JanOgren.net

Printed and bound in the United States of America.
Text set in Times New Roman
*Designed and edited by Kemari Howell*
*Cover design by Lisa A. Wiggins*

ISBN: 13:978-1456541415
ISBN-10: 1456541412
LCCN: 2011906689

# Dedication

*To all those who believe
in the reality
of a global consciousness shift.*

# Contents

# Contents

# Prologue

*Skyweb peered down at the gathering humans as she floated six feet above a graceful grove of cedar trees. For the last twenty centuries, she had been observing and waiting, patience drifting through her essence like a raincloud over a desert. Sighing deeply, she noticed that a murky haze obscured each new arrival, as though a child had taken every color of paint, spun them all together, then smeared the mixture over each person. A metallic, blue cocoon rolling on four wheels along a fused black-rock path snatched her attention away from the humans. The cocoon came to rest next to a lone fir tree and a human crawled out of it, her body clearly visible, ringed in soft rainbows, with only a few foggy patches around her head and back. Relief fluttered through Skyweb's essence. Her form thickened and she started drifting down toward the earth, calling to the other guardians, telling them she had found one who might listen.*

# Chapter 1

## *Future Pharmaceutical*

Miranda gazed at the ancient fir tree soaring above her sky-blue electric car. A cool, rejuvenating scent wafted around her as her eyes traveled up the trunk and out the branches to the emerald web of needles.

Behind her, a sign flapped as a gust of wind passed by. She turned and read the bold black letters. *2020: The Decade for Mastering Behavior through Neurochemicals*. Above that, was the name *Future Pharmaceutical* and a red arrow pointing toward a massive gray structure that towered over a concrete entrance. She scanned the other buildings in the complex; each had a matching set of guards standing at attention in their camouflage uniforms.

Miranda hesitated another minute, looking longingly at the hints of gold in the sky that promised a majestic sunset. Sighing, she turned away from the tree and sky and followed the other people marching toward the building.

Briefcases bumped against her legs as she slipped inside the conference center, squeezing into the line of people waiting to check in. The tall, white entry hall trembled with the vibrations of one-sided conversations while people wearing somber business suits and dresses shouted into their cell phones.

The line shifted uneasily as people were distracted from their conversations by the need to pick up informational packets and badges.

By the time Miranda arrived at the long tables, the name tags were in disarray. She searched for several minutes, then decided her badge must have flown off to a more hospitable realm.

Spying a young woman wearing a staff badge, Miranda tentatively approached her. "Excuse me. I'm sorry to bother you, but I can't find my name tag."

The woman gave her an exasperated glance. "Did you pre-register?"

"Yes, but it was just four days ago. The guards at the gate had my name."

"Of course they did or you wouldn't have gotten this far. Name?"

She started to give it when she felt the wisp of a voice above her. She stole a quick peek over her shoulder, but feeling the intensity of the crowd overflowing the massive foyer, she assumed it had been nothing more than their turmoil that had touched her.

Turning back to the woman, she said loudly, trying to be heard over the reverberating conversations, "My name's Miranda Williams."

"What company are you with?" The woman shouted back.

"None. I came on my own."

"Oh, I'm so sorry, I didn't recognize you." The woman looked more attentively at her, leaning closer. "Which company do you own? Is it food or pharmaceutical?"

"Neither. I'm not with a company. I understood individuals could enroll in this conference."

"Oh, yes, of course. You'll need to go over to that table at the far end." The woman waved in a vague direction, then turned away.

Miranda let herself be jostled through the crowd until she came out the other side. She noticed a small table where a young man was sitting, head bent, shifting through sheets of paper.

"Excuse me, I'm trying to check in—as an individual. I'm not with a company. Is this the right place?"

The man looked up and smiled. "Yes it is. What's your name, please?"

She gave her name again, biting her lip, and hoping for better results this time.

As he searched through several short lists, he began to shake his head. "That's odd. I can't seem to find you anywhere. When did you register?"

"Just four days ago."

"Let me check another list."

As she waited, Miranda again felt a presence above her, as though a cloud, trapped in the building, was searching for the sky. Tensing her brow and forming her thoughts clearly, she mentally sent a question into the realm beyond the physical world where her spirit guide lived. *:Adnarim, is that you? I came to the conference as you suggested. Will you tell me why I'm here now?:*

"Ah, here you are!" exclaimed the young man, brandishing a large manila envelope in triumph. "Someone had you backwards. You were under 'M' instead of 'W.'"

"Thank you." She grabbed the heavy packet, grateful for any sign confirming that she was supposed to be at the conference.

The man held onto it, looking closely at the information identifying her. "You work at a hospice?"

Miranda nodded and tried to pull away but he stood up, drawing closer to her.

"We don't usually get people who work for hospice coming to these conferences. Are you here professionally or for personal interest?"

She hesitated, unsure which would lead to the least questions. She looked around, hoping someone would walk up and distract him, but everyone else seemed to be at the sign-in tables for company affiliations.

Turning back, she shrugged and smiled. "It just sounded interesting."

"How did you hear about it?"

"The web."

He smiled at her, leaning closer. "We like to make sure everyone is satisfied with the conference. What specifically are you hoping to accomplish this weekend?"

*Getting away from you,* Miranda thought, keeping her smile firmly pasted on her face. She gave her envelope a sharp tug, dislodging it from the man's grasp.

"I'm sure I'll enjoy it," she told him as she backed away from the table, sidestepping a group of determined women who swept by.

She glanced back and noticed the man was making a note on a small pad. When he looked back up at her, her stomach twisted and she hurried to get farther away.

Searching for an empty space from which to survey the gathering, she slipped down a corridor leading away from the main hall. She came to rest opposite a sign that showed a woman running through a field of flowers. Below the picture was the slogan "Your happiness is our concern," followed by information about a new antidepressant drug.

As a herd of staff swarmed by, Miranda ducked her head, pretending to focus on the packet while listening for any response from Adnarim, her elusive spirit guide.

She felt energetic stirrings, which she again attributed to the intensity of the crowd. But from Adnarim, there was nothing but a void that felt like standing alone in a crowded railway station, not knowing which train to take.

She'd heard nothing from her since she'd been browsing the web five days ago, searching for ideas on how to ecologically control garden pests. Her screen had gone blank, then the website announcing this conference had appeared. There had been a shimmer in the corner of the room, which had manifested as a tall golden-skinned woman in a burgundy shawl. Adnarim had emphatically instructed her to sign up for the weekend, then disappeared back into a swirl of tiny lights when Miranda tried to question her.

Despite repeated attempts by Miranda, her guide had offered no explanation as to why she should spend her entire weekend away from home and Chris just to listen to lectures on neuroscience. She didn't even know if the reason for her being here had anything to do with the subject of the conference.

Standing against the wall, she wondered if this was going to become another annoying treasure hunt: another book and folder incident, or BFI, as Miranda had first named them. Most of the time, BFI ended up meaning a Big F-ing Irritation.

Fifteen years ago, when she first began conversing with guides, she tried to use their extrasensory awareness for practical purposes. One morning before leaving for hospice, where she worked as an administrator, she asked Adnarim if there was anything special she should remember to take with her. Her guide promptly told her to take a book on communication styles she'd borrowed from a board member. She dismissed the suggestion, informing Adnarim that the board meeting wasn't for two days and she hadn't finished reading it yet. Miranda repeated her request, asking if there was anything else she should remember, but Adnarim continued emphasizing the book, which she didn't take. As soon as she arrived at work, the nursing director asked for the folder containing applications for the new RN position, which Miranda had promised to bring that day. She was forced to drive home to retrieve the folder, annoyed at her guide for reminding her of the wrong item.

After some frustrating hunting, she finally found the folder, underneath the book Adnarim had insisted she take. That first time set the tone for future help from her guides: valuable but irritatingly vague.

Standing against the wall, Miranda stared at the poster of the woman in the field of flowers. *I wish my happiness were Adnarim's concern. What does she want me to find here? I don't have time for another BFI!*

Resisting the urge to throw the heavy envelope at the poster, she turned it over and started to open it.

*I guess I'd better start searching for clues on my own since she's not going to help.* Inside she discovered a name tag, a schedule of events, a list of companies participating in the conference, and a book-sized pamphlet entitled *2020: The Decade for Mastering Behavior through Neurochemicals.*

She scanned the hundreds of respectably attired women and men now moving about the main hall, wondering how each of them fit into the theme of the conference. Some were standing stiffly next to displays of hors d'oeuvres and bountiful beverage tables. A few were conversing with other people, but most of them were still shouting into their cell phones. *Looking at it this way isn't going to show anything. Maybe Cat Vision will help me find that presence I felt earlier.*

Growing up, she'd always been fascinated with how dogs and cats could sense when someone was approaching the house, or when a family member was getting close to home. She never noticed any obvious clues the animals were receiving until Merawl, her feline guide, taught her to use Cat Vision. Seeing with it was like stepping back from her eyes and raising a periscope from her heart. Her feelings came through as images integrated into the scene she was viewing, allowing her to perceive the strength and direction of energy connections and to be aware of things farther away than her vision could see.

Leaning back against the wall and trying to relax as much as possible, she looked around the room again, seeing it as a cat would see it. In addition to the physical objects and people, Cat Vision highlighted a mass of thin threads whipping about the large conference room.

She could see slightly denser energy lines extending beyond the physical walls, illuminating how most of the participants were focused on talking to people outside the room.

Underneath the conference chamber, the earth pulsated with connections thick and deep, like roots of a tree. Above the earth, the people's energy connections were like gray cotton candy: masses of thin strands but no substance. They were numerous enough that it made detecting any other energy sources above the ground difficult.

*The planet is more alive here than the people are. But that's no surprise.* She returned to the information she had been given, skimming the pages of participants. She didn't recognize the names, but the food and pharmaceutical companies they represented were familiar from everyday ads she encountered in magazines, television, and the Internet.

As she peered at the organizational biographies, still searching for clues as to why she was here, her stomach rumbled. Enticing aromas were drifting from the hors d'oeuvres tables, reminding her that she had worked through lunch in order to get off early for the conference.

Reluctantly, she pinned on the name tag that declared she was Miranda Williams from Whole Life Hospice in Whetherton, Washington. She was sure this information would mean nothing to anyone, except possibly to inform them that she lived close by.

As she headed toward the expansive main hall, she noticed the light from the evening sun was painting red and gold murals on the cream-colored walls as it drifted through the windows arranged high above the circular room.

As she approached the crowds, she pasted on a smile and nodded to people as they glanced at her, scanning her badge of identity before returning to their conversations. Slipping past them, she filled a plate with small puffed pastries, and sculptured carrots and cucumbers.

She stopped by the wine table and picked up a glass of sparkling water before finally emerging on the other side of the crowd. Looking around, she spied an unoccupied sofa near the back of the room and headed towards it.

Carefully perching on the corner of the couch, arms drawn in, head down, Miranda munched on her delectables as she monitored the advance of two older people. The woman was grimacing as she gripped the man's arm. His suit hung on him as though it had been thrown on as an afterthought. His face was drawn in tense lines, topped by a pelt of white unkempt hair. Both were teetering, he on bowed legs, she on a three-legged cane as she cautiously finished crossing the room, staring at the couch as though it was a life raft bobbing in rough seas.

The man smiled down at Miranda. "Is there anyone sitting here?"

She shook her head as she shifted over to the other side of the couch, self-consciously adjusting her skirt as she tried to disappear into the fabric of the furniture.

She'd dressed carefully: a beige silk blouse with a light brown jacket and skirt to compliment her olive skin and wavy black hair. A new pair of brown dress shoes added an extra inch to her slightly below average height. Her medium build usually allowed her a measure of invisibility, but tonight she was feeling extremely conspicuous.

The man assisted his delicate companion into the corner of the couch, then instead of sitting in the middle, he crossed in front of Miranda, claiming an armchair next to her. After taking a long look at Miranda, he held out his hand.

"I'm Peter, and this is my wife, Sonya. What brings you to this conference? Are you a presenter or participant?"

She accepted Peter's offered hand and tried to shake it firmly, yet carefully, her mind racing as it created and discarded numerous scenarios to explain why she was at the conference.

"I'm Miranda. I thought I'd come since it sounded so interesting. I'm just a participant, but I've always been curious about brain neurochemistry." She winced at how lame her response sounded, but it was better than admitting she didn't know why she was here.

She placed a smile over her nervousness and returned the question. "Why are you here?"

Peter nodded, accepting her response.

"I used to teach physics at Seaside University in Seattle. You know the old 'publish or perish' problem." He smiled and patted her hand. "I wrote enough papers that they finally realized they have to understand the physics of the brain in addition to the chemical make-up to determine behavioral changes. So now I'm in demand by all these companies." He swept his arm, indicating the people in the room. "So much for retirement. Sonya insisted I come. Future Pharmaceutical wants to give me an award for something."

Miranda glanced at Sonya who was rubbing her hip, ignoring Peter's remarks. *How important is he? What's he mean about the physics and chemical make-up of the brain?* As she turned back and saw Peter grinning at her, Miranda relaxed a tiny amount. *Maybe he can help me figure out why I'm here.*

Pulling out the list of sponsoring companies, she asked him, "I understand why the pharmaceuticals are here, but why are there so many food companies listed?"

"Ah, that's where the real money is. Think about how valuable a chemical that can stimulate hunger is for a company that manufactures snacks. Or how about a dessert company that could produce an additive that convinces the body that sugar doesn't create calories?"

Miranda swallowed and looked at her empty plate, feeling queasy as she wondered what chemicals were now circulating in her body. "Wouldn't that be illegal?"

Peter gave a disgusted laugh. "And who's supposed to monitor all that?"

"Now, Peter," Sonya waved a hand at him. "You promised to be pleasant tonight."

"I'm always pleasant," Peter replied, raising his voice. "I'm just being honest."

Miranda noticed that an impeccably dressed man, his ebony suit complimenting his dark complexion, had broken away from the main group and was quickly approaching her. She started to grip the edges of the couch, preparing to rise, when the man opened his arms indicating her two companions.

"Peter, Sonya, I'm so glad you could make it! When I heard about Sonya's latest surgery I wasn't sure I'd see you this weekend." He leaned over and gave Peter an enthusiastic embrace.

As the new arrival turned toward Sonya, Peter grabbed Miranda's arm, pulling her closer to the edge of the couch and giving more space for the large man to slip in between her and Sonya. Miranda wondered what illness was troubling Sonya, as she scrunched further into the end of the couch.

"Van, this is Miranda." Peter nodded to each of them.

Van smiled at her. "Pleased to meet you. Are you another protégé of Peter's? What field are you in?" She smiled, giving him a blank look, unsure how to respond.

"We just met," Peter announced. "Haven't even found out where she works yet." He reached across her and clapped a hand onto Van's knee.

"I lent him my expertise to obtain a grant for investigating the side effects of psychotropic medications on adolescents."

Miranda nodded at Peter, who was now reclining back in his armchair, smiling proudly. "That's nice you could do that. I always hear them listing possible reactions to medications in their advertisements." She turned to Van. "I'm glad to know you'll be studying them."

"Yes, I was pleased to receive the grant. Medications can be so helpful, lifesaving even. But sometimes the side effects are worse than the symptoms they're created to cure."

Leaning closer, Van examined her name tag. "Whole Life Hospice. What type of work do you do there?"

They all stared at her, waiting while she hesitated, proud of the work she did, yet worried it would lead to further questions about why she was at the conference.

:Greetings you, who speak with all beings:

Miranda swung around, praying she would discover a physical basis for the unfamiliar ethereal alto voice that had just dropped words into her head so candidly. The closest person was a young woman walking backwards through a swinging door leading to the kitchen, balancing a tray of abandoned glasses, but she didn't seem a likely candidate for the telepathic communication Miranda had just received.

Surveying the area behind her once more, she swallowed, pushing down the lava in her gut, hoping ardently that it had only been her imagination and that she was not going to have to spend another evening conversing with disembodied voices. Scrunching her eyebrows together and forming her words as clearly as she could, she sent a message to the mysterious voice that had spoken to her. :What did you say?:

When she turned back, the three people were all looking at her with perplexed expressions on their faces.

"Are you okay, dear?" Sonya asked.

"Oh, I'm fine. I just thought I heard something."

Peter waved at the crowd. "It's so noisy in here you probably heard everything. You were going to tell us what you did at hospice."

"Oh, um . . . I'm the administrator: a glorified go-fer for whatever people need. We serve the city of Whetherton. It's about thirty miles east of Seattle so it's very close. I live just twenty minutes away from here."

Van smiled and nodded. "That makes it very convenient for you. Do you attend events here often?"

More words slowly drifted through the air, nudging her awareness. :*Greetings you, who speak with all beings. We have been waiting for one to hear us:*

"Ah . . . actually it's my first time." Staring at Sonya, Peter, and Van, Miranda scrutinized their faces, searching for some sign that they too had heard the mysterious message. They showed no indication of hearing the airy voice, so she gave them a half-smile and added, "I didn't even realize Future Pharmaceutical's plant was here, until I heard about the conference." Then she tensed her forehead and sent another telepathic question. :*Who are you?:*

Sonya peered around Van, "We live just outside Whetherton, north of Community Expressway. Where do you live?"

:*I, who am Skyweb. We, who are guardians of this place. We, who have been waiting many Earth cycles for one to hear us:*

Miranda's gaze was drawn to the window behind the couch, above the peoples' heads, revealing a patchwork rock and flower slope, ascending from the patio of the conference center to a circle of cedars clustering at the top. She fervently wished she could ignore her companions long enough to use Cat Vision, so she could discover who or what the voice was.

Staring intently out the window, she resigned herself to sending her thoughts into an unfamiliar realm and to beings, she didn't know. :*Skyweb, why do you wish to speak to me?:*

"Miranda dear, I didn't hear where you live." Sonya was bending farther over, cupping a hand around her ear.

"What? Oh, um, I live in the southeast section."

*:You hear us. You, who are the first to listen:*

"Excuse me, do you remember me?"

Miranda spun around, hoping the spirit voice had solidified and was going to manifest for all to see and hear. But instead, she saw a purely physical woman in a blue sarong standing next to Peter, her dark straight hair framing a friendly grin and sparkling cinnamon-colored eyes.

The woman was speaking to Sonya. "We met at the psychobiology conference last year, when our husbands were both presenting."

"Kamini!" Sonya flung her arms wide. "Of course I remember you."

The new arrival gracefully squeezed past Miranda and Van. She knelt in front of Sonya, hugging her carefully then sitting back on her heels. "I'm so glad you are here. I was afraid you wouldn't be well enough to come. Are you still writing? Are you working on another book? I loved your last one."

Miranda peered at the older woman's name tag. "You're Sonya Bloom! The author of *Speaking with Spirits*!"

"Yes, dear, but that was a long time ago. I'm surprised anyone remembers that book."

Miranda tried to act casual, but the author equivalent to Santa Claus had just materialized in front of her.

"Your book was an immeasurable gift to me. The way you wrote about talking to other beings as though it was so natural made me feel less alone in the world. When I was a kid, I was able to converse with my cat. Then when I grew up, spirits started showing up and I was hearing all these voices, and I was afraid someday the authorities would come and take me away to a mental hospital because I was crazy. I . . . I . . ." She stopped herself, realizing she had just admitted to hearing voices in front a group of unknown people, one of whom was an expert in non-physical communication. Her heart raced, as she feared she may have inadvertently offended her idol by her unrehearsed ramblings, and she had no idea what the others would think of her now.

Before she could concentrate more on their possible reactions to her blathering, the unknown voice continued, swirling the words around her, like leaves blown by a sentient wind. *:We, who have waited thousands of Earth cycles. Waiting for a human who will converse. Who will connect. Who will complete the circle with us:*

Sonya looked questioningly at her. When Miranda didn't continue she offered, "I'm glad my book helped you become comfortable talking with spirits."

Miranda's attention was stretched between the older woman sitting on the couch and the cedar grove at the top of the hill. Luckily, Kamini engaged Sonya in an intense conversation, giving Miranda the opportunity to use Cat Vision. Leaning back into the couch, she took a couple of breaths and peered out the window. The grove danced with waves of swirling green energy, but she couldn't distinguish any actual forms who might be talking to her.

When she refocused on her companions, Kamini was talking to Peter. "I read your latest article in the *Psychic Physics Press*. It sounded so dismal. Do you really think we have so little chance of surviving this environmental crisis?"

A wind of words blew around Miranda *:The world is opening. Opportunities are approaching. Potentials long asleep soon begin to grow. A healing possible:*

Peter nodded solemnly. "From a purely biochemical perspective, we've passed the point of no return. The scientific evidence is overwhelming, even if the acknowledgement of it by the commercial community is underwhelming. I predict that in less than fifty years humans will become an endangered species."

"Why do you think that?" Miranda asked, her stomach clenching as Peter voiced her own fears about the survival capacity of humans on Earth. Responding to the hope offered by the non-human voice, she tensed her brow, adding a psychic question *:What do you mean 'a healing possible?':*

*:Why we are here. Why you are here. A healing possible:* The words came like fresh air blown into a room too long isolated from nature.

"Let's not talk about the destruction of the world tonight. My husband can be so depressing sometimes," Sonya said, gesturing toward Peter. "Kamini, how is your project with Women's Financial Future coming along in India?"

"Can I have your attention please?" A luminous tenor voice echoed through the room.

Peter nudged Miranda's arm, pointing out a man dressed in a tan suit, standing on the stairs leading to the dining room. "That's Dr. Steven Westin, he's the president of Future Pharmaceutical. They wanted me to work for them, but I don't need their blood money so I—"

"Shh," Sonya waved a hand at Peter's mouth. "Be nice. Steven was very polite. And Bruce didn't think the project was that bad."

"Well, I'm not Bruce and—"

"Shh," Sonya insisted again, pointing toward the president. "He's trying to get our attention."

Dr. Westin repeated his plea for quiet while tapping on a wine glass, which sent a melodic ring throughout the room, hushing the discussions.

"They were interested in my biophysical findings on neurotransmitters," Peter told Miranda in a loud whisper. "Future Pharmaceutical is owned by Ben Zero Financial. They wanted me to help them create a new happy pill so no one will worry about the environmental crimes BZF is committing."

Sonya leaned over Van and thumped Peter on the knee with her purse. He harrumphed, folded his arms against his chest, and sat silently as Dr. Westin welcomed everyone to the weekend.

Miranda sighed and sank into the couch. She hadn't been sure how to respond to Peter. She agreed that BZF's disregard for environmental safety was appalling, but she was more concerned with Sonya and what impression she was making on her favorite author. Glancing to her right, she noticed that Sonya seemed to be completely focused on what Dr. Westin was saying. She relaxed slightly, relieved that all the attention was now on one person, rather than so many conversations ricocheting around her.

It appeared that the president was going to speak for a while so she let her attention focus inward, allowing the room around her to blur while her concentration spiraled down, helping her become aware of the earth underneath the building. Pulling energy from the ground below her, she sent out as strong a telepathic plea as she could to her guide. :*Adnarim, why am I here? Is it because Sonya Bloom is here? What about those guardians? Who are they? Am I supposed to connect with them?*:

No response.

Miranda breathed slowly, counting five breaths, then tried again. :*Adnarim! Why did you want me to come here? What should I do?*:

Silence.

Miranda directed the next question to herself. *Why is it I can always hear voices I don't want to hear, but I can never hear the voices I do want to hear?*

She shook her head in resignation and annoyance, then jerked it still, fearing the president might have said something to which she should've been nodding, not shaking her head to, and that Sonya Bloom would think her impolite.

Holding her breath, she sent a final message out to the spirit world. :*Adnarim! Come on, you're the one who wanted me at this meeting, where I have to talk with all these people who have a 'real' reason to be here. The least you can do is tell me what to do—you're my guide after all!*:

Receiving no better response than her previous attempts had produced, and after verifying that the president was still immersed in talking, Miranda re-centered within herself. Pulling more energy from the earth, she sent her spirit away from the gathering of people, toward the hill outside the window, which had drawn her attention when the guardians were talking to her. Now in spirit form, Miranda could feel that the grove of cedars was emitting a distinctive pull, as though a psychic road sign had been placed at the bottom informing her to "climb here."

Drifting further away from the conference room, she found herself at the top of the hill standing in a circle, facing north with three beings who appeared in human form.

The spirit woman directly across from Miranda had her arms crossed over her chest, each hand holding a rattle, with strands of white feathers and tan-colored shells dangling from the handles. A brilliant white cloth was wrapped around her black straight hair, pulling it back from her face, then flowing over her shoulders. She wore a brown buckskin dress, tied with a cream-colored beaded belt. At her feet was a woven grass basket holding smooth white stones.

In the center of the circle was a rough round stone, reminding Miranda of the story of a boulder, that when lifted, exposed a staircase leading down into the earth. She turned her attention away from the stone and back to the woman waiting patiently across the circle from her.

:*Welcome:* An earthy, calm voice greeted her. :*We, who are honored. You, who have come. Who join us:*

Miranda gave her a slight bow. :*I am honored to talk with you. Who are you?:*

:*We, who are guardians. We, who are of this land. We, who have been here long before the pale humans. You, who may call me Earthweb. You, who may call me Northern Grandmother:* The words felt like stepping stones, solid and slowly leading along a path.

:*These, who are my sisters. She, who is Fireweb, who is Eastern Grandmother. She, who is Waterweb, who is Western Grandmother:* Earthweb's penetrating black eyes stared steadily at Miranda, while her head tilted left then right, indicating the two spirit beings not fully coalesced on either side of her. She raised her chin toward Miranda and added, :*She, who is Skyweb. She, who first talked. Who is Southern Grandmother:*

Miranda was puzzled, since she herself occupied the southern section of the circle. Where was the one with the ethereal alto voice, who had first spoken to her?

Earthweb continued speaking, her words heavy and slow. :*We, who need. We, who have waited many Earth turnings. You, who will—:*

"Would you like to join us for dinner?" Miranda stifled her urge to yelp as she turned and stared at Sonya, who had placed her hand on Miranda's arm.

"Van reserved one of the central tables, but it seats eight so there'll be plenty of room if you haven't already made plans to visit with someone else."

Miranda took a deep breath, giving herself a moment to remember she was attending a conference and that she had just met Sonya Bloom, the author of *Speaking with Spirits*, who was inviting her to join them for dinner. Now that she was back in her body, she remembered she was hungry so she nodded at Sonya. "Thank you. That would be lovely."

As she rose from the couch, she glanced up the hill, momentarily pulled back to the circle of cedar trees. She swayed slightly, trying to balance the need to be both in the physical world, preparing to eat dinner, and in the spirit world, finishing her conversation with the grandmothers. *:Sorry, you were saying something about why you wanted to communicate with me:*

Earthweb's words appeared in her mind at an annoyingly slow pace. *:We, who need a human. You, who will talk. We, who will talk. Who will—:*

"So, dear, you're an administrator for a hospice organization?"

Miranda's attention was drawn back to Sonya who was peering up at her. "Ah, yeah . . . I am." She chewed on her lower lip, wanting to ask Sonya about the guardians but unsure how to do it. "And you can . . . I mean . . . you're an expert in talking with spirits."

"Oh, I wouldn't call myself an expert. Right now I'm just an old woman who can't even get off this couch on her own." She raised her left hand toward Miranda, as her right hand gripped her cane.

Miranda noticed that Peter, Van, and Kamini were now all standing with their backs to the couch, intently conversing together, so she bent down and offered Sonya her arm.

As the older woman rose shakily from the couch, she tried again to start a conversation about guides. "How are you able to—"

"Sonya, are you okay?" Peter hobbled over looking concerned. "Do you want me to get you a plate? Van can help you to the table." He glanced at Miranda. "Or do you want her to help you?"

Sonya waved him off. "I'm fine. Miranda is going to join us for dinner. So if she doesn't mind going with me through the line, I'd like to pick out my own food. And I'm sure together we can manage to balance two plates."

As they approached the buffet line, the people at the front moved aside and motioned for Sonya to go ahead of them. Miranda found herself at a place of honor as Dr. Westin handed them two plates and motioned them forward. Dr. Westin's eyes flickered expertly over her name tag as he said, "Ms. Williams, I'm so glad you could come to this conference. I'd be interested in hearing how our exploration of neuroscience relates to your work at hospice."

Miranda was distracted by Skyweb's voice floating around her. *:We, who are waiting. We, who are speaking to you, who hear us:*

Miranda swore inwardly. *Damn, why is everyone talking to me at once? And where is Adnarim? She got me into this.*

Sonya rescued her by tapping on her hand. "Can you give me some of the marinated chicken please? And I'd love a helping of the mashed sweet potatoes."

"Here, let me assist you." The president balanced his wine glass between two fingers and started serving both women from the diverse array of delicacies on the table. Ignoring Miranda's protestations that she could return and help herself, he continued to assist both of them. Carrying their plates, he escorted them to a center table. As he slipped away, he told her, "I'll make sure we have time to talk over the weekend. I do want to hear about your interest in psychotropic medications and what brought you to this conference."

Sonya sat down at the table. "I'm glad you'll get a chance to visit with Steven later, he's very nice. I hope you'll forgive me but I wanted to get to a table before my hip gave out."

"I'm glad you said something. I wouldn't have wanted you to be in pain while I talked with Dr. Westin." *And I'm glad I didn't have to explain anything to him. Now if I can just avoid him for the rest of the conference. Or until I figure out why I'm here—so I can leave. If only the grandmothers would talk faster and clearer.*

Sonya interrupted her worries by tapping her plate. "Go ahead and start eating, dear. Don't wait for Peter. I'm sure he'll get involved speaking with other people before he makes it here to join us."

"That's fine, I'd love to hear more about your speaking with guides. How did you learn to do it?"

"Oh, that's a long story, dear. Why don't you tell me about your work at hospice? How do people know when to call? Do they do it or do their doctors make the referral?"

Miranda hesitated, she wanted to be polite and answer Sonya's questions, but she needed guidance about the grandmothers, and Adnarim still hadn't shown up.

"Aha, I found you!" Peter bent down and kissed Sonya on the cheek before placing his plate next to hers.

"Sorry to keep you waiting. They had to talk to me about the presentation tomorrow." He nodded at Miranda. "Thank you for helping my lovely wife."

"It was my pleasure. I've been an admirer of hers for years."

"Is someone sitting here?" Kamini, the woman in the blue sarong, came up to Miranda's right.

"No, no, sit down." Sonya waved to the empty place. "Join us. I want to hear all about your trip. Are you staying in the United States long?"

Three more people sat down across the table next to Van, introducing themselves and the scientific research programs they were coordinating for Future Pharmaceutical. Miranda, engulfed by the animated conversations flying around the table, strained to hear any words from the grandmothers, but all she was able to detect were vague murmurings from the hill.

In spite of being able to sit next to Sonya Bloom, she was relieved when the dinner was finally over.

# Chapter 2

## *Chris and Merawl*

Finally, the first evening of the conference ended and Miranda was able to crawl into her familiar blue car and let the radio serenade her with smooth jazz. The dinner had extended beyond the promised end time, then there had been speeches and a video presentation on the latest biochemical behavioral studies.

It was close to ten thirty by the time she drove up her driveway, pressing the garage door opener and pulling her car into the garage. The door to their home swung open, and Chris stood silhouetted by the soft light from their living room. Miranda's shoulders lowered two inches as she gazed at her lover, envisioning a gazelle on a vast African plain, poised but powerful. She parked, climbed out of her car, and melted into Chris's arms. *I should go to conferences more often if this is what I get.*

Gently lifting her head up and back, Chris gave her a kiss, then asked, "I thought you said you'd be home by ten? I've been listening for the garage to open."

"It went on forever. I was at a table right in the middle so I couldn't sneak away."

"So how was the event? Did you meet anyone interesting?"

"Interesting is an understatement. I sat next to Sonya Bloom at dinner!"

"The author of *Speaking with Spirits*? You must have been in heaven. Did BB and Merawl enjoy talking with her?"

Miranda hesitated on her way up the stairs into the house. "No, that's odd. They didn't even show up. I tried to contact Adnarim, but you know how elusive she can be. I never even thought of BB or Merawl. They should have been ecstatic to talk with Sonya, but they didn't say a word all evening."

She felt a well-known presence behind her, and looking over her right shoulder, she saw a large brown bear lounging on top of her car. She took a breath, scrunched up her forehead, and asked telepathically, :*What's up with that? Where were you, BB?*:

"Hey, I know what that face means. I want another hug before you start talking with them and excluding me." Chris pulled her up the last three steps and gave her a bear hug, which led to a lengthy kiss.

:*Humph:* the word pushed at Miranda's back, as BB psychically nudged her. :*Ask me a question and then ignore me:*

Miranda broke out of Chris's embrace and twirled around in time to watch BB disappearing. She squinted at the empty air, thinking quickly. :*Don't go. I'm sorry. I still want to know why you weren't there to talk to Sonya:*

Chris drew her into the hallway and closed the door behind her. "If you are going to talk to my invisible competition, at least do it out loud so I can hear half the conversation."

"If you'd open up more you could hear and see them too." Chris's mouth tightened into a straight line as they walked into the living room.

Turning around, Chris sighed, looking pleadingly at Miranda. "We've been through that before. You're the mystical, magical one. I'm the mundane cook, gourmet gardener, and love slave."

The last two words were accompanied by a caress down Miranda's side that made her shiver and decide she was lucky she could drive home each evening, when only an hour earlier she had been so tired she'd been jealous of the other attendees who were spending the night at the conference center.

She plopped down on the couch and opened her arms to Chris, but instead of her lover, a gray, tiger-striped cat appeared on her lap. "Merawl!"

*:You wanted to talk to me?:*

Miranda glanced up at Chris and continued the conversation out loud. "I was wondering why you weren't there tonight. But you can tell me tomorrow morning on the drive back to the conference."

Chris forced a smile. "Go ahead, and talk with him now. I was just finishing up something in the kitchen." Chris headed off, then swung around, brandishing a finger toward Miranda's lap. "Just remind him the bedroom is off limits and you are all mine later."

Miranda looked pleadingly between the two, but her partner was already disappearing into the kitchen as Merawl rose, stretched, and meandered off Miranda's lap. Finding a place on the couch to his liking, he circled a few times, eventually curling up, and looking expectantly at her. "Okay, Merawl, you heard Chris. We can talk now but then no coming into the bedroom." His gray tail whisked back and forth, and Miranda imagined he was saying, "You can't tell a cat what to do, especially a spirit one who can go anywhere." Miranda breathed deeply into her gut, focusing on increasing her energetic connection to Merawl, enabling him to enter the material realm more fully, then she reached over and scratched his chin.

"Stop your tail twitching and tell me what you came to say."

*:I didn't come to say anything. You asked me a question:*

"You're right. I was wondering about this evening. Why did those guardian spirits say they'd been waiting to talk to someone? Sonya was there. They should have talked to her. Why did they pick me?"

"What guardian spirits?" Chris called from around the corner.

"While I was at the gathering tonight some spirits, the main one, who called herself Earthweave—no, it was Earthweb—or Northern Grandmother, seemed to be saying that they hadn't been able to talk with other humans before. But that can't be right. I'm nothing special."

"Hey, that's my girlfriend you're talking about." Chris walked back into the living room folding a dishtowel into a precise package. "And why wouldn't they speak to you? Everything else invisible does."

"It's not that I'm surprised they spoke to me. But why just me? Sonya Bloom was there and I don't think they were even trying to speak to her. At least she didn't say anything was communicating with her."

Merawl's voice popped into Miranda's mind, sounding like a teacher lecturing to a foolish student. *:She didn't hear them because she doesn't know how to listen to them. And they don't know how to talk to her:*

"That's ridiculous; she wrote the book on talking with spirits."

"What's ridiculous?" Chris asked, squinting at an empty section of couch where the air seemed to be swirling, as if a tiny gray fog bank was trying to grow ears and a tail. "What did Merawl say?"

The cat yawned and spoke again. *:The spirits must not have read Sonya's book. Maybe if you took them a copy next time they'd realize they were supposed to talk to her and not to you—even though you obviously can hear them:*

"Don't mock Sonya. Her book is amazing. And I sounded like such an idiot in front of her!"

She turned away from both of them, ramming down the tears that were making it hard for her to talk. *Why didn't Adnarim warn me that Sonya would be there? I've always dreamed of meeting her and now I went and ruined it by my stupid ramblings.*

Careful to leave plenty of room for Merawl, Chris squeezed in next to her, pulling her into an embrace.

"It's okay, cry a bit. It must have been an overwhelming evening, meeting Sonya Bloom, then having those guardians single you out, and not having a single spirit pal to aid you."

Merawl reached out a paw and putting extra heavy energy into it, swung it through Chris's arm, provoking a jump and a curse. Miranda relaxed, allowing herself to sink against her lover's side, as she watched the normal banter between her loyal allies.

Merawl walked across his rival's legs and curled onto Miranda's lap, his purr a deep psychic murmur reaching into her core, releasing the tension stuffed there. *:You are special. I keep telling you, for a human you are amazingly open and bright. It's no surprise the grandmothers waited and wanted to converse with you:*

"But I'm afraid I won't be able to accomplish what they need me to do."

"What have they asked you to do?" Chris used a tissue to dab at the tears running down Miranda's cheeks.

"I'm not sure. Talking to Earthweb was like conversing with trees. They're so rooted in the earth, their wisdom's deep, but their words are so deliberate and excruciatingly slow. If only she'd talked faster and clearer. She did convey that whatever it is, it's really, really important. That's why I don't understand why they picked me. I'm nobody."

"You are not! What about all the people who come to your Sunday meetings? They get a great deal from listening to you talk about guides. They're always trying to persuade you to meet with them individually, like you used to, before you had me to come home to."

"Yeah . . . but . . . you wouldn't know since you never come to the meetings. I'm always referring to Sonya's book. It's not like I have any wisdom myself. And besides, I only schedule people on the evenings when you teach your cooking classes. It was an emergency when I saw Rhonda last Tuesday night."

Chris reached for her hand, pausing before responding. "I wasn't trying to bring that up again. I'm just trying to reassure you that you are special."

"Okay, sorry. I'm just worried."

Chris gripped her hand tighter. "They aren't asking you to do anything dangerous are they? What is it they want you to do?"

"I don't know what they want! That's the problem."

"Promise me you won't agree to do anything if it's risky."

"How can I do that when I don't know what they want?"

Chris took a long breath, then asked through gritted teeth, "What specifically *have* they asked you to do?"

"So far, all they've asked me to do is just listen. I haven't really gotten a good chance to talk with them yet. I'm hoping during the breaks tomorrow I'll be able to speak to them more."

"You're going back tomorrow? I thought you said it was just tonight."

"I said I *hoped* it would just be tonight. Don't get so upset. I'd rather be here with you. But I have to find out why Adnarim wanted me to go there. And now there are these guardians giving me riddles. And I need to see if I can't talk with Sonya more—maybe even sound somewhat intelligent this time." Turning away from Chris's hurt expression, she looked down at her cat guide. "Merawl, what do you think I should do?"

Merawl turned his green-gold eyes toward her. *:I think it would be purrfectly intelligent to wait to worry until you actually know why they want to talk to you:* He jumped off her lap and headed toward the bedroom. As he crossed the threshold, he slowly began to disappear, starting with his pink nose and whiskers, and ending with the tip of his tail that twitched as it vanished. Miranda smiled weakly at his technical obedience of Chris's request not to enter their bedroom.

Chris shook her shoulder gently. "What did he say?"

"That I should wait to worry until I actually have something to worry about." She felt as if Merawl had just opened a door in her brain, exposing shelves over-laden with jars of pernicious possibilities, which she compulsively stored there.

Chris reached an arm around her. "That's a great idea. I think you should listen to your wise-ass guide. And if you are going to be gone all day tomorrow, rather than arguing tonight, we should have our Saturday afternoon love feast now." Her lover stood up, pulling Miranda toward the bedroom, unknowingly following Merawl, but unlike the cat, neither human dissolved as they hurried through the doorway heading toward their bed.

# Chapter 3

# *A Hole at the Top of the Hill*

The next morning, Miranda stole out of the bedroom, clothes clutched in her hand. Crouching in the chilly living room, she pulled a beige sweater over her head, then carefully stepped into a black skirt, fastening it around her waist, adding a matching blazer and an onyx necklace. She looked longingly at a pair of jeans hanging over the back of the couch, but sighed, resigning herself to dressing professionally on a Saturday.

She made her way to the kitchen where the coffee pot, whose timer had started twenty minutes ago, was sending an enticing aroma throughout the house. She added "setting up coffee" to her list of why she loved living with Chris.

A smile played around her lips as she sipped the hot liquid, remembering the passion they shared last night. She yawned, then fighting the urge to return to bed, she poured the rest of her coffee into a travel mug and headed out the door.

Backing out of the garage, she chose the Santana programming on her car's sound system, cranking the music up deafeningly loud to keep herself awake.

Humming along with *Black Magic Woman*, she forgot her plan to talk with BB and Merawl on the drive down. She flashed her conference badge to the solemn guards at the gate and they waved her through. As she was stepping out of her car at the conference center, her attention was drawn to the hill with the cedar trees on top.

*Damn, Merawl was supposed to tell me what to do about the guardians.* While she was staring up at the grove of trees, the man she had talked to at the check-in table the evening before spied her and started walking over.

Miranda felt words wafting around her like a welcoming warm breeze as Skyweb's airy voice greeted her. *:You, who came last sun leaving. You, who have returned:*

She breathed deep into her center, preparing to send out a telepathic reply when she heard leaves crunch behind her.

"Ms. Williams, good morning. Welcome back. Did you enjoy the dinner presentation last night?" The staff member stopped next to her car and held out his hand.

Miranda's shoulders shot up toward her ears and the coffee curdled in her stomach. *Oh, no. Not you again.*

*:Yes, I am here. I greet you again:*

"Sorry, did I startle you?" He pulled his hand back to his side, but leaned closer to her.

"Yeah, I haven't really woken up yet." *Be careful what I'm thinking.* She pulled her thoughts in tightly, concentrating on sending only her chosen words to the spirit.

*:Grandmother, I am happy to hear you again. Thank you for talking with me:*

"Let me escort you into breakfast. I think you'll find the coffee is excellent here." He extended his hand again, this time motioning her to precede him as he stepped closer, herding her toward the building. Miranda wanted to swing back toward the hill, but she didn't want to give him any reason to question her more, so faking a few yawns, she hurried ahead of him.

She heard a flutter of words from Skyweb but she could only catch "you," "listen," and "who." Once inside she joined the lines moving toward a luxurious display of breads, hot egg-and-vegetable dishes, and large bowls of fresh fruit. She was relieved when another staff person intercepted her unwanted shepherd, dragging him into another room.

Miranda filled a plate with five times her customary breakfast fare, then found a place at a table with people conversing intently through their cell phones. *Good, no one will bother me if I try to talk to the grandmothers while I eat.*

She took a deep breath, closing her eyes and trying to center. The aroma of apples, spices, and fresh bread flowed into her body, causing her stomach to rumble. *Be quiet body, you don't usually get anything this early.*

Instead of her mind forming words to send to the grandmothers, it overflowed with images of quiches, fruit tarts, and fresh coffee. After a few more futile attempts to concentrate, Miranda opened her eyes and picked up her fork, promising herself she'd find another opportunity to talk with the grandmothers.

The first presentation after breakfast involved many slides and videos. When they dimmed the lights, Miranda took several slow centering breaths. She felt an urgent pull from the cedar grove she had visited the prior evening. She quieted her mind, then let her spirit drift up and away from the conference room. When she reached the top of the hill, she found three of the four grandmothers standing in a half circle in the center of the cedar grove.

Earthweb's strong presence dominated the northern portion of the circle. Fireweb illuminated the east and Waterweb flowed gently in the west, but there was a gap in the south. Miranda searched for Skyweb, realizing she had not seen that grandmother yet, only heard her voice. The opening in the south tugged at her spirit and she slipped into the empty space, completing the circle.

:*Welcome:* Fireweb said. She was holding a pipe stem in her left hand, while her right hand caressed a red, stone pipe bowl carved in the shape of a bear's head. She wore a buckskin dress and her black hair was tied with a crimson ribbon.

*:I, who am Eastern Grandmother. I, who tell the* when's. *I, who tell you now the* when *of our being here. The long before* when:

Miranda turned to her right, drawn by the warm voice that wrapped the words around her like a blanket. Fireweb looked at her, black eyes dancing with fire. As Miranda waited for the words explaining how the grandmothers had come to be here, her mind jumped ahead, imagining scenarios of ancient ceremonies on the hilltop, illuminated by firelight and full moon. Absorbed in her mental wandering, she missed the beginning of Fireweb's next words.

*:—each wanting control of this hill. Each desiring the power implied in the conquest—:*

*:What? I'm sorry, I missed what you said. Please, can you repeat it?:* Miranda berated herself for filling her head with her own thoughts when she was so anxious to hear what the grandmothers wanted from her. Fireweb nodded and began her explanation again as Miranda frantically pushed her self-criticisms out of her mind in order to have space to hear the grandmother's words.

*:The when was before. Before those, who have your pale skin. Before those, who came from afar to walk this land:* The words paraded clearly into Miranda's mind, like candles being lit, each phrase illuminating more of the image Fireweb was conveying. *:It was a when of warring. Those of every tribe against those of every other tribe. Fighting for this hill. Desiring the earth sun energy here. Those striving for power were like locusts in human form:*

An image of elders circling around a fire on the top of the hill blazed into Miranda's awareness. *:We, who saw there was no safety. Never safety while so many two-leggeds wanted supremacy, not connection. We, who were able to perceive the life-force that dwells in this place. We, who listened to that life-force hid the rays of the sun and warmth of the earth that springs from the top of this hill. We made smaller places of earth sun far away on mountains, in rivers, and on beaches to attract those who wanted power. The fighters, who desired the life-force for their own went away. Left our space in peace:*

Miranda felt a warm calm spread through her as Fireweb described the change from the times of violence to the times of tranquility. Her mind drifted to thoughts of the present world and the wars occurring across the planet against both other humans and against nature.

:*Thank you for sharing that. How were you able to hide the power and create the peace?*:

:*We, who saw the need, gave of ourselves becoming spirit guardians of this place:*

Fireweb paused. Miranda felt the guardian's words flaming brightly inside her, illuminating the meaning of Fireweb's message. Forming her thoughts as clearly as she could, she asked, :*This place was so important to you that you died to protect it?:*

:*It was a when of change, not a when of death. We, who gave of our physical forms did not die. We, who were once as you are now have been waiting. We have waited as many Earth cycles as leaves on a tree:* An image flashed into Miranda's mind of a tree growing one leaf a year until it was thousands of years old and bursting with foliage.

:*Then we, who have been watching, saw those like you, with skin the color of sand, come to this land killing the ones who lived here before. Cutting the forests, poisoning the water, and now, poisoning the air:*

Miranda shivered, yanking her spirit back to the conference auditorium. Momentarily disoriented, she looked at the people surrounding her, sipping coffee from their Styrofoam cups inside a building made of the earth, but dedicated only to advancing human objectives. She felt shame thinking of how her ancestors had treated the native people and of how some of her species were raping the earth. She didn't want to return and face the grandmothers, but Fireweb's words continued to shine in her mind.

:*You, who have come to listen to us, who do not need blame for what others, who have made other choices, have done. Everyone has a path. Some choose to walk it. Some believe they can take others' paths. But they are never a substitute for one's own, never satisfying, always leading to sorrow:*

Fireweb's support helped Miranda to send her spirit back to join the circle, which was silent as Miranda tried to clarify her thoughts.

*They're saying this is some type of power spot that they've been guarding for countless centuries. They sacrificed their lives to protect it and they're still guarding it with their spirits. But why are they telling me about it now?*

Miranda's musing must have been noticeable to the Eastern Grandmother, or else it was a coincidence that she started saying, *:Now is near. The when, when the world must change. Become anew. You, who have witnessed, who have aided in growing roots for this when. You, who helped a human transform his physical form to a new form:*

Miranda's concentration stumbled as she realized Fireweb was referring to Don's death. Don, her best bud from college, her soul brother, her confidante, and clown extraordinaire. Her stomach clenched and tears burned her eyes, pulling her spirit back to her body in the conference room.

She struggled to send her spirit back to the circle but her mind ricocheted between memories: Don's first call, heralding his pancreatic cancer; his spirit and hope, while her world inverted; his ardent struggle with chemotherapy, ending with two weeks at home supported by hospice; and then the last morning, holding his hand as it grew slowly cold.

Her mind flew to the scene at the crematorium where she had been instructed by Adnarim to help transform the energy of his physical body, as it was released by the fire, into a ball of pure energy, like a tiny planet waiting to be born.

Over the last six years, she'd let that memory slip, but now it overwhelmed her senses. Once again, she was at the crematorium, staggering out of the room dominated by the massive oven and back into the chapel and into Chris's welcoming arms.

Her thoughts swirled around the many questions she had asked her spirit friends about that experience, but none would explain it to her. Now Fireweb was referring to it as serenely as if she was reciting the food Miranda had eaten for breakfast that morning.

Miranda mentally shook herself and tried to refocus on Fireweb, hoping she could discover why the grandmother had spoken of Don's death. But as she tried to send her spirit back to the circle, the grief gripping her gut kept pulling her back. She thrashed about, floating halfway between the circle and the building, grasping at Fireweb's words, which were dancing around her like fireflies. :*Indication . . . Time . . . Divide . . . When . . . Who:*

Miranda tried to open her spirit wider to receive more of the message and was able to see more words, flickering at the edge of her awareness :*The when. You, who will perform the task. Know the when. Transform:* The words stopped.

:*What when? What task? What's going to happen?:* Miranda felt her heart rate accelerate, her alarm increasing as she began losing her connection to the grandmothers. She fought to calm her body but her mind was racing, yelling at herself to relax, building a wall of worries between herself and the circle, imprisoning herself in her quaking body, confining herself in the crowded conference auditorium. Miranda could no longer hear Fireweb's words, only her own voice echoed in her head. *Damn! What did she say? I can't believe I let myself get so distracted I missed what the grandmother was telling me. I shouldn't get so nervous talking to spirits! Now I've ruined any chance to find out more. I have got to learn to relax better!*

:*Aye lass, and berating yerself will certainly help:*

"Agh!" Miranda twisted to the right as an Irishman appeared beside her, wearing a cap, knickers with suspenders, and a gray flannel shirt. :*McNally! I wish you wouldn't scare me like that:* Miranda covered her mouth with her hand pretending she had just coughed instead of exclaiming at what others would perceive as an empty aisle. :*Doesn't anyone else see or hear you?:* She glanced around the room where people were still listening to the lecture, or texting on their phones.

:*'Ere in your N-World? Not 'lessen I want-em to. After all, now that ye's back in yer "normal" world, spirits like me certainly wouldna appear:* McNally sat down in mid air, pretending there was a chair in the aisle for him. Crossing one leg over the other, he peered at the presenter. :*Fascinatin',*

*What's she sayin' about alterin' states a reality? Is she tryin' to tell ya that's possible?:*

Miranda squirmed in her seat, knowing McNally was always good for a humorous reminder to not take life so seriously, which was easy for him since he wasn't living in the N-World anymore, as he liked to refer to physical reality. She remained quiet, not wanting to let him know how upset she actually was and subject herself to more teasing.

To distract herself she focused on the presenter who was making her final concluding remarks: "While the brain is a highly discriminatory organ it can't tell whether input comes from the outside or from inside its own neural strata. This means a chemical, properly introduced, carries the same emotional and physical stimulation as witnessing an actual external event. Most importantly, it means an induced event will evoke a reaction within the brain that is indiscriminate from an actual event. Are there any questions?"

A woman from the far side raised her hand. "By 'induced event' are you referring to personal delusions, or drug-induced hallucinations?"

"Both." The presenter replied. "The brain cannot discriminate the origin of the input. But we are not focusing on hallucinatory experience here—but on creating corrective brain functioning." She swept her gaze across the audience checking for more questions.

McNally waved at her. *:Are ya includin' ghosts as correct brain functionin'? Or are we ta be merely disappointin' personal delusions?:*

The presenter shook her head, then squinted hard at the open aisle next to Miranda. McNally smiled and waved again. The woman took off her glasses, sat down, and began to fumble through her briefcase. After several moments, she withdrew a cloth and small bottle. She wiped her glasses carefully, then set them firmly back on her face. Staring at the empty space to Miranda's right she sighed heavily, then called on the next question from the back of the room.

*:Ah . . . I bin removed by a dab a cleaner and a mere hankie:* McNally sighed dramatically and disappeared.

Miranda smiled to herself and noticed her anxieties had softened while paying attention to McNally's antics. He could be infuriating in his disregard for what she considered crucial; however, as he often reminded her, everyone dabbling in the spirit world needed an Irish ghost to keep them humble. Her heart was now serenely drumming in her chest. She glanced at the clock, then checked her schedule. The presenter had allowed half an hour for questions, then there was another hour presentation before lunch, so Miranda closed her eyes and calmly sent her spirit back to visit with the grandmothers.

Miranda entered the circle from the south, toes pointing at the center rock, eyes sweeping the crest, searching for the grandmothers, but the top of the hill was empty.

Down below, the conference buildings, instead of being a dull gray color, appeared a forest green through her spirit eyes, but the people milling around outside were obscured by a splotchy, mud-colored haze.

Miranda felt her attention being pulled back to the circle, so she hastily turned away from the buildings and humans, expecting to see the grandmothers, but they had not reappeared. Instead, Miranda's gaze was drawn to her feet, which were now inches away from a gaping hole. The center stone had vanished, as if the earth's mouth had opened and was now calling her to enter. She knelt down, reaching out her hands to feel an invitingly bubbly energy emanating from the hole. Glancing around once more, but still not seeing the grandmothers, Miranda allowed her spirit to drift down into the tunnel.

The tunnel took her past roots, rocks, and layers of Earth. As she descended, an opening appeared below her, until she slowly drifted down into an egg-shaped cave. She felt her feet touch the floor as her hands reached out to the walls.

*:Is anyone here?:* Miranda sent out a call, but there was no response.

Bending down, she ran her fingers along a thin crack in the rock that traveled over the floor, up the far wall, and across the ceiling which was now all stone, with no passageway visible.

Miranda's heart started to race as she realized she was completely entombed in rock. *Don't worry. I'm okay.* She tried to calm her emotions so that they wouldn't drag her spirit back to her body, which was sitting in the N-World conference room. She wanted to discover more about the purpose of the tunnel and the cave, but part of her thought it would be infinitely smarter to leave this rock-encased tomb immediately. To keep herself from fleeing, she focused on filling her heart with images of Merawl and Chris and their love for her. *I'm okay. I'm not alone. I'm not physically here so I'm not in danger.*

:No . . . danger is . . . not . . . yet: A cool, calm voice flowed into the chamber and Miranda turned to see Waterweb, the Western Grandmother standing to her left. She wore a buckskin dress with a coral-colored shawl around her shoulders, and was holding a drum with a striking stick, which had a ball of leather secured at the end by a sapphire ribbon.

Miranda was relieved to no longer be alone in the cave, except the grandmother had alluded to there being a time when she would be in danger, so hesitantly she asked, :*When will that time be?*:

:*Fireweb, Eastern Grandmother, explained the* when:

:*But I didn't hear—*:

:*I, who will show you* where *it will all occur*:

:*But how?*:

:*Earthweb, Northern Grandmother, will explain the* how: Waterweb's message came like a heavy mist into the chamber; the words slowly coalescing until they fell like drops of rain for Miranda to capture, so that she could drink in their meaning. :*See. Here. It is*:

Waterweb raised her left arm, her fingers pointing to the crack that traversed the chamber, which Miranda had been tracing until her fear distracted her. The grandmother's arm moved, following the split as it traversed the ceiling, dripped down the far wall and flowed back to the center of the floor. Miranda felt as if she was inside an enormous egg that a giant could cut open, separating the two halves along the line, which bisected the cave so precisely. Waterweb nodded at her. :*This is the where*:

*:Where what will happen! Please explain! What are you talking about?:* Miranda wanted to shout her questions at the Western Grandmother, but her years of experience conversing with spirits had taught her patience was prudent.

*:The changing. The transforming. Opening. Leaving one for another:* Waterweb looked up at the line on the ceiling then rolled her head as her eyes followed the thin mark around the entire cave. *:The where, here, is power:*

Miranda's spirit tingled as though she was standing inside a giant electrical transformer. *:I can feel power here. Is that what you are saying? It's like a hum, or a vibration through the rock. What am I supposed to do with the power here?:*

The watery words continued. *:Northern Grandmother will explain the how. The opening. I show you—:*

"Miranda?"

"What?" Miranda jerked, her eyes flying open to reveal Peter leaning over her.

"It was pretty boring, huh? I don't blame you for falling asleep. But everyone else has headed over for lunch, so Sonya said I should come over and let you know."

Miranda looked around at the empty room. The clock on the wall now declared it was twelve thirty. It had only been ten thirty when she had left the N-World to visit the grandmothers.

*What happened to all the time? It felt like I was only there a few minutes.* Miranda sighed, thinking of Waterweb. *I hope she still isn't in that egg-like cavern explaining the where, like the other Grandmother kept talking about the when, not realizing I couldn't hear her anymore.*

"Are you okay? Would you like to go to lunch with us?"

Miranda looked up at Peter, who was staring at her so intently that he was scrunching his eyebrows together; making the two, white furry lines appear as if they were battling each other. Miranda lowered her head to stifle her laughter and ended up coughing awkwardly.

Peter placed a hand on her shoulder. "Are you ill? Do you want to find a place to lie down?"

*Stupid. What am I doing? That's Sonya Bloom's husband I'm acting the idiot in front of.*

"I'm fine. Just having a hard time waking up." *What's wrong with me? That's the second time today I've lied about being sleepy so I don't appear crazy.* Miranda stood up and smiled hesitantly at Peter. "Lunch sounds great. Is it in the same room as breakfast?"

"Yes. Yes it is. Let me get Sonya. Then we can all walk over together."

As Miranda watched Peter shuffle across the room toward Sonya, her mind raced around in different directions. *Should I try to contact that grandmother to let her know I'm not hearing her anymore?—No, better not. They'll be back here soon. It wouldn't take too long just to let her know I'll be gone for awhile. But what if I drift off and lose track of time? I can't pretend I fell asleep standing up. Wait—didn't Sonya write something about that being possible?* Miranda continued her inner argument until the Blooms reached her.

"Good afternoon, Miranda. I didn't see you at breakfast. I'm glad you'll be joining us for lunch." Sonya reached out and squeezed Miranda's hand in greeting.

"Thanks for thinking of me." Miranda felt a warmth spread up her arm from where Sonya had touched her. She was grateful the older woman was kind enough not to ask her about the conference, since it was obvious she hadn't been paying any attention to it.

Peter wasn't as considerate. "You missed a great rationalization for chemical behavioral modification. Wish I could've slept through it. I couldn't believe they used MSG as a positive example to support their arguments." He turned and studied Miranda. "Do you know what MSG is?"

Miranda glanced at Sonya who was scanning the room, apparently trying to ascertain if Peter's comments were going to bother anyone. They were the only three left in the conference room, so she gave Miranda a nod, as if to say: "Go ahead and humor him."

Miranda turned back to Peter. "Yes, MSG stands for Monosodium Glutamate. They use it a lot in Chinese food. I like the flavor of it." Miranda felt proud that she knew what it was.

"No, you don't," Peter stated.

"I don't what?" Miranda asked.

"You don't like the flavor of MSG."

"Yes, I do."

"No, you don't." Peter was looking very smug.

She was starting to get annoyed. She and Chris had argued about MSG many times. Chris always tried to go to restaurants that didn't use it, but Miranda thought the food didn't taste as good there and tried to insist they go half the time to restaurants that did use it.

"Go ahead and tell her, dear. Lunch will get cold if you keep baiting her much longer." Sonya was leaning against her cane, apparently resigned to waiting until Peter had finished his lecture before going to lunch.

"You don't like the flavor of MSG, because it has no flavor." Peter stated loudly. Miranda remained silent, deciding he probably didn't really need her input to keep talking.

"MSG has no flavor, because it isn't a food. It's a neurotransmitter. It's a drug."

"A drug?" Miranda was shocked out of her compliant state. "It can't be a drug. I can taste it on food. It's really good. I've eaten dishes with it."

Peter wagged a finger at her. "No. It coerces the brain into convincing you that the food is tasty. But it adds no flavor."

"I don't understand. How can it tell the brain to make flavor if it doesn't have flavor itself."

"There are thousands of chemicals that instruct the brain in different behaviors. MSG fools the gustatory senses into thinking that what you're eating is good. If you don't believe me just put a dose of it on something you don't like. Or try it on dog food—and I guarantee you'll think it's wonderful."

Miranda thought back to her arguments with Chris. What had seemed like a chef's snobbery, were now making more sense to her. "Wow, I had no idea it did that." Miranda's thoughts bounced around in her mind.

*It sounds deadly and I've been arguing for it? And why are we talking about MSG anyway? I should be trying to remember what that grandmother was telling me. She was saying something about some danger that I'll be involved in.*

*And what's the meaning of that line she was tracing in the cavern?*

Sonya took Peter's arm and started moving toward the door. "Well, dear, now that you've made your point, shall we go and join the rest of the people? Van said he'd save us a place, and I'm sure he'll want to hear your critique of the morning's workshops." She turned to Miranda. "It's hard for Peter to sit through a lecture after all his years of teaching. He always needs to give someone a little lecture himself afterwards. He never feels quite himself until he does. I hope you didn't mind."

"I don't *need* to lecture. If they'd get it right in the first place I wouldn't need to say a word."

Peter and Sonya kept a loving banter going all the way to lunch, allowing Miranda to focus on remembering what the grandmothers were trying to tell her. All she was able to figure out was that something important was going to happen. It was some kind of healing, it could be dangerous, and it involved her and that strange underground cave.

Before the lunch ended, Dr. Westin came by their table to talk with Peter. As he finished he turned to Miranda. "How are you enjoying the presentations, Ms. Williams?"

"It's very interesting," she said, hoping Peter wouldn't say anything about her appearing to fall asleep during the morning lectures.

Dr. Westin bent closer to her. "I'm interested in learning why you chose to come to this particular conference. Are you here representing Whole Life Hospice or your own interest?"

"Just for myself." *Quit asking me why I'm here. I don't know yet.* Miranda's gut clenched, upsetting her stomach that was overstuffed with lunch. "Excuse me, I'll be right back." Miranda took the opportunity her body was giving her to make a quick exit to the bathroom. When she returned she was relieved to see that Dr. Westin had left.

Peter leaned over when she sat down. "Don't let Steven upset you. He just worries if there's anything he can't control or decipher. And he can't figure out why you're here."

*That makes two of us.* "I don't understand why my being here concerns him so much. I'm not with a company or anything—just here by myself."

"That's exactly why he's worried. You're not in the pay of some company he knows. Steven's concerned that you might be here investigating some pattern of deaths that have shown up in your hospice."

"What? Pattern of deaths? I don't understand."

"Oh, these big pharmaceuticals are always afraid that someone will discover some correlation between their drug and a fatal condition."

"Peter! What tall tales are you scaring Miranda with?" Sonya was trying to give Peter a stern look, but she appeared to be having trouble not laughing. "Honestly, I think you watch too many movies. Thinking Steven is worried that Miranda is some kind of spy. He's just being polite since it's her first time here. Now help me get up or we'll be late for the next workshops." Sonya poked Peter with her cane, ending the conversation.


The afternoon sessions were too noisy for Miranda to continue her conversations with the grandmothers, so her head filled with conflicting worries instead.

*How can I prove I'm not here spying for hospice when I can't say why I'm really here?—Stop thinking about the conference and start finding out what the grandmothers want. It'd better not be anything too dangerous or Chris will really be mad. What if I can't do what they want me to do? Why didn't they choose Sonya? She's the one who knows everything.*

Miranda was feeling glum by the end of the afternoon. As she walked out of the conference room, Sonya motioned her to come over. "How are you doing, Miranda? You don't look like you're enjoying the conference. Would you like to join us for dinner again?"

*I was going to get out of here and go home to Chris. But I can't miss a chance to talk with you again.* "I'm fine, just a long day of sitting and listening. I'd love to join you for dinner. Thank you for thinking of me."

During dinner, Sonya and Kamini were discussing Sonya's latest book, *Just Me,* an exploration of her journey from a girl who loved gardens, to a world recognized medium, to an older woman finally finding herself. Miranda wanted to join the women's conversation, but Van and Peter were seated between her and Sonya. Van politely tried to include her in their passionate discussion concerning the accuracy of the afternoon presentations, but she declined, pretending to be fascinated with her food. *Why did I bother staying? I'm not getting anywhere with the grandmothers' message. Maybe they're talking with Sonya and she's not telling me. After all, why would she tell me if she was? And I haven't been able to tell her I'm hearing them.*

As people were finishing their desserts, Dr. Westin stood up and began tapping his wine glass. "May I have your attention please?" he called out as the conversations in the room diminished. "We have the honor this evening of acknowledging a leader in the field of neurophysiology." Miranda's mind drifted as he read out an extensive list of publications and scientific studies. She was surprised when he came to the end and announced: "Dr. Peter Bloom, would you please come forward." The crowd surged to their feet in exuberant applause. Miranda struggled to rise quickly, acutely aware that all eyes in the room were focused on her table. Peter ambled past her, shaking hands as he went until he was standing at the podium next to Dr. Westin.

After saying a few more words and handing Peter a plaque, Dr. Westin raised a champagne glass full of amber liquid. As everyone else in the room followed his example, Miranda noticed there was a glass of champagne in front of her. *How did that get there?* Before she was able to reach for her water glass, Van swept up the champagne glass, and making an elaborate bow, handed it to her with a smile. "Ah, thanks." Miranda accepted the glass, holding it away from her with no intention of drinking it.

"To Dr. Peter Bloom," Dr. Westin called out and everyone, except Miranda, raised their glasses and drank.

Sonya reached over, clinking glasses with her. "Drink dear, it's excellent champagne."

Miranda raised her glass toward her mouth, hesitating.

*Oh, man! What do I do? I can't admit to Sonya Bloom that I'm an alcoholic. She was very clear in her book about the difference between actually conversing with spirits and alcohol-pseudo-voices.*

Sonya continued to hold her glass up to Miranda, a puzzled look in her kind eyes. *I'll explain being an alcoholic to her later. One little drink now can't hurt. It's been eight years since I quit.*

Miranda tried to smile as she took a slight sip of the champagne. Sonya took a swallow from her glass, nodded, and turned to drink with others who were coming up to her to applaud Peter's achievements. More people came over to Miranda clinking and drinking. Her glass was empty surprisingly fast but she proudly refused a refill, and when she spotted several people filling their champagne glasses with sparkling pear juice, she gladly grabbed some for herself. *There, no harm done.*

# Chapter 4

# *Berkeley Grad*

Miranda flopped onto the sofa, work clothes exchanged for jeans and a sweater. It was Monday evening and half an hour of possibilities existed before Chris was expected home, so she pulled her phone out of her briefcase and dialed a familiar number. "Hey, Susan, how's the Berkeley grad doing?"

"I haven't achieved graduate status yet. And, if I don't get my shit together soon, I'll become an unemployed social pariah in January."

"Your language! Berkeley's been an even worse influence than I was." Miranda smiled, remembering the subdued teenager who was dragged to see Miranda by her father. He demanded she fix his daughter's craziness and make her as normal as her very animated, socially acceptable sisters. She'd been successful, if you considered Susan's changing from hearing voices, to actively conversing with spirit guides an improvement. "So how are your classes going?"

"Forget college and classes. What've you been doing?

Merawl take you on any amazing adventures lately? Mesmerize you with any mystical meanderings?"

"I've been on some adventures but it wasn't Merawl's doing. Remember, I told you how I was going to have to go to that neurobiology conference over the weekend? And how uncomfortable I felt having to go, yet how emphatic Adnarim was that I should attend it?"

"Yeah."

"I met Sonya Bloom, the author of *Speaking with Spirits* there. I also met some grandmother guardian spirits, but it was hard to talk with them with so many people about."

"Uh-huh."

Miranda heard shuffling in the background. She imagined Susan: freckled face scrunched in concentration, head cocked to one side, her short, curly, auburn hair entwined around a cell phone, which was propped up by her shoulder as she sorted through her overburdened desk, the central feature of her cramped studio apartment.

"Did I call at a bad time?"

"No, I just misplaced my political science notebook. It's got to be around here somewhere. Go ahead—tell me about that nervy-neuro conference you were at."

"While the head of the conference was giving an introduction, I was able to do some spirit traveling to meet the guardians. I discovered these grandmothers want my help, but I'm not sure what they want me to do. It's hard to hear them."

"So why don't you just talk to them now?"

"It's not that easy. They're tied to that place, they don't seem able to travel around and I can't seem to reach them from here. They did tell me that they're guarding some ancient power spot. But it's underneath Future Pharmaceutical, so I can't just go back there whenever I want to."

"Cool, so you're saying these spirits have their own drug company? Do you think they'd want to make some special psycho-spirit drugs for us humans at Berkeley? Tell them I'd be happy to be their sales rep, for a small commission of course."

Miranda sighed as she stood up and started to unload her briefcase onto her desk. *Maybe Susan's got the right attitude. I'm getting way too wrapped up in the grandmothers and their messages.* "So what've you been doing?"

"Waiting to hear about my internship with Assemblyman Daniels."

"With who?"

"Daniels—haven't you been paying any attention to what I've been telling you the last weeks? He's the leader in environmental legislation for California. It's my dream career to work for him."

"Didn't you tell me he's got a youth ecology-corp or something like that? I'd think they'd always be recruiting."

"Yeah, he's the one that supports Earth Youth Corp. But I don't want to give make-overs to dilapidated buildings or sweep stream beds . . . I mean, not that that's an unworthy endeavor but . . . well, you know."

Miranda pushed her worries aside and tried to focus more on Susan. "You want more."

"Yeah! I want to be in the heart of things, working on the political aspects. That's why I want the internship with their legal team. It's my *gath*."

Miranda shook her head, flinging her black hair out of her eyes. "It's still hard for me to imagine you *gathing* politics." Miranda liked the term Susan invented to mean *guided* on one's *path*. It was useful as both a noun and a verb and simplified the need to justify when an action felt like the right thing to do, when there were no rational reasons substantiating the decision.

"Someone has to gath politics, or the chaos crap will expand even faster; and this world needs more problems as much as my sisters need more boyfriends."

"No argument there. I just remember when you thought following a religious path was your gath; back when you were quiet and didn't want any attention focused on you."

"I'll take all the attention I can get, especially from Daniels."

"Well, if it really is your gath, you know something will materialize. But that doesn't mean you don't have to do your share of the work creating it."

"Fair enough, oh gath guide of mine. You've led me wisely through family, religion, and college—now just help me get this internship. There must be some guide you can contact who can put in a good word for me. And once you've done that, it'll be time for you to start settling down to some real business by gathing us a winning lottery ticket."

Miranda joined in as they created their customary lottery wish list, and then asked about Susan's plans to come back to the Seattle area over the Christmas holidays. They continued talking, until Susan had to head off to class.

After Miranda hung up, she plugged in her phone to recharge it, then collapsed back on the couch. *What am I going to do about those grandmother guardians? What do they want?*

# Chapter 5

## *Whole Life Hospice*

"Hey, Miranda! Ya got a call from Sonya Bloom on line seven," Stephanie hollered down the row of cubicles to where Miranda was conferring with Grace, the lead hospice nurse. Grace looked up from her desk, giving Miranda a wry smile.

"I see your talks with Stephanie about receptionist etiquette and decorum have been very beneficial." They both laughed.

As Miranda turned to leave, Grace reached for her arm. "Wait a minute, is that Sonya Bloom the psychic author? How do you know her?"

"I met her last fall at a conference I attended. I'll tell you more later, but I'd better go get this call now, before Stephanie bellows at me again."

Miranda strode down the row of desks, ignoring the smiles and laughs from the other staff. Avoiding Stephanie, while promising herself to have another talk with her soon, Miranda went into her office and closed the door.

Even though one wall of her office was glass and faced the cubicle hallway, it still gave her the feeling of privacy, and she didn't want to be disturbed.

*Why's Sonya calling me? Has she been talking to the grandmothers? It's been months since that conference. I should have found a way to talk with them by now. Maybe they gave up on me and contacted her.*

She picked up the phone and punched the flashing button.

"Hello, Mrs. Bloom. This is Miranda."

"Heavens dear, call me Sonya. I'm feeling old enough as it is."

"How's your hip doing?"

"It's fine. Thanks for remembering."

"When I met you at the conference you'd just had surgery and were using a cane to get around."

"I finally had to graduate to a walker. I was too off balance with a cane. And enough people would say I'm off-balance anyway." Sonya laughed. "Using that silly thing lets me get around easier. But it's hard not to put pride before pain and stuff it in a corner."

"I'd never call you off-balance. It was a great honor meeting you last fall. I recommend your books to people all the time." *Should I tell her I lead groups about talking with spirits? But what if she thinks I'm not qualified to do it?*

"I'm very glad I met you at that conference. I've been dreading this call, but it makes it a little easier to know the person on the other end. The doctors have been encouraging me to call for the last few weeks, but I was putting it off. Then Peter slipped in the shower yesterday and I had to ask friends to come over, since I wasn't able to help him to get up by myself." Sonya paused, but Miranda could hear her struggling to control her breathing.

"I'm really sorry to hear that. Take your time. I can tell this is hard to talk about. You said the doctors have been suggesting you call hospice? Can you tell me what's happening with Peter?"

Sonya began describing the situation while Miranda made notes. Any thoughts about spirits or the grandmothers were left behind as Miranda slid into her professional role.

After the phone call, she looked at the intake form: hospital bed, walker, nurses for medication, assistants for personal care, and volunteer support to give Sonya respite. She jotted a few more notes, and filled out two contact cards with Sonya's number and address. As she was heading for the door, a tall woman in a blue-sequined dress flashed into her office. Miranda swung around to confront the intruder, who promptly disappeared.

*:Adnarim!:* Miranda ground her teeth together, hoping no one had seen her swing around so abruptly in her office. Trying to act natural, Miranda pretended she had turned around quickly because she needed to return to her desk. Sitting down in her chair, she acted as if she was searching for a paper while her mind was searching for calm. She breathed slowly, stilling her heart, reminding herself that when she looked directly at Adnarim she would disappear; an infuriating practice since Adnarim would habitually appear in intriguing forms making the temptation to stare intensely distracting. Miranda didn't fully understand why she couldn't look directly at her guide, but it involved some spirit rule that two pieces of the same spirit-essence couldn't connect too closely. Like two magnets, that when brought close together push each other away.

Adnarim was a part of Miranda's spirit-essence that had not entered the N-World when she was born. Miranda thought of her as her troublesome twin, literally separated at birth. When Miranda was not being totally frustrated by her, she acknowledged it was probably as difficult for her spirit-twin to understand Miranda's everyday N-World reality as it was to understand how Adnarim lived separately from the physical world.

Her elusive, frustrating guide had informed Miranda years ago that all humans had a piece of their spirit-essence that did not incarnate, but most people were not aware of their parallel spirit sides. Miranda tried to consider herself fortunate that Adnarim was so involved in her life, but all she felt was impatience while she waited for her to reappear. She shuffled more papers, noting the long list of crucial phone calls that needed to be made before the end of the day.

Tensing her brow and thinking loudly she sent a message into the non-physical realm. *:Okay, Adnarim. I'm relaxed now. I won't look at you. You can come back and tell me what you came for. Adnarim?:*

Gradually she felt a presence to her left. Still focusing on shifting through papers Miranda glimpsed in her peripheral vision a tall, dark-haired woman, draped in a neon orange shawl over green flowered pants, standing next to her desk. *:I'll never understand why you show up in such outlandish outfits when you don't want me to look directly at you:*

There was a vibration of air, like a fog drifting in and out, then a small, brown-skinned man in a khaki shirt and pants was standing next to her. *:Is this a better costume?:*

*:Sure, whatever. So tell me, is this why you made me go to that neurobiology conference? Was I supposed to meet Sonya there, because she was going to need to call hospice later? Is this why you didn't invent a quieter way for me to meet the grandmothers, rather than going to a conference where I had to justify my presence to everyone?:*

*:Yes. Yes, yes. Yes, yes:* Adnarim's reply sounded like an echo of yes's rebounding off Miranda's office walls.

Miranda struggled between wanting to ask more about the grandmothers and needing to get back to her N-World job as soon as she could decipher why Adnarim had shown up at work.

*:Well, what do you want to tell me this time? Is it about Sonya and Peter?:*

*:Now is the time to connect with them. Yes:*

*:Yes what?:*

*:Yes, my coming is about Sonya and Peter:*

*:That's obvious, you just said so:*

*:And you asked, 'is it about Sonya and Peter?' I answered yes:*

*:Okay, you're right, I did ask:* Miranda consciously lowered her shoulders and unclenched her hands, reminding herself the more tense she got the harder it would be to convey her thoughts clearly to Adnarim or to listen to her replies.

Forming each word slowly she tried to direct the conversation in a useful direction. *:Since you've been so good in the past, letting me know which staff would be best to help a new client, and you obviously think Sonya and Peter are important, who would you recommend as a nurse for them?:*

*:Yourself:*

*:I'm no nurse. I was thinking of Maria. She's very thorough and kind. Do you think she would be best for them?:*

*:The call came to you. This is part of your path to walk— your gath. So that you will be, where you will be, when the time is, to be where you are. No:*

Miranda sighed, not wanting to spend too much time deciphering Adnarim's cryptic reply, but the 'no' had been in response to her question about Maria being the best, so she did want to try to clarify that. She was also becoming increasingly distracted by Stephanie, who instead of being at her desk, was standing in front of Miranda's office window chatting with John, the good-looking new home health aide.

*One problem at a time*, she reminded herself, then projected her thoughts toward Adnarim. *:So Maria would not be a good nurse for them? Do you have another suggestion? Because they need a nurse. I'm the administrator, as you know, so don't play mystical with me. Just help me get them the best match:*

*:Maria would be a good nurse. No. They need who is best for them and you are the best for them. I know you are the administrator. It is not mystical. She called you. You were called. I am helping you make the best match:* The air shimmered and when Miranda carefully used her peripheral vision to check, there was no one there.

She let a sigh roll through her body, then slowly stood up and opened her door, wondering if her difficulty in getting cooperation from her guides related in any way to her inability to control her office receptionist.

Walking out of her office, she stared directly at Stephanie, who instead of disappearing back to her desk continued conversing with John.

*I'm not avoiding the situation,* Miranda told herself. *I just don't want to embarrass Stephanie in front of John. I'll bring it up to her later. I talk to strange spirits all the time. I run an agency with 135 employees. I'm certainly not nervous about confronting one receptionist about how she's doing her job, even if she is the daughter of our most wealthy board member and I never should have agreed to hire her in the first place.*

By the time Miranda's inner diatribe was finished she was back at Grace's desk. Grace glanced up at Miranda, then looked down the hall to where John and Stephanie were still conversing.

Before Grace could make a comment, Miranda handed her the intake form. "Can you follow up on this? Sonya was calling for her husband Peter, whose lung cancer has metastasized to the bone. They're a very devoted couple, been married sixty-one years. Sonya's been struggling, trying to care for him, but she has her own medical issues and is overwhelmed at this point, both physically and emotionally." She laid the paper on Grace's desk and added, "Try Maria, I think she'll be a good match."

"Right, I'll check her schedule, your hunches are usually right on." A call came for Grace before she could say more, so Miranda took a left down cubicle row heading for the volunteer coordinator, Lydia, who also happened to be on the telephone.

As Miranda waited quietly, she gazed at a poster hanging behind Lydia's desk of a kitten dangling from a branch. Instead of the familiar "Hang in there," it read "All you need is a little help from your friends." Miranda smiled. *I bet whoever designed that poster was not thinking of enigmatic, elusive spirit guides when they created it.*

Lydia hung up the phone, looked up, and asked, "To what do I owe the pleasure of your company, fair maiden?" Her eyes were sparkling, but they would have been bulging if she could've seen the Irishman in a gray shirt, suspenders, and knickers who materialized next to Miranda.

*:Aye now, there's a lass who knows how to greet one:*

*:McNally! What are you doing here?:* Miranda sent a mental question at the ghost, while trying to pretend she was just gathering her thoughts before answering Lydia.

*:A fair maiden calls and I am at yer service:* McNally swept his cap off his head, stepped back and bowed. The dramatic effect was lost as a nurse came striding along the aisle way, passing through the space he was occupying, and causing McNally to vanish. The nurse jumped sideways, then looked around her. Upon seeing Miranda, she straightened, nodded nervously and continued walking.

"I wonder what that was all about?" Lydia asked, looking down the hallway at the nurse.

"No idea. Sorry to bother you Lydia, but I just got a call from a new client who could benefit from having a volunteer give her some respite. She's caring for her husband, who has advanced cancer, and is overwhelmed trying to do everything right now. We haven't done a full intake yet but I wanted to pass this along to you so you could start finding someone."

Lydia reached for the information sheet, scanning it carefully. "Hand delivered by the boss, must be a special case. Any idea who would be a good match?"

"Actually, I was thinking of myself." Lydia's startled look matched Miranda's as she realized what she had just verbalized.

"I'd heard you used to volunteer once in a while when the agency was small, but I never realized you still did. Are you sure you have the time? I could easily find someone since we just did that new round of volunteer training." Miranda stood silent, trying to calculate if she could do it and when and how often. Lydia looked closer at the note. "You mentioned here that she would like someone three or four times a week. Maybe you could do one or two times in the evening or weekend and I could find someone to do a couple daytimes each week."

"That's a great suggestion. I wasn't sure how I could manage it. But I would like to be involved in this case . . . as a volunteer I mean." Miranda blushed as she stumbled over her words. "Chris works late on Thursdays so I could stop by after work, then go over on Saturday morning for a few hours."

"Okay, I'll give her a call . . . or do you want to? Or did you already arrange it with her when she called?" Lydia looked up, wanting clarification that Miranda didn't have.

"Um, why don't you call? No, I'll call, then I could arrange to go over tomorrow . . . but you'd better call to arrange the other volunteer. Wait, I'm not even sure she would be comfortable with me as the volunteer, or that Peter would. I didn't mention it when we were talking."

Lydia reached out a hand and laid it on Miranda's arm as she was trying to squiggle down the address and phone number from the sheet. "How do you know this couple? Are you sure it's a wise decision to be a volunteer for them?"

Miranda tried to pull back into her administrator-self but she was distracted as a form began appearing beside and slightly behind her wearing a rose cape and purple top hat. *:Adnarim! Not now, I'm trying to figure out how to manage this case:*

Adnarim's voice emerged clearly in Miranda's mind. *:It is not a case. It is your gath to walk with Sonya and Peter now:*

*:But volunteers are not supposed to become involved in a case if they know the people. It's a conflict of interest:* Miranda was experiencing a conflict in interest as she tried to argue with Adnarim and answer Lydia's questions.

Her troublesome twin continued calmly and confidently. *:The interest should be to match the person with whom they are supposed to be with; the conflict would be to ignore what you were supposed to do:*

*:It's not that simple, we have rules in the N-World we have to—:*

"Miranda? Do you want to take some time to think about this?" Lydia interrupted the telepathic disagreement. "I can give her a call and start working on getting them a volunteer so they'll have a primary one, and then you can call and offer to do some extra visits when and if it works out."

"That sounds great." Miranda let out the breath she'd been holding, relieved that Lydia had found a solution that didn't require her having to explain anything.

Miranda was able to call Sonya and work it out so that when she left work on Thursday, instead of driving directly home, she headed toward the Blooms' house. She had to stop for a red light, so she used the time to send out a telepathic plea.

*:Okay Adnarim, I'm going over to Sonya and Peter's. Now are you going to tell me why this is my gath?:* A young boy in a rainbow, tie-dyed T-shirt and cut-offs, with what looked like a ball and mitt, materialized in the seat next to her. Miranda kept her eyes glued on the traffic signal to avoid looking too directly at Adnarim and causing her to disappear.

Adnarim's voice resounded with the enthusiasm and the high pitch of a young boy. *:It will be fun talking to them. Peter is a physicist so he can explain the universe to me:*

*:You're not going to challenge him are you? He's dying after all:*

*:No. What better time to talk about life, death, and all the rest? This should be an optimal opportunity for him to become aware of his own parallel-spirit side:*

From the corner of her eye, Miranda could see Adnarim tossing the ball into the air, where it would disappear at the top of the arc, then reappear back in the mitt, ready to be released airborne again.

*:Just what he needs—his own troublesome twin. Don't forget, Adnarim, Sonya is the expert in talking with guides. She'll have already helped Peter connect with his parallel-spirit side and any other guides who will be helping him make the transition:*

*:Well then lass, they'll be expectin' me:*

Miranda rolled her eyes heavenward as she felt McNally's presence in the back seat. *:NO, they won't. I'm going over to offer some respite for Sonya. It's WORK related. She called about hospice help. She's not one of the people who come to my Sunday afternoon meetings wanting to contact weird spirit beings:*

*:Aye, now t'ere's a fun group. It was good ya started getting people ta-gether so you could 'xplain how to talk ta weird spirit beings. Even if it is only once a month:*

The light was still red and a brown bear with white-feathered angel wings was now flying back and forth in front of the car, adding her own comments. *:Maybe they believe in angels? Do you think Sonya will talk with me if I polish my halo and fluff up my wings and you introduce us politely?:*

*:BB, what are you doing? And why can't I go yet? I thought you were supposed to make the lights green for me, not red:*

BB swung her head down, her small black eyes, two beads staring at Miranda. *:Seems to me you're the one intent on impeding the process. We're all ready to go when you are:*

Miranda sighed through clenched teeth. *:Okay, you can all come. I'll even see if it's possible to introduce you to them:*

BB clapped her paws together exactly as the light turned green, then vanished as Miranda drove through the space where she had been floating.


Sonya met her at the door pushing a walker. "Welcome, it's so good to see you again." She patted her walker. "As you can see, I'm attempting to take care of myself. And of course Peter insisted I get the deluxe model: padded seat, wheels, cushioned hand grips, the works! Any more doo-das on it and the silly thing would be pushing me around." Sonya was interrupted as barking exploded from the back of the house. "Come on in and close the door. Peter's got a hold of Doogie so he won't run out."

As they headed for the living room, a boisterously bouncing, barking dog met them half way. The small poodle followed them around as Peter and Sonya eagerly showed her their home of over forty years. Miranda noticed it was a merger of scientific books, magazines, and journals piled on end tables and stuffed in bookcases; along with dream catchers, crystals, and sculptured goddess figures displayed on walls and arrayed along the tops of the bookcases.

After the tour they took their places in the living room: Peter in his recliner, Miranda on the side of the sofa, and Sonya hovering on the edge of her easy chair. A heavy silence filled the room. Even Doogie was quiet.

After a few moments, Miranda cleared her throat. "It's good to see both of you again. I'm sorry it has to be because of Peter's cancer."

"Oh dear, I forgot the drinks." Sonya jumped up and headed for the kitchen.

"I'll help you carry the tray." Peter levered himself out of his chair and followed his wife.

While they were gone, Miranda's mind whirled.

*I hate bringing up the cancer, but I've got to do my job. They didn't invite me here just to talk. I wish we could talk about guides. If only I could ask Sonya some questions. I bet she'd understand what the grandmothers want. Maybe if I asked her in general . . . I could try to . . . No—Stupid! That's what Lydia was worried about. I'm here to help them, not have them help me. I've got to keep my boundaries straight or I'll mess everything up.*

Sonya wheeled herself back in, followed by Peter who was balancing a tray with three wine glasses and a bottle of Chardonnay. *Oh, no—wine. What am I going to do?* Miranda's stomach tensed as her body froze. *Sonya saw me drink that glass of champagne when Peter received his award. I can't admit I'm an alcoholic now.*

Sonya filled the three glasses with wine, then offered one to Miranda, who felt herself smile and nod as her arm mechanically reached for the glass.

*It'll be fine. I didn't have any ill effects with the champagne. I'll just have one glass now to help them feel more comfortable talking about his cancer.*

She raised her glass in a salute to them. "Here's to the both of you. May hospice help support you with love and grace as you enter this very difficult time of your lives together." They all took a sip of the wine, then slowly began talking about the reason for Miranda's visit.

Over the next two hours, during which Sonya refilled Miranda's glass twice, she learned that this cancer was a resurgence of an earlier lung cancer they thought had been cured. Peter tried to joke his way through the details, while Sonya kept reminding them that even though they were on hospice they had to stay open for a miracle cure. Miranda listened carefully to the fear and sadness beneath their words, knowing from years of experience how difficult it was making the decision to call hospice. After hearing how little time Sonya had for getting out of the house, she arranged to come back Saturday at noon to allow Sonya to have lunch with some friends.

When Miranda returned on Saturday, Peter took her into his study, proudly pointing out the books he had authored.

Miranda picked out a few and read their titles: *Primary Principles of Physics and Quantum Chemistry, Neurobiology and Physics* and *Theoretical Physics Basics for Beginners.* "So you taught at Seaside University? I used to go there for concerts and services at the Chapel of the Colors."

"I taught there thirty years and never once went inside the chapel. Heard it was beautiful though. I almost didn't go to my niece's wedding when they decided to have it in a church." Peter grinned at Miranda, then reached over and picked up a slim paperback entitled *Rational Thought for the Rational Man.* "I took this in with me. I figured it would keep me safe. It did too. No celestial voices called to me and I never felt any urge to roll on the ground and speak nonsense." Peter swayed slightly, wincing in pain. Miranda guided him back toward the living room to discover a large brown bear was sitting in his chair.

BB, dressed in wings and a halo, waved a paw at Miranda, while Peter continued talking about his disdain for the irrational in religion. Miranda gave BB a stern look, motioning with her chin for her to vacate Peter's chair. She flapped her wings, lifting into the air and fluttering over a few feet to allow them to pass.

Miranda settled Peter into his chair as he launched into a lecture on the superiority of reason, waving his hands in emphasis. BB dropped to the ground and donned a three-piece suit, bowler hat, and spectacles, then started waving her paws in an exact imitation of his movements.

Peter stopped talking and looked intently at Miranda who was pretending to cough, as she tried to hide a grin behind her hand. He squared his shoulders and gave her his best instructor voice. "And what do you find so funny about rationality? I suppose you're one of those people who listen to 'guides' and believe anything they tell you."

"No, no. I'm sorry." Miranda glared over Peter's shoulder at BB, sending her an annoyed inquiry. *:Why are you doing this? I'm trying to connect and build trust with Peter, and now you made me insult him:* Looking at Peter she added, "Actually I think that 'guide' wisdom is vastly over-rated."

BB scrunched her muzzle in an imitation of a pout and disappeared. "I wasn't laughing at you. I was just thinking . . . about . . . well . . . I was wondering how you and Sonya balance it all out. I mean with her writing about spirit guides and you writing about physics."

Peter smiled and allowed his shoulders to drift back down. "We get asked that a lot. And we do have some very interesting conversations. I've actually consulted on many scientific studies of metaphysical phenomenon. Some of the latest theories of quantum energy fields and how they integrate with mental processes are quite intriguing. That's how I ended up at the conference where we met and where they gave me an award."

Miranda nodded, then felt guilty that she had been more concerned with the champagne and making a good impression on Sonya than on why Peter was receiving an award.

"I'd prefer to study the interaction of quantum fields and the brain's electromagnetic states directly. But they only *give* money if you can substantiate some kind of a chemical connection so they can *make* money." He shook his head slowly, then returned to the original issue. "Sonya and I are both interested in exploring metaphysics. The difference is, Sonya tends to jump in and follow her intuition; I prefer a logical course of inquiry. I've never seen a statistically significant outcome from a study that has clearly demonstrated to me that these phenomena that she so adamantly believes in are true."

He reached over and touched his finger to the outstretched hand of one of the goddess figures balanced atop a stack of mathematical journals.

"I'm not sure this is a dispute I want to win. Sonya seems to get more solace from her faith than I achieve through my reasoning." He sighed, staring at the figure a few moments, then swung back toward Miranda shaking his finger and looking at her sternly. "Don't mistake me; I'm not the type of person to believe in something just to feel better now that I'm dying. I'm not going to give up a lifetime of logic for a little relief at the end."

He turned and glared out the window where Merawl was perched on the sill taking a bath. "But if there is something to this spirit-guide stuff, which some of the newest advances in physics make surprisingly possible, I don't want to ignore it."

Merawl stopped washing his tail and looked at Peter. *:I'm glad. I'm not particularly fond of being ignored:*

Miranda started to lean forward toward Merawl, then pulled herself back into her chair. *:Can he hear you?:*

*:Why don't you ask him?:*

Miranda started to shift herself back to speaking verbally, but before she could decide on a question for Peter, he continued.

"So am I boring you with all this old man's chatter? Why don't you tell me more about yourself? You said you'd read Sonya's books. What do you think of this spirit stuff?"

Miranda glanced back and forth between Peter and Merawl, who was stretching into a cat arc, then stepping down from the windowsill onto a precarious pile of books.

Peter swung his head back and forth following Miranda's lead. "What are you looking at? Is there something outside the window?"

"No . . . not *outside* the window. I just . . . well, I have talked with others who have had experiences seeing beings that are not completely rooted in the physical world. For myself I believe there is more than the physical reality, and we are more than our bodies."

"We have electro-magnetic energy fields that extend beyond the physical body; there are numerous machines that can record that, but that doesn't mean one should make the jump to assume that we have spirits or that we will exist after death."

Merawl leapt off the stack of books causing Miranda to gasp in expectation of an extremely difficult-to-explain crash. But the pile remained intact as Merawl landed in the middle of the room then strolled over to Peter's chair, turning back to twitch his whiskers at Miranda.

*:Why don't you try making it more personal and less theoretical? Ask him why he gets solace from Sonya's belief in us non-physical manifestations of electro-magnetic energy:*

"You said you wouldn't mind losing the argument with Sonya about there being something else in the world. What would that mean for you if Sonya was right?"

"It would mean something more than my books and the memories of those who knew me would continue on after my death, and I would be able to still explore this great mystery of the universe called life."

"How would it affect you while you're still alive?"

Peter looked down at his hands, rough and dotted with age spots. He rubbed them back and forth then pulled on his fingers. He resumed talking so softly Miranda had to lean forward to hear him. "I would know death wasn't the end and I wouldn't be so afraid."

Miranda sat quietly absorbing his words until Merawl warned her that Sonya was getting close to home. "I'd certainly like to help you discover a connection to something beyond the material world that would decrease your fears, and maybe even tie in to some of what you have discovered in your exploration of quantum physics." Peter looked up at her, hope and incredulousness warring across his face. "How about if I come by every Saturday and Sonya can know it is her time to get together with friends or run errands?" Peter nodded, then they both turned as they heard the garage door going up.

As Miranda greeted Sonya, she felt appreciation for the sharing Peter had gifted her. She wondered how Sonya would react to knowing Peter secretly wanted her to win their on-going debate concerning the spirit world.

# Chapter 6

# *Merawl's Mishap*

"Hello?" Miranda stuffed the phone under her ear, scrunched up her shoulder to prevent it from slipping, and continued hunting for the house key in her briefcase.

"Hi, this is Susan. Got time to talk?"

Miranda leveraged the door open, dumping her work accessories on the couch. "Sure, how often does the busy political intern ever deign to call her woefully neglected friends?"

"Be careful or I'll cite you for harassment or blackmail or something legal like that. It's only been a month since I started this job."

"And in January we talked every week. You're going to make me regret asking my guides to help you get that internship."

"That's the best thing you ever did for me! Well, besides helping me become comfortable conversing with Angel . . . and you did convince both my family and me that I wasn't a lunatic.

I suppose encouraging me to pursue what I wanted and not what my Dad expected was pretty great too."

Images of Susan flashed through Miranda's mind: progressing from an excruciatingly timid teenager, whose only confidante was her angel guide, to a confident young woman boldly heading off to Berkeley to study law. "I'm glad BB gave you that tip so you were able to connect with Assemblyman Daniels's aide. It certainly seems to be your gath; though I had hoped you'd return to the Seattle area, rather than staying in California."

"When are you going to learn to space travel like your guides? Merawl appeared in my bedroom last week; you should have come with him."

"Sorry, I still find myself confined to some N-World norms." Miranda plopped herself onto the couch. "What'd Merawl want?"

"It was kind of odd. He wouldn't admit it of course, being a cat and all, but it appeared as though he hadn't intended to come into the N-World through my apartment. He kept looking around and seemed unnerved to see me instead of you."

"That's disturbing. What'd he say?"

"Oh, he recovered fast enough, said he was just making the rounds, checking on the *namens*, then he disappeared without asking me anything."

"Well he does like to keep track of us natural humans, but then he should have actually engaged with you, not just popped in and out. Except for once when I was with Peter, I haven't seen him much, which is inconvenient since I need his advice in deciphering what the grandmother guardians need me to do."

"Haven't you been able to contact them yet? You really should learn to loosen up more; exorcise those vicious inner voices and learn that you can do anything!"

"I can't contact them from here and I can't just waltz back to that conference center and ask to hang around until some magical grandmothers talk to me."

"Why not? You're always telling me not to limit myself. Now you're coming up with limitless limitations for why you can't contact those spirits and why you can't zap over here and visit me."

"Great, now that Merawl is absent you're going to start lecturing me on how to journey and how to talk to non-physical beings?"

Susan laughed. "I wouldn't dare advise the great, first *namen*—"

"There is no 'first' namen," Miranda interrupted impatiently. "All namens are equal, we're just humans who can't ignore our connection with nature, but right now I wouldn't mind ignoring mine, if I could. Merawl's acting weird, my gath is all twisted up with these grandmothers who talk in riddles and show up in my dreams at the most inconvenient—"

"What dreams?"

Miranda fought her urge to snap at Susan for interrupting, and focused on pushing down her fear and panic that were threatening to overwhelm her as she remembered her disturbing nightmares.

"I keep dreaming I'm in that rock-encased, egg-like cavern. The three grandmothers are there: Waterweb is reminding me that the event will happen here, Fireweb is explaining when it will happen, and Earthweb is clarifying exactly how I must do my part. I try to reach out to them but they disappear. I'm left alone, with the realization that I can't remember any specifics of what they just said. All I have is this gnawing sense of urgency, that whatever I have to do is crucial for the future of the world. Then the line bisecting the cave starts splitting apart, it gets wider and wider. I'm trying to balance between the two sides but it becomes slippery and I start to slide through, then I'm falling into a chasm and I know, like you just have that knowing in dreams, that I will never be able to escape from the abyss." Miranda shuddered just thinking about the dream.

Susan's tone got more serious. "That's really heavy. Do you think it's a psychic dream or a worry dream?"

"If I knew that I wouldn't need Merawl!" Miranda answered crossly, then immediately regretted it. "I'm sorry. I don't mean to snap at you. It's just been weighing on me since meeting the grandmothers last fall. I have such a strong sense that it is my gath, and such a sketchy awareness of what I'm supposed to do. I just wish I could talk to those spirit guardians again."

"If you can't get back to that conference center, why don't you just contact them from where you are? Do some awesome astral adventuring. Then you can be conscious, or as much as astral is conscious, instead of in a dreaming, semi-consciousness."

"I told you before, I've tried and I can't do it!" Miranda closed her eyes and rested her head against the back of the couch.

"You always say the benefit of having spirit friends is that they can be everywhere and anywhere, so you're never alone—"

"This isn't the same. They aren't guides like Angel is for you and BB, Merawl, and Adnarim are for me. They're guardians of the land." Now that Miranda had someone to talk to, her reasoning mind was slowly calming her fearful parts. "It's probably because they're so tied to that place that I can't reach them from here. That's why I had to go there for them to first contact me."

"Are there other workshops you could attend so that you could go to the conference center again?"

"I've checked but Future Pharmaceutical only offers workshops geared toward people who can prescribe their drugs, like physicians. That conference was unique. They might not have another one like that for years and I can't wait years to learn what the grandmothers want me to do."

"You could pretend you're a doctor."

"I was lousy at faking I had a reason to be there last time. No way could I pretend to be a doctor. Besides, the sign-in forms all had places for license information. How am I going to fake that? They were suspicious enough just because I wasn't from a company." Miranda shuddered, remembering the president questioning her about why she was there.

"They must sell drugs for pain that relates to hospice. You could go to a workshop that promotes pain drugs."

"I don't know. I felt so uncomfortable last time, so alone and out of place. My uneasiness probably interfered with my ability to hear the grandmothers clearly."

"I could go with you when I'm back for Easter vacation."

Miranda felt a brief glimmer of hope, then discarded it. "Oh, great. If they weren't suspicious enough of me before, showing up with a lawyer will certainly make them more accepting of my being there."

"Okay, so that's not the best idea. But maybe I can use being a lawyer, or wishing I was one."

The phone went silent, so Miranda stood up and started unloading her briefcase, breathing slowly and focusing on placing her papers neatly on the desk while waiting for Susan to continue.

"Hey, I got it! What if I approached them about an internship? Not that I'd really want to learn to find legal loopholes for pushing chemicals on innocent people, but I'm sure they've got a team of lawyers and I could pretend I wanted an internship with them. I could say I'm trying to find one back in the Seattle area for next year while I study for my bar exams. I could set up a meeting when I'm back over the Easter holidays. Then you could drive me and wait in the car. You should have at least an hour to contact the grandmothers. We could even go early and I could get lost in the building to give you more time."

Miranda started to discount Susan's idea, then she listened closer as her mind replayed the significant points. "That might just work. Since you're up from Berkeley it would make sense that you wouldn't have a car. We could just say I'm a friend of the family. Which is actually true since it was your father who found me and decided I could 'cure' you of hearing voices." Miranda relaxed as she remembered the scene, then she refocused on their plan. "I could bring a book and sit in the car holding it while I contact the grandmothers. I don't think anyone would hang out in the parking lot long enough to notice I wasn't turning the pages."

"Great. I'll hit Future Pharmaceutical's web site and figure out who to contact to set up a meeting. Hang on while I memo myself."

Miranda heard clicking and imagined Susan holding her phone out, a satisfied smile on her face as she typed in her message.

Susan's voice continued again, clear and confident. "Okay, now that we've solved your paralyzing predicament, can we get back to the debilitating dilemma that I called you about?"

"Are you having perplexing problems with mystifying messages from elusive guides too?" Miranda felt relaxed enough to join Susan in her alliteration word play.

"No, I don't have spirit problems, I have boy problems."

"Someone you're interested in?"

"No, someone I'm not interested in, but who thinks I'm the Goddess incarnate."

"Well, at least he's got good taste. Who is it?"

"His name is Thomas Chin, but I call him TMSC, because he always prefaces everything with 'This might sound crazy but . . .' Then he talks about something that really isn't that strange."

"Maybe not to you, but other people have a less expansive view of normal."

"I bet he's actually a namen. He's starting to share some non N-World experiences with me. Though I can just hear TMSC if BB ever showed up and talked with him. He'd say in his rational tenor monotone: 'This might sound crazy but there's a bear over there.' That's why I decided Thomas C really stands for TMSC."

"I like that. I've got a few 'This might sound crazy' friends too. But wait, are you talking about Chin, as in the son of Mike Chin, the guy BB helped you hook up with?"

"Now you've journeyed over! That's my problem. BB's idea to contact my Dad's old buddy was brilliant, but she should have warned me the connection came with baggage. TMSC thinks I bathe in moonlight and eat stardust for breakfast. Only he wants to be there at night and in the morning to watch me."

"That's awkward, considering Mike Chin arranged your internship with Representative Daniels."

"That's how he knew about the internship, because his son was doing it. Add in TMSC is nice, in a clunky sweet way, and probably a namen too so I don't want to hurt him, but no way am I interested in anything more than friends."

Privately, Miranda didn't think Susan would ever be interested in any man, but given Susan's religious upbringing she didn't want to be the one to suggest it. Susan had managed to overcome her homophobic upbringing when it related to others, but it would be a different reality adjustment to think about herself in those terms.

"How about if you suggest some friends he could date? That way you'd be saying both: you're not interested, and you think he's nice enough that you'd recommend him to your girl friends. You could even arrange to get together in threesomes. If he wants to go out and do something, just make sure to invite some available woman with you."

"That's a great idea. That's been my problem. We have similar interests so he's always inviting me to do things I'd really like to do but I don't want to give him the wrong impression by accepting and going out like it's a date or something. And there are plenty of women I know—I can think of three right now that work in the office who would probably be interested in hanging out with us. Thanks. My mind always seems to go into pause mode around these guy kind of things, but the thought of asking some women to join us feels easy. I'll exercise my options and give it a try. So how is Chris doing?"

"As annoyingly irresistible as ever. It's wonderful having a chef as a partner, but sometimes I just wish I could come home and have a peanut butter and jelly sandwich."

"A PB&J for dinner! I'm shocked. I thought you always craved crème à la cream sauce de jour. Or a perfect pear parfait with chicken à la Chris."

"Yeah, yeah. Anyway now that Chris is teaching cooking, we have more of our evenings together so that works well."

They talked for another twenty minutes, then Chris came home and Miranda got off the phone and into an impassioned embrace, feeling lighter than she had since first meeting the grandmothers.

# Chapter 7

## *Nasty Neighbors*

When Miranda arrived for her fourth visit, Peter threw open the door, almost swinging himself off balance as he brandished a registered letter at her.

"Look at what *they* did! Made me sign for it and everything! If I'd known it was from *them* I'd have never accepted it."

Miranda took the letter Peter was waving erratically in the air, along with his arm and guided him back to his chair, where his walker was parked uselessly beside it. Miranda sighed inwardly, thankful he hadn't fallen on his way to the door, and resigning herself to another visit focused on Peter's neighbors, instead of on the spiritual issues she had hoped to explore with him.

Two years ago, a couple bought the house next door. It was a small house and soon they wanted to expand and build a granny unit on top of their garage. But they needed the agreement of their neighbors before the city would allow them to build it.

Peter and Sonya had gladly agreed, wanting to be good neighbors. They hadn't expected the new structure to become a looming two bedroom house, perched on a dilapidated, detached two car garage. Peter berated himself for not having checked the building's design before agreeing to the neighbors' plans. Now they had a three-story, make-shift monstrosity towering over their fence and the neighbors were insisting that Peter and Sonya cut down their liquid amber tree that was growing near their new structure.

As Peter collapsed into his chair, he jabbed a finger at the letter in Miranda's hand. "They've hired some goddamn lawyer to threaten us if we don't cut down our tree. Our tree! It's on *our* side of the fence. We planted it when Sam was just a baby, watched the two grow up together, as he played in the branches." Peter's eyes misted over and his voice thickened. "I can still see him swinging upside down from the lower limb. Only it's not so low anymore. That tree must be over fifty years old. Sam would have been forty-eight this year if that drunk driver hadn't . . ."

Miranda pulled her chair over and put her hand on Peter's arm as he lapsed into silence. When she saw the tears starting to run down his face, she handed him a tissue and encouraged him to talk about Sam, helping him put words to his horrendous loss. Sam's death was resurfacing as Peter faced his own death without the support of his only child, who was killed in an auto accident when he was twenty-six.

Miranda left an hour later, fuming at the neighbors and their insensitivity. "Why can't they see how much that tree means to Sonya and Peter?" she demanded while steering her car toward home.

*:Are you asking me?:* Merawl appeared in the passenger seat, his paws on the door handle as he scrutinized the passing traffic.

"I wasn't asking anyone in particular, but if you have an answer I'd love to hear it."

*:They're greemens:*

Miranda tightened her grip on the wheel. "Of course they're *greemens*! With their hatred for trees, they certainly aren't namens. Greed is all they care about. Greemens!

Damn, stupid greemens!" Miranda felt a slight satisfaction in spitting out the term Susan had invented for greedy humans, who were the opposite of namens: nature humans.

Merawl bobbed his head, laid his ears against his skull and hissed. Miranda continued her tirade until she got home and into Chris's arms. "I just wish I could do something," she moaned collapsing onto the sofa and dragging her partner with her. "Why can't their neighbors see how hard it is for them right now, having to deal with Peter's cancer?"

"Do they know about it?"

"Practical as ever." Miranda shook her head, relaxing slightly at the hope her lover offered. "I don't know if they're aware of Peter's illness."

"Maybe next time you visit you could go over to the neighbors and talk to them. Use all your good administrator skills and I'm sure you can reach an understanding."

Miranda smiled, "Thanks, you're my anchor." She gave Chris a hug and focused on enjoying the rest of the weekend together.

Next Saturday, Miranda visited Peter while Chris waited anxiously, hoping the suggestion to talk with the neighbors proved helpful. When Miranda pushed the front door open with a force that rebounded it off the wall, all hope for an easy solution evaporated.

"I'm going to kill them!" Miranda threw her backpack against the sofa and stripped off her jacket.

"What happened?" Chris asked, forgoing the usual hug and stepping back to give Miranda room as she swung her arms wide, pacing up and down the room.

"Those jackals! When they heard about Peter's cancer and how preoccupied Sonya is with his illness, they began planning more atrocities. They started talking about the other two trees and how concerned they are that they might fall and hurt the house. House! That was only supposed to be a room above a garage!" Miranda continued to give every excruciating detail of her meeting with the people until finally Chris was able to get her to sit on the couch and allow her shoulders to be rubbed.

"I'm so sorry they're proving unreasonable!"

"Unreasonable! They were rude. The guy kept blowing smoke in my face as I stood in the entry way. They didn't even invite me in. She sat in a chair with her back towards me, talking to him as though I wasn't even there, saying how they should insist on the other trees being cut down and they have been living with the danger of them falling for far too long."

"Hey, I hate to interrupt this, but I do have the meeting at the school at three. Will you be okay if I leave?"

"Sure, go ahead. I think I'll take a walk, blow off some steam."

"That's a great idea. I won't be too late."

Ten minutes later Miranda was striding past Last Stop Market, the local convenience store. She noticed they had a sale on Stormer's beer, which used to be her favorite before she quit drinking.

While she walked, she remembered how calming a good cold brew could be and how she'd had wine a few times at the Blooms with no ill effects. She strode a few more blocks then decided it would be more productive to burn off her energy cleaning the house, so she turned around and headed back towards home.

As she passed Last Stop Market she wandered in, intent on buying Chris some sparkling pear juice, as a thank you for the hours spent listening to her rant about Peter and Sonya's neighbors.

On the way to the cash register her hand reached for a six-pack of Stormer's, following the neuromuscular pathways encoded through years of daily drinking, which now seemed only a day away, rather than eight careful years of sobriety.

After cleaning the bathroom and living room, the cold beers were satisfying, but she kept having the sensation she was being watched while she drank. She put the empty bottles in the neighborhood recycling bin, rather than the one they kept in their house. She reassured herself that this was a one time, extraordinary circumstance and she was only hiding the beer bottles to be considerate.

Early in their relationship her drinking had been a major source of conflict, and she didn't want it to be a problem again.


The following Saturday afternoon Miranda was back at the Blooms, but instead of Sonya leaving to visit friends she lingered by Peter's chair asking him a multitude of questions about his health and needs. Finally, she sat down in her chair complaining of hip pain.

"Why don't you stay and visit with us?" Miranda suggested, sensing Sonya's need to be with Peter was greater than her need for respite. "It's not that nice a day to go out anyway."

"That's a great idea," Sonya stated, bounding out of her chair. "I'll just get us something to drink and I think I have some leftover cookies too." Sonya poured them all wine while they listened to the rain splattering against the window.

As they talked, Miranda tried to take the opportunity of Sonya's being with them, to turn the conversation to spiritual issues. She was hoping to bring out the aspects of Sonya's faith that Peter wished for himself, but he kept pulling the topic back to the neighbors.

They had followed through with their threat and now wanted all three trees removed from the fence line. Miranda tried to play negotiator between Peter, who wanted to hire their own lawyer, and Sonya, who thought it best to be agreeable and cut down the trees. Miranda was pulled between her own resentment of the neighbors, and Sonya's reasoning that there were more important issues: mainly Peter's dying, to focus on. Eventually Sonya's persistence prevailed and Miranda agreed to search for an arborist who could remove the trees.

Driving home, Miranda marveled at Sonya's ability to be calm, while being challenged by Peter's cancer, the neighbors' callousness, and her own physical pain. Wanting to know Sonya better, she had bought her latest book, *Just Me*, an autobiography chronicling how Sonya had first started to speak with spirits, and her life-long journey teaching others to communicate with non-physical beings.

*I wonder how it is for her that she has helped so many people, but she can't help Peter in that way?* Miranda mused to herself. *Here I am a stranger, and he's more open with me than with Sonya. He's shared with me his desire to know there is something beyond the N-World and I don't think he's ever admitted it to Sonya.*

Miranda stopped for a light just as Merawl traveled through the car door and landed in the passenger seat. He swung around, ears and tail up, then crouched ready to spring away again. Miranda quickly called to him, "Hey wait, what's up? What are you doing?"

*:Traveling around. Checking on things:* Merawl sat down on the seat, wrapping his tail around his body, while his head swung from side to side, as though trying to orient himself.

Miranda switched to sending her thoughts out telepathically, in case anyone noticed her talking to what in the N-World would appear to be an empty seat. *:Did you mean to show up here, right now? Susan said you showed up at her place by mistake once:*

*:That wasn't a mistake. She was mistaken in her assumption concerning my behavior. I've been checking up on you namens:*

*:Then why were you going to leave right away without talking to me?:*

Merawl flicked a paw toward the light, which turned green. *:You can go now:*

Taking her foot off the brake Miranda eased forward, checking to make sure no one was trying to run the red light. When she was able to look at the passenger seat again Merawl was gone. *:Merawl, come back! What's happening? What's wrong?:* But she remained alone in the car for the remainder of the trip home.

Driving up to their townhouse, she pushed the garage door opener and was relieved to see Chris's car. She had been afraid she was going to come home to an empty house and she was in need of her lover's steadfastness. She was greeted at the door with a warm embrace, a kiss, and an explanation.

"I got a call from my Mom, then I really didn't feel like hiking anymore so I came home early. How's your day going?"

"It feels like the world is unraveling. The neighbors are going to get their way. Sonya insisted we agree to cut down the trees, so now I have to find a tree murderer. Then Merawl showed up in the car on the way home, acting weird. I'm sure he didn't intend to materialize in the passenger seat but he disappeared again before I could find out what was going on." Silently Miranda thought the only thing that had been feeling normal lately was drinking the wine with the Blooms and when she had the beers last week, but she didn't want to admit to Chris that she was finding comfort in drinking alcohol again. She brushed past her partner and walked into the living room.

Chris sighed, shrugged, and slowly followed after Miranda. "I'm sorry about the neighbors getting their way. I know that's frustrating for you. What was that about Merawl showing up when he didn't intend to? I thought everything that cat did was accomplished with style and complete control. He certainly likes to give that impression."

"A few weeks ago, when I was talking with Susan, she told me Merawl had appeared in her apartment, and then seemed confused, as though he hadn't planned on visiting her. Just now it seemed like he did the same thing with me when I was driving home."

Chris wrapped an arm around her. "Maybe he's just experiencing some minor spirit technical difficulties. Tell him to get Scotty to adjust his transporter beam, or have Geordi rebalance his anti-matter mix."

Miranda smiled weakly. "You're mixing your Star Treks again. Scott was the engineer for the original series; Geordi was the engineer in Next Generation." She pulled out of the embrace and walked over to the desk, pretending interest in the advertisements that had accumulated in the mail the last few days.

Chris walked up behind her and said softly, "My Mom had to go pick up my father again."

"What?"

"I told you my Mom called. That's why I cut short my hiking. Marco wouldn't let my Dad drive home last night. He took his keys so Mom had to go get him."

"I suppose that's pretty considerate for a bartender."

"If he was really caring he wouldn't serve him alcohol at all."

"That's not the bartender's job to decide—"

"Hey, whose side are you on? What's with—"

"I'm on your side," Miranda shouted, her face flushed with frustration. "I just don't think you should blame the bartender for your Dad's drinking. Or your Mom deciding to run after him every time he's drunk." *Damn, stupid idiot. He has no control. I made sure not to drink so much that I couldn't drive myself home today. Now Chris is going to be super sensitive about alcohol. I won't be able to say anything about my ability to drink socially.* Miranda let out an annoyed sigh and turned back to the mail.

Her partner paced the length of the living room several times then walked up behind her and started massaging her neck. "I'm sorry, I don't want to fight. I just hate hearing my Mom so upset. Why can't she just leave him, and have her own life for once?"

Miranda forced her shoulders to relax. "I'm sorry too. I should be more understanding. I'm just worried about Merawl."

"Why, what's happening?"

"It just isn't like him to be nervous. He was trying to hide it, but I could tell he was upset, and Susan got the same feeling from him. I've been noticing he hasn't been taking me to other worlds like he used to. I thought it was just because I'd learned what I needed to from those other dimensions, but now I'm beginning to wonder if there isn't something larger going on. I wouldn't want him ending up somewhere bad, or where there're bad things that could harm him."

"If he's having difficulties journeying between destinations I'm glad he's not taking you with him. Tell him I won't mind his showing up at our home whenever he wants to, as long as he doesn't take my girl friend astral traveling until it's absolutely safe. I don't want anything happening to you."

Chris gently spun Miranda around, giving her a stern, concerned look. "Promise me you won't do anything dangerous."

Miranda shrugged out of her lover's arms and started pacing. "That's not what's worrying me. It's Merawl and his behavior.

Why is he having difficulty? If he actually is—which he tried to tell me he wasn't—but he certainly seemed surprised to be in my car and in a hurry to get back to wherever he had intended to go. When I think about it, all my guide friends seem a little off and strange in their behavior."

"Normally, I'd make some wisecrack about how can you tell when they're strange? But I'm serious." Chris stood in front of Miranda causing her to halt her anxious walking. "What if they took you somewhere and you couldn't get back? Please don't do anything until you know it's safe."

"But if it's my gath—I have to follow it."

"Not if it would harm you. What if following your gath killed you?"

Miranda's alarm started dissipating, as Chris's anxiety loomed so large. "Lover, everyone's gath ends in dying. That's what humans do."

"Don't be flip. You know what I mean." Chris's face showed a mixture of a tight, determined mouth and eyes filling with tears. "What about that time at the crematorium when you had trouble returning to the N-World? I thought I was going to lose both you and Don then. It took you days to recover from that experience."

Miranda's mind flew back to when she was at the conference and Fireweb was referring to her experience after Don died: when she helped his physical body transform into a ball of pure energy, like a new world being born. For six years, she had been trying to puzzle out the purpose of that, and now she felt closer to uncovering an explanation for that extraordinary event.

"Miranda!" Her partner's voice, tightly strung with fear and pain, broke through her mental meanderings. "You're doing it now! Where were you? Were you talking to one of your guides?"

"No. I was thinking about Don's death and that time at the crematorium. It's odd that you mentioned it. Did I tell you that when I was at that neurobiology conference one of the grandmothers referred to Don's death and what I experienced when his physical body transformed?"

"No, you said everything was pretty fuzzy when you were trying to communicate with them. But that's not the point."

Miranda plopped onto the couch. "It was hard to understand them. All I have is a hand full of puzzle pieces and no idea what the picture looks like that I'm trying to create."

Her arms mapped the air as though she was moving pieces in a three-dimensional jigsaw puzzle. "One thing I know is that whenever I focus on the grandmothers I get that gath-like internal sense that whatever it is, it is something very important, crucial, probably the most important thing I've ever done. That's why I have to try to figure out what it is the grandmothers are asking me to do."

Chris crouched in front of Miranda, grabbing her hands in an attempt to hold her attention. "Why does it have to be you? Why do you always have to be the one chosen to do something? Can't someone else do it?"

"They only talk to me. I don't know why they didn't choose someone else. There are so many people doing so much more to try to rebalance the world, but I'm the one they're giving their message to." Miranda stared hard at her partner while her mind raced. "If I can help in any small way, I have to. We can't go on like this. Humans are destroying the planet. A change has to happen now or it'll be too late. I can feel that something tremendous is about to happen and somehow I'm part of it. I have to try to help the world!"

"I know; I'm a namen too. I might not be as strong of a nature-human as you are, but I'm namen enough to see the imbalance between humans and the natural world. I feel how close we are to a crisis."

"Then you know I have to do what I can. Whatever my gath is calling me to do to help heal the world."

"What if my gath is to protect you from doing something dangerous?"

Miranda shook her head. "You're confusing gathing with worrying. Gath means walking your guided path in this world. If everyone followed their gath, then humans would be in balance, like nature is in balance. Everyone's gath is unique, yet they all interweave to create a complete, healthy pattern for the world."

Chris stood up and backed away. "Don't lecture me on gaths!

I have as much right to say what my internal sense of purpose is as you do!" Tears started flowing down Chris's cheeks. "Ever since you went to that conference and spoke with the grandmothers you've been different and I don't understand why."

"Don't be so upset. I'll figure it out. In fact, Susan's working on a way that I'll be able to go back to the Future Pharmaceutical complex. She's going to set up an interview there that I'll drive her to. Then while I wait in the car, I'll have the opportunity to journey to the grandmothers' circle and get clear on what they want me to do in that cavern."

"You're going back there? And journeying again on your own before you even know what's interfering with Merawl? He's a spirit guide! If he's having problems you could really be in danger."

Miranda pushed herself off the couch and began to walk over to comfort her partner when a furry, gray-striped figure appeared between them. *:Since you have been deciding my life and troubles for me, I thought I should show up to set everything straight:*

"Merawl!" Miranda remembered to speak out loud. "Can you tell me now what happened when you showed up in the car today?"

*:Thank the chef for the invitation to show up anytime. Not that I ever limited myself, but it's always nice to be welcomed:*

Silently Miranda sent what she hoped would be a warning, *:Chris is worrying that I might put myself in too much danger by following my gath with the grandmothers:*

*:And you think your gath couldn't lead you into a dangerous situation?:*

*:Well, yeah actually. I did think gathing was always following my most healthy course through life. I wanted you to tell me something to reassure Chris, not scare me!:*

"Hey, what's going on? Are you talking to Merawl privately? Why did he have that problem materializing? What's he saying? Why aren't you including me?" Chris backed away, firing off questions, but sounding more anxious than actually desiring answers.

"That's what I'm trying to find out! Just give me a second to converse with Merawl, okay?"

Chris turned and walked out of the room.

"Don't act like that; I'm trying to ask him about your fears concerning my working with the grandmothers." Miranda sat back on the couch, troubled by her partner's behavior, but also relieved she could now talk privately with Merawl without having to translate something that might upset Chris further.

In the back of her mind was a nagging desire to get out of the house and go by Last Stop Market for some Stormer's beer, but she pushed it aside, not wanting to make things worse between them right now. *One thing at a time,* she told herself, as she turned toward her furry feline guide.

*:Okay, Merawl, can you please explain what's going on with traveling between realities?:*

*:It isn't like it used to be:*

*:That's obvious, but what's happened?:*

Merawl swished his tail but was silent. Miranda could tell he wouldn't answer her questions without the right prodding, so she leaned back and reached for the paper, pretending to read a front page story, as if it was more interesting than what a mystical cat could tell her.

She glanced over at Merawl, but he was still silently swishing his tail. She decided she would need some heavier ammunition.

*:It's okay, I didn't mean to put you on the spot. If it's too complicated to explain, I can ask BB next time I see her:*

Merawl's tail accelerated and his ears laid flat against his head. He growled low, almost inaudibly, but it started Miranda's spine shaking.

*:It used to be I could aim and jump right to the Green-world or to the Mountain-world. Now the worlds are changing. I can't be sure where I'll end up. BB is no better. I found her wandering in a parallel N-World, not even aware that she'd gotten lost and wasn't in the right one:*

*:What's happened to change it all?:*

*:That's what the grandmothers are working on. It's all coming to a whisker point and the balance is very delicate right now. So many different interactions and paths to balance.*

*In the middle of it all, humans are creating separate realities within the N-World. That's not supposed to happen. Humans may be the greatest creative experiment that ever happened in this reality, but the paths are supposed to interlock not separate:*

*:What happens if they separate?:*

Merawl went back to silent tail swishing.

*:You don't know, do you?:* Miranda felt her stomach sink into a well of dark forebodings. She thought of the many times she and Chris had mentioned that certain greemens felt like they were living in another world. Even humans who weren't trying to destroy the earth, but just held divergent world views, felt alien. Even on the subject of love, which should be a uniting theme, opposing beliefs were tearing families and communities apart as some people believed all couples should have the right to marry and others saw marriage equality as an abomination and evil.

Miranda sighed, trying to swim out of her tangle of thoughts, and refocus on Merawl. *:So these conflicting views are making it hard to travel between different worlds?:*

Merawl's whiskers twitched as he contemplated Miranda's question. *:Actually, it's only coming or going in the N-World that is giving me difficulty. I am not having any mishaps between other worlds. I think it's the lack of human gathing that might be causing it:*

*:You've got to at least try to explain that to me:*

Merawl raised a paw, extending his claws, then swung it through the air leaving five gray lines hanging there. He continued moving his claws deliberately back and forth, then up and down, and finally forward and back until a three dimensional pattern floated in the air.

*:When all creatures are following their gaths there is a pattern:*

Now he turned his back to the image and from the end of his tail he shot out a beam of gray fuzzy light. The light threaded a path through the lines from one side to the other.

*:It's possible to get from one place to another because there is predictability. I can follow my own gath, because my gath is supported by others. When they walk the pattern that fits for them, it creates space for others to flow their own gath lines:*

Miranda stared at the lines, pushing down her fear and anxiety to better comprehend what Merawl was showing her. :*This relates to what you explained before about gaths—right? That gathing is not about predestination, where everything is predetermined, and you just follow along. Everyone's gath develops and changes in relation to others. So, when everyone is living the lives that fit for them then it creates an overall weaving, which makes sense and is healthy:*

:*Yes, you've found the mouse in the hole:*

Now Merawl used his paw to separate certain lines from others, forming a void in the middle where no lines intersected.

:*This is what happens when humans stop following their gaths and create islands of beliefs that exclude others:*

:*You mean prejudice? When people believe they're better, or separate from other humans?:*

:*Yes. Separate and above nature. That's the big one: when humans exclude themselves from the natural world they live in. Then they try to create their own vision separate from everything else that exists in the N-World. It messes with every other species, plant, and especially the minerals, since they keep mining and transforming them:*

Merawl tried to create a gray path of light through the mass of lines again. This time when it reached the gap it had no support in its travels and it wavered then shot across arriving randomly on the other side.

Miranda studied the two pictures. :*I think I've got it. When you travel between places in the N-World now, there are so many voids in this reality you aren't sure where you'll end up:*

:*Since I'm not physical, I'm more vulnerable to the nuances of others' unfulfilled gaths:*

:*So I wouldn't necessarily have that problem if I went to visit the grandmothers?:* Miranda felt hopeful that she had discovered something she could offer to Chris.

:*Your anchor is in this world so even if you did end up somewhere unexpected you could pull yourself back. But eventually it'll cause every namen problems as humans continue pulling so far away from each other and from the natural world.*

*It's affecting BB, me, and the other spirit beings now when we try to travel. But it could create openings between this world and others that some weirdness might take advantage of:*

Miranda shook her shoulders, trying to rid herself of the idea of bad things happening between worlds, or terrible creatures showing up in the N-World. She tried to refocus Merawl on some specifics. *:Where were you trying to go when you popped into my car today?:*

*:I was actually going to visit you, but in your house two days ago:*

*:Two days ago?:* Her mind jolted, endangering her latest understanding. *:I'd better hang out with what you just explained. If you start adding time travel to it, my mind is going to divide up, just like your picture there. Besides, I need to get back to Chris, before the gap between us gets too wide:*

Merawl swiped his paw through the air, dissipating his diagrams.

*:Be careful with the grandmothers, they're at the heart of this. Be very clear when you leave your body; follow your gath as carefully as you can. Yours is a strong gath. If you can follow it, you will help others weave theirs:*

Miranda watched him disappear while she pondered his caution. She couldn't remember in all the years of connection with him that he had ever warned her like that before. He'd always challenged her, pushing her limits. His warning made her want to hide in a closet and forget she had a mystical gath— forget she had ever heard any voices other than the multitude within her own head, like the ones currently fighting within her. Half of her inner assembly was screaming in fear, while the other half scolded about responsibility, with plenty of guilt and confusion mixed in.

"Well, I think that's all I'm going to get from Merawl." Stating her sentiment out loud helped her orient more firmly into the N-World, pushing aside her inner struggles as she prepared to go in search of Chris. Then she added a non-verbal encouragement. *I can do this. I can be there for Chris, I can figure out what the grandmothers want, I can follow my gath, and I can help Sonya and Peter. I can make this all work. I can do it.* Mentally fortified, Miranda headed toward the bedroom.

"Hey, Merawl is gone," she called as she entered. She heard fumbling from the bedside, and when she got fully into the room saw Chris perched on the bed, absorbed in a book. As Miranda got closer, she noticed the book was upside down. Her heart hurt realizing how upset her lover was, while her mind was amused, and wanted to make a smart remark. But instead of commenting on the book, Miranda sat on the bed, laid her hand on Chris's leg and said, "I'm sorry for all this."

Chris lowered the book, exposing red eyes and a stuffy nose. "I'm sorry too. Sometimes I just feel so frightened. I don't understand what it is you do, or why you have to do it." Chris took Miranda's hand and squeezed it. "I love you so much it scares me, especially when I think of losing you."

She squeezed back. "I love you too and I don't want to do anything that hurts you."

"Promise me you'll be careful around the grandmothers."

Miranda thought of Merawl's warning and responded sincerely, "I will, I promise." Then she remembered his explanation and added, "He said I shouldn't have the problems he's having. It's because he isn't physically based in this world that makes him more vulnerable."

They sat in silence for a few more awkward moments, both absorbed in their own thoughts, both wanting to avoid any further conflict. Then they simultaneously turned and said, "Do you want to—"

Miranda laughed and Chris genuinely smiled. "What were you—" they said at the same time.

Chris gestured toward Miranda. "You first. What were you going to ask?"

"I was going to suggest going for a walk. What were you going to say?"

Her lover peered out the window. "It's still raining pretty heavy. I was going to suggest we go out for dinner. After I get presentable, of course."

"That sounds great." She glanced at the clock, which proclaimed it was only 4:30. "Do you mind if I make a couple phone calls before we go? That will give you some time to get ready."

Chris agreed, but neither one moved. Miranda twisted her toes into the carpet, staring hard at the random brown and beige design. Finally, she inhaled deeply and asked, "Do you want to hear more about what Merawl told me?" Before Chris had a chance to respond, she hurried on. "You don't have to, if you don't want to. It wasn't like he explained anything really clearly or anything. I did want to offer, if it would help, but I don't want to . . ."

"Upset me?" Chris finished the thought Miranda left dangling.

"Yeah."

"Go ahead. I promise not to get upset. It's probably better if you let me know and keep me informed. I do want to be supportive of you and your gath, even if it does scare me."

"It wasn't much. Not anything you're not already aware of. You know how you'll be reading something in the paper and exclaim that some group must be from another planet, because their views seem so opposite to ours?" Chris nodded. "Our gaths are supposed to be interconnecting, so when they're so divergent it pulls the world apart, leaving gaps in the fabric of reality and it's harder for him to travel between two places in the N-World."

"But that's been happening a long time, different nations fighting wars. Why is it affecting Merawl now?"

"It's never occurred to this extent before. Even when two nations fight, they're fighting for something that both recognize: like land, power, or resources. I think the danger now is that people are holding such radically different views of reality. I ran into someone at a hospice fundraiser who believed sincerely that pollution was part of God's plan and we shouldn't interfere with it."

"They said that?"

"Well, they didn't call it pollution, but when I pointed out the recycling container, after she had tossed her bottle into the trash, she said something to the effect that we need to have better faith in God's plan for us and not get so worked up about where we put our bottles or believe the hype about global warming. Evidently she thinks the climate change is all just a media conspiracy."

"I would have problems finding something in common with someone like that. I could see how finding any connecting thread that would link yours and her reality together would be hard for Merawl." Chris grinned weakly. "But how can you be sure this isn't just about his never getting over the fall of the Egyptian dynasties? That must have been a terrible blow for him when cats lost their God status."

"Yeah, you're probably right. He's just upset we don't worship him anymore." Miranda smiled, glad to have her lover joking about the spirit world again. "How about I go make those phone calls, you get yourself ready, and then we can go have a nice dinner?"

"Sounds good." Chris pulled her in for a kiss, then let her go and headed for the bathroom.

# Chapter 8

# *Bear Comes for a Visit*

Miranda shoved her front door open, tossed her briefcase on the sofa, kicked her stifling shoes across the room, and allowed her shoulders to relax, knowing it was finally Friday. Collapsing on the couch, she pulled out her phone and dialed Susan.

"Hey, Susan, did I tell you I finally got a chance to talk spiritual with Peter?"

"No, you've been ignoring me again."

"Yeah, right. And you've been giving my phone seizures making it ring so much. Anyway, last night when I was over at the Blooms, Peter started opening up more. Now that Sonya convinced him that they needed to cut down the trees, all the visits aren't about what to do about those blasted neighbors anymore."

"That's great. You'll make a namen out of him in no time."

"Well, it was actually more about how he was raised by a religion that discouraged questioning and encouraged blind belief and how he distrusts anything that even sounds religious now."

"Oh, did I mention I was able to arrange an interview with Future Pharmaceutical? I couldn't get the time off for Easter. So I set it up for Wednesday, May 19$^{th}$. I could probably change it if I needed . . ."

"No, that's great! Thanks so much." Miranda bounced off the couch, feeling like she could fly around the room. "I'll figure something out with work. I don't want to miss a chance to finally discover what the grandmothers want from me."

"Well, I hope it isn't anything too dangerous."

"Now you're sounding like Chris."

"So? Aren't we the two namens that care about you the most?"

"Yes, and you'll be the first to know what they want me to do."

"Good."

There was a silence over the phone, which gave Miranda a chance to realize Susan was sounding much more subdued than usual. "So what's up, Susan? Do you need to get back to your work? We can talk more next week if you want to."

"No, that's not it. I just . . . well, I had a very . . . um . . . strange weekend."

"Hey, I thought we'd been through all that. Strange is normal and of course normal is very strange. So tell me, what happened?"

"It started because TMSC wanted to . . ."

"Who?"

"TMSC. It's what I call Thomas Chin. Before he shares anything namen-ish, he always prefaces it by saying: This might sound crazy."

"Uh huh," Miranda replied as her mind flashed back to the conversation three weeks ago, when Susan was describing Thomas.

Miranda's grunt was enough to allow Susan to continue in her story. "So, TMSC wanted to go to this powwow. I'd always wanted to go to one and your suggestion to get girl friends to go along with us works well. Though Sheila was off doing her own thing most of the time."

"But at least it wasn't just the two of you going somewhere together. Hopefully he's getting the idea now that you're not interested."

"Nope. He still thinks we're fated to be soul mates. It's annoying, but I don't know what else to do . . ."

There was silence on the other end again so Miranda returned to Susan's original subject.

"So you went to this powwow with TMSC. What happened that was so strange?"

"Well . . . I'm minding my own navel, looking at the jewelry booths, when this old guy in jeans, a beaded denim jacket, and a cowboy hat starts chattering at me in a language I can't understand. I just shrug, smile, and try to move on, but he grabs my hand, pulls me around behind his table, then drags me over to the back of his pickup truck that looks like a chimpanzee's playpen. I'm just standing there as he's rummaging around, tossing hides and scattering feathers until you won't believe what he pulls out."

The line was silent for several seconds.

"I can't believe it 'til you tell me. Then I promise I'll believe it."

"A bear's head."

"A what?"

"A grizzly bear's head. Huge! With the teeth still in the mouth, which is gaping open like it's ready to bite someone. It looks ancient and it isn't made to be hung on a wall like a trophy or anything, because it's got this black felt on the underside of its chin so it can rest on a table. It's got dark brown fur, so it looks like BB when she lays her head over the back of the sofa."

"Okay, you got me. That is strange. What'd the guy do with it?"

"He thrusts it at me. I try to grab it, but the fur is slippery and while I'm struggling to get a grip on it, trying to make sure neither hand slips into its toothy orifice, he's ushering me back to the other side of his booth. Then he pats me on the back and walks away as though handing out bear heads was as normal as giving away Tender Teddies from Toy Town."

Another silence left Miranda feeling both impatient and incredulous.

"Susan, come on, don't leave me hanging. What happened next?"

"I tried to return it to him but he kept repeating: 'It yours. It yours.' At first, I thought he was trying to sell it to me, so I told him I wasn't interested in it, but he couldn't understand me any better than I could understand him. Then he takes a big piece of red cloth from underneath his table, wraps the head in it, dumps it back into my arms, and pushes me out into the stream of people wandering past the booths. I tried to get someone to help me but whenever I showed anyone the head they'd just shush me and instruct me to keep it covered since they aren't allowed to sell animal heads of endangered species, like grizzly bears, at a public powwow."

Miranda closed her eyes, trying to visualize the scene Susan was describing. "So what'd you do then?"

"Went looking for TMSC who, for once, didn't think this might sound crazy, even though I had just been given a bear head. All he was interested in was going to see the dancing, so I just lugged it around to the different shows; then later I went back to try to return it to the guy again, but I couldn't find him. In fact, the women in the booths next to where he'd been didn't remember him at all. They acted like I was crazy talking about this man with a pickup truck that had been parked next to them. But that figment of my imagination gave me a very large, real bear head. "

"That is very weird."

"I'm glad you finally journeyed over and acknowledged that fact. Could you ask BB what I'm supposed to do with it?"

"Okay, I'll check." Miranda looked around the room.

*:BB? Are you here?:*

A very large brown bear standing erect, with a silver ridge running down her back, materialized to Miranda's right. BB shook her paw, which was holding a small silver bell.

*:You rang?:*

*:What's up with Susan and this bear head?:*

*:Bear head? Is there a bear around here who's missing her head?:* BB pulled her head off, and holding it between her paws swung it around, scanning the room. *:I don't see any bear heads here. Tell Susan she'll have to find one somewhere else:*

Miranda sighed and shook her head.

*:Are you going to tell me anything useful? Or is this one of those just-gotta-go-with-the-flow-and-see-what-happens kind of adventures?:*

BB placed her head back on her neck and batted her eyes at Miranda. *:I don't know what you mean by that:*

"Susan, are you still there? I don't think I'm going to get any useful information from BB."

"It's a Go-Flow?"

"Yep, so far this definitely looks like what you like to call a Go-Flow. But you can always try asking her directly."

"That's okay, maybe I will later. Thanks for trying."

Miranda scrunched up her forehead, trying to think of more suggestions for Susan. "Have you tried looking at it with Cat Vision?"

"Are you implying that I forgot your teachings from Mystical Viewing 101? Rule number 63 ½: Always check the energy lines running between all beings, places, and objects to identify and try to understand the connections between yourself and everything else. That's exactly what's got me nervous. When I look at the head through Cat Vision, it appears so alive I'd swear I was looking at a living bear, not a century-old decapitated head. It's connected to someone else I know, but I can't tell who it is. I was hoping it might be you, but it doesn't sound like you're getting psychic associations with it."

"No, 'fraid not. If I get any hits about it, I'll definitely let you know."

"Thanks. I did check with Angel and the impression I got from him was one of pleasure and rightness. Not that that helps explain anything, but it does make me feel a tiny bit better living with this toothy paperweight in my apartment."

"Angel's your main guide, so it should be okay. Keep me posted. I'd better get going. Talk to you next week?"

"Sure. If the bear hasn't eaten me, if my job hasn't piled even more bureaucratic drudgery on top of me, or if the world hasn't come to an end yet, we'll talk."

"Okay, take care. I love you."

"Love you too. Bye." Susan ended the call, then sighed, slipped her phone into her pocket, and turned to gaze resignedly at the grizzly bear head, which was staring at her.

"So what am I going to do with you?" The bear was silent. Susan pushed herself out of her chair, moving deliberately across the room until she was standing looking down at the bear head. "Well, Ms. Bear Head, since you're here and it appears you'll be staying for awhile, may I ask you to assist me with my *bear-ly* manageable workload?" Susan picked up a folder from her desk and waved it at the bear head. "I have to author an audacious argument as an addendum to this stream preservation bill Assemblyman Daniels is sponsoring. Maybe this is why you showed up. After all, the addendum does have to deal with California Grizzly Bears."

Susan opened the folder, flipping through the pages as she held them in front of her new roommate. "Do you realize you were born about a hundred years too early? You should have waited until this summer to show up. If I'm successful in writing a politically poignant piece of prose, the California legislature might vote to give California grizzlies permanent protective status: granting you the right to exist. That is, if I'm ever able to figure out how to wordsmith it so that it appeals to the sentimentality of the assemblymen. It's supposed to make them feel good about the bill, so they won't listen to the miners who want to destroy the streams in Fresno County. So what do you say? Want to help?"

The bear's eyes started to glow brighter. Susan gasped and stepped back from the head. "This is getting too weird. Not only am I talking to a bear head but I just imagined you responded to me." Susan shook her head and took a deep breath.

"Well, whatever is going on I have to get back to work. If you do have any magic about you, assist me with all this legal word-weirdness: facilitate my faculties flowing with factual data. Help me stop humans from killing our home nest." Susan plopped down at her desk, scattering the papers. She continued talking to the bear head, complaining about all the pressures of her internship while gathering the courage to write down ideas for the bill that was going before the State Assembly next week.

# Chapter 9

## *Merawl's Journey*

When Miranda arrived at the Blooms after work on Thursday, she let herself in as usual, expecting Peter to be waiting in his chair. Instead, the chair was empty. Clutching the doorframe tightly, Miranda felt fear welling up inside her.

She called out hesitantly, "Peter? It's Miranda, are you here?"

"Miranda, is that you?" Sonya called from the kitchen.

"Yes, I'm here for my Thursday night visit," Miranda responded, walking quickly into the kitchen where Sonya was unloading the dishwasher. "Is Peter okay?"

Sonya set down a stack of bowls and opened her arms, inviting Miranda in for a hug. She gave her a firm embrace, then patted her on the back before releasing her and finally giving her the words she'd been waiting for. "He's fine. He's just in the bedroom taking a nap."

*Oh, thank God. I'm not ready for him to be too sick, too soon.* "If he's tired I can come back on Saturday."

"No, dear, Peter so looks forward to your visits. He'd hate to have missed you. If you don't mind waiting a little bit I'm sure he'll wake up soon."

"Sure, no problem." Miranda looked around, feeling uncomfortable and unsure of what to do. "How about if I help you with the dishes while I wait?"

"I can finish them later. I need to take a break. Why don't I get us both a glass of sherry and we can sit down in the living room." Sonya turned and leaning heavily on her walker, headed toward the corner of the kitchen where she kept the wine glasses. Miranda trailed behind her. *I should've told her right away that I don't drink alcohol. She looks so tired tonight, and she's obviously not planning to get together with friends, so the least I can do is join her for one drink. I'll explain it all later.*

"Here you go." Sonya handed Miranda both glasses of sherry. "Today has been so hectic. I've hardly had a chance to sit down all day."

"What was happening today?"

"First, Peter had a bad night. We couldn't seem to find him a comfortable position so that he could sleep." Sonya wheeled her walker into the living room and sat down in her chair.

Miranda handed her a glass, then perched on the couch sipping on her sherry. "That means you didn't get much sleep either."

"Oh, that doesn't matter. But it's getting harder to help him up at night. I'm afraid we're going to need that hospital bed you've been suggesting from the beginning."

"I know you'd hoped to do it on your own, but those beds make it so much easier. All you need to do is just push a lever to get him sitting up in bed, or to lower the bed. He can even adjust it himself when he needs to change positions. I'll let Maria know and she'll arrange one for you."

"Thank you, dear. I'm sure it will help Peter. And that's the important thing."

Miranda noticed how small and fragile Sonya looked sitting in her recliner. *I wish I could do more for them.* When Sonya finished her sherry, Miranda jumped up and refilled both their glasses. "What else happened today to make it so hard?"

"The people came to take down the trees." Sonya paused as Miranda had trouble swallowing her sherry and started choking. She got it under control and looked over at Sonya to see how she was taking it. "I know you felt like Peter. That we should've fought them more. But now that it's done I'm glad it's over."

"I just hated to see you lose something as precious to you as those trees, especially the one that Sam used to play on. You've had enough to deal with—your hip surgery and now Peter's cancer."

Sonya's phone rang. She glanced at the screen then turned back to Miranda. "It's a friend of mine returning my call. Do you mind if I answer it? I shouldn't be long."

"No, go ahead. I'll just go outside for a little bit." Miranda stood up, and taking her glass with her, wandered out into the Blooms' backyard. She was acutely aware of the tree stumps rising like tombstones alongside the fence. Looking down the row of houses, she could see stately trees growing in the other yards, some towering majestically over the people's houses. Only the neighbors on the other side of the fence had no visible trees. Their large, boxy building stood out harshly against the blue-black of the sky.

Numbly, Miranda stumbled over toward the fence, until she was standing in front of the middle stump, then she collapsed cross-legged onto the bark-strewn ground. Feeling a presence to her left, she turned as Merawl leapt onto the stump.

Swishing his tail back and forth in rhythm with his words, he proclaimed, *:Poor trees. Respected on one side of the fence, detested on the other. Viewed as old friends on this side, adversaries on that side. Encouraged to grow here, ordered to be cut down and lumbered there. Stupid greemens!:* Merawl ended with a fierce hiss that Miranda agreed with completely.

*:Unfortunately, those greedy humans have the N-World power backing them:* Miranda responded mentally, not wanting the neighbors to hear her. *:After their loathsome lawyer got the city to support their request, there wasn't anything we could do. Even though the trees were precious to them, it was too much for Sonya and Peter to try to fight it, with his cancer and all:*

"Miranda, are you out there? I'm off the phone." Sonya slid the patio door open, allowing Doogie to scamper out yapping. "Doogie! Stop that, you'll annoy the neighbors."

Doogie rushed out into the yard, enthusiastically accompanying each of his bounces with a bark, until he landed at the base of the farthest stump. Then he flung his front paws up as high as he could and serenaded Merawl at full volume.

"Shut that dog up!" a gruff voice bellowed through the fence. Miranda winced, hearing the man's voice and remembering her painful personal encounter with him and his wife, when she had attempted to promote compassion from the other side of the fence.

Merawl swiped an immaterial paw through Doogie's head causing him to dance around yapping louder. Then the cat leaned over and bit the dog's tail causing it to fly through the top of Merawl's head.

Miranda turned away from the scene on the stump. :Merawl, stop it. It makes my stomach churn when you do that:

"Doogie, what's wrong with you. Hush!" Sonya called, struggling across the lawn towards them, trying to use her walker on the rough path.

"Stop that racket or I'll stop it myself!" Floodlights stabbed through the fence, forcing Miranda to cover her twilight-attentive eyes.

"Damn, all we need is more problems from them," Miranda muttered, turning toward Sonya, while raising her hand behind her back, her middle finger extended high toward the fence. "Sonya, be careful, there are remains of the trees scattered all over the yard. I don't want you to fall. I'll bring Doogie in; you go back to the house. "

:You take care of the nice woman; I'll see what I can do about the nasty neighbors: Merawl leapt off the stump and sailed through the fence, heading towards the neighbors' backyard. As he steered toward a landing spot behind the man, he felt his paws slipping off the energy stream he'd used to travel from the Blooms' backyard. The stream disappeared completely and there were no energy paths left for him to follow. He thrashed about in the void, unable to find a connection that would allow him to land in the neighbors' yard.

A powerful rope of energy whipped across the void carrying Merawl along it. The spirit cat tumbled along, unable to break free as he passed through numerous N-World scenes. Then the new energy stream ended abruptly, dumping him into an alley.

He spun around, surrounded by tall buildings, shadowy trashcans, and dented cars.

*Dog drool! Where am I now?* He sniffed, then muffled his nose in his paw as stale beer, tobacco, exhaust fumes, and the remnants of panic-drenched human sweat overwhelmed him. He turned around, looking at the wall he just passed through when traveling from the Blooms' yard to what he had expected to be the neighbors' yard.

*Scratch that—the pathways are all torn apart again. If I jump somewhere else it might get worse.* He swished his tail in frustration. *I guess I'd better deal with this fur ball of a mess now. So what distortion brought me here?*

*:Tasty tasty kitty kitty kill kill:* A heavy, cracked voice echoed through the alley, dripping malevolence like an overflowing sewer emptying into a still lake.

Merawl used Cat Vision to peer around the alley. Three gremlins were on the other side of a brick wall to his left. They had their elongated, bumpy arms around each other, scratching each other's massively hairy ears, which were perched on top of oblong faces with gashes for mouths full of misshapen fangs.

*:What are you doing here?:* Merawl countered. *:This is a human world:*

*:They invited us, us. Asked us, us:* replied the middle gremlin, slightly larger than the other two, with a jagged scar across his face, which was displaying a disgustingly self-congratulatory grin. *:Yes. Yes. Here us, us:*

Merawl extended his Cat Vision further, searching for a human wizard, or would-be wizard who was in trouble, and who might have opened a doorway that allowed the gremlins access to the N-World. *:Who let you in?:*

*:Here us, us:* The central gremlin pointed to its two compatriots then jabbed an oozing claw at Merawl. *:Dinner! Food. Kill, kill!:* Two more gremlins appeared to Merawl's right lounging on top of a car.

Merawl backed further into the alley as five more materialized in the street in front of him. *:You're not allowed in the N-World. How did you get here?:*

The largest gremlin broke away from the other two and swaggered through the wall. *:Open here, like here:* The gremlin threw the words at Merawl as it strutted closer, red drool cascading down from its gaping mouth.

*Pigeon poop! There's no wizard energy around here so there's only one other way gremlins got in the N-World.* Merawl crouched low, compressing the springs in his back legs.

All the gremlins started moving closer, chanting, *:Kill kitty, kill kitty:*

*:Not unless you get smarter and quicker:* Merawl yowled, as he sprang straight at the largest group of gremlins, crammed together in the center of the alley.

The two grotesque groups on either side launched themselves into the middle of the alley as he twisted low, slipping under the arms of the gremlins in the center group who were soon swallowed up by the side groups in their attempt to catch Merawl. He cruised past the last gremlin as the entire mass collapsed in a spiky pile of green-pitted arms, scratched torsos, and malformed legs. The gremlins thrashed around vainly as Merawl dashed down the alley. As he spun around the corner he called back, *:Bigger isn't always stronger and it's definitely not faster:*

*:Kill! Kill!:* screeched the leader as he crawled over the pile of filthy gremlin bodies, leaving yellow oozing gouges across exposed backs and heads. Two of the attackers didn't move when the rest disentangled themselves, so three of them stayed behind to gorge on their former companions, while the rest raced after Merawl.

Merawl tried dodging between cars but the gremlins just ran through them gaining on him as he raced out into an intersection with a larger street. Merawl looked to the left, spying a group of humans in identical gray overalls who were striding down the middle of the street. After a cursory survey of the other direction, he sprinted toward the humans projecting his yowling into the N-World as loudly as he could.

Telepathically he sent a last message to the gremlins. *:Tough luck you grotesque ghosts. These working humans are too solid to ever see your hairy faces:*

"Did you hear something?" One of the men asked the other three.

The closest one to Merawl turned around scanning the garbage cans and dilapidated cars. "Sounded like an animal to me. Look around, maybe it's hurt."

Merawl slid out from under a car just as the lead gremlin made a grab for his tail, which he whipped in close to his body as he landed next to the man's feet.

"Here it is. It's a big gray Tom." The human leaned down to inspect Merawl, unaware of the grimy gremlin arm whipping around from underneath the car. The cat moved closer to the man, purring as noticeably as he could.

The man knelt down, holding out his hand toward him. "Nice kitty, don't be afraid."

The gremlins came out from around the cars and surrounded the humans, swiping their claws through the air as they chanted, *:Death, death:*

Merawl situated himself in the middle of the men, weaving through their legs, looking up and telling them: *:You want to pet me. You feel good seeing a cat. I'm a happy cat. All you see is a friendly cat. That's all that's here:* Merawl nearly levitated with the intensity of the energy he was generating, as he attempted to appear as an ordinary N-World stray cat to the men.

The men knelt down around Merawl, each reaching out and stroking him. "What a pretty cat. He reminds me of one I had as a kid."

"My kids would love this cat, but we can't afford an animal."

"He's probably a good mouser. He must have a home though; he's too friendly for a warehouse stray."

A gremlin darted in, attempting to strike Merawl. One of the humans reached out to pet the cat and his elbow inadvertently touched the gremlin's putrid torso, causing the monster to dematerialize. The man shuddered, rubbing his arm. Then he quickly picked up Merawl, and started down the street. "Come on, let's get out of this place. It's giving me the creeps."

*:Kill you,:* chanted the gremlins, following the men who were glancing over their shoulders nervously as they moved away.

Merawl purred louder, adding some meows for encouragement. *:There's nothing there, just the wind. You want to get home and be with your families:*

"Did you see something over there?" one man asked, peering in the direction of the trailing gremlins.

"It's the wind blowing paper around," said the man carrying Merawl. "Come on, I want to get home. You're just seeing things. It's late and we're all tired."

The gremlins hung back as the men entered a busier street.

A large woman pushing an overflowing shopping cart made an abrupt right turn into one of the gremlins who promptly popped out of existence.

Two more chance encounters with hurrying humans and there was only the lead gremlin left, who snarled at Merawl, *:Kill kitty:* He thrust a paw full of claws at Merawl, while dodging an umbrella-wielding human.

Merawl curled deeper into the man's arms, trying to ignore the gremlin, who slunk back into the quieter alley.

As the man continued carrying Merawl farther away from the gremlin, Merawl began to relax, lulled by the gentle swaying of the man's arms. He sent out a final soft purr and melted away.

"What happened to the cat?" the man called in alarm. He stopped so suddenly the man walking behind him collided with him.

"Hey, what's ya doing?" the second man complained.

"The cat disappeared. It was in my arms one second and the next it was gone."

"It just jumped down and you didn't notice," reasoned another man.

"No, I swear. He vanished. I felt him one moment, then the next the air felt thick and there was no cat."

"You're getting thick in the head," one of the men patted him on the back, propelling him along the street. "We all need to get home and get some rest."

The man who had been carrying Merawl started to protest again, then fell silent. He followed his friends down the city street.


Two weeks later Miranda came home late after work to discover a tiger-striped cat napping on her sofa.

:*Merawl, where've you been? It's been weeks! What happened with the neighbors? Did you scare them?*:

Merawl yawned, and stretched, then sat down and stuck his hind leg into the air, preparing to wash himself.

:*Come on, tell me what's up? We haven't heard anything from the neighbors, but Peter is worse so I haven't been paying attention to them. They got what they wanted anyway, the trees are down. Damn selfish idiot greemens! So what happened when you went through the fence that night?*:

Merawl continued licking his leg. Miranda looked closer at him, noticing he was dimmer than usual. She could see the brown pattern of the couch through his gray fur. She opened a spiritual channel to him, sending him love and energy, then resigned herself to waiting until he had settled himself more solidly into the N-World, before receiving any response to her inquiries.

She wandered into the kitchen to greet Chris, who enthusiastically responded to her returning home. When she returned to the living room, after changing into jeans and a t-shirt, Merawl was still focused on his bath so she plopped down beside him and reached for the newspaper. He continued methodically washing every hair until he reached the very tip of his bushy tail.

:*The world is getting crazier:* he finally offered in answer to her earlier questions.

"You're telling me." Miranda spoke out loud for Chris's benefit. "There's an oil company suing Seattle for the right to drill in Puget Sound."

"You're kidding," her partner called from the kitchen.

"No, it's true. Typical greemens. And what's worse is they're citing the original treaty we used to steal the land and water from the native people as a basis for their cause."

"But that's dangerous. A spill, or even a small leak, would wreck the local environment." Chris came in carrying a plate of apples, cheese, and crackers and started to sit on top of Merawl.

"Don't sit there. Sit over here." Miranda urgently indicated the empty space on her left.

Chris glanced at the empty couch and sighing loudly moved over. "Who's there?"

"Merawl."

The gray cat stood up and stretched, arching his back and swishing his tail. :*What is dangerous is humans inviting gremlins into the world:*

"Gremlins?"

"Gremlins?" echoed Chris.

:*Yes, gremlins. I was chased by ten of them. If I hadn't found a group of men getting off work, who were too sane to see them, I'd be a dead spirit cat right now:*

"But you can't die! You're not alive."

Merawl gave Miranda an exasperated look, then found a place on his hind foot he needed to lick again.

Chris pulled on Miranda's arm. "Who's dying? What's Merawl talking about?"

"In addition to greemens trying to destroy Puget Sound, evidently they're also allowing gremlins into the N-World."

"No way, the N-World can't be normal if there're gremlins in it."

Merawl twitched his ears at Chris. :*That's the whole point. Only what's 'normal' to humans can exist in this world. I've been trying to determine exactly how they entered the N-World. This wasn't because some idiot human, pretending to be a wizard, opened a door between the worlds. I'm afraid it's because too many humans keep watching horror movies. They see so many weirdling things on the screen that they're getting used to them—they're becoming normal so they're becoming part of the N-World:*

Miranda's stomach clenched at Merawl's words, but Chris was tugging on her arm again so she tried to translate Merawl's explanation.

"It won't be the N-World we're used to, but according to Merawl, if too many humans believe in something it can materialize here."

"Well, I'm going to believe in rainbows, butterflies, and people loving everyone, and that's the world I want to live in." Chris punctuated the sentence with a kiss on Miranda's cheek and a one-armed hug. She returned the affection but was distracted by Merawl's message and worried that he wasn't sharing everything with her. She wanted to question Merawl further, but was afraid of upsetting Chris and didn't want to start another argument about the potential dangerousness of her gathing.

Chris stood up, pulling her off the couch and away from Merawl. "Come on, I've been holding dinner for you. Sherry called today and wanted to see if we were free to get together in the city this weekend. The Burke Museum is having a new exhibit called *Weaving through the Centuries*. They're boasting some original textile masterpieces and demos on making rugs on a loom."

Chris continued chatting as Miranda allowed herself to be led to the dining table. She wanted to stay and talk with Merawl, but she was feeling guilty for coming home late today, after going out for a couple of beers with some nurses from work. She pasted on a smile, wrapped an arm around Chris, and promised herself if she couldn't find Merawl the next day, she'd a least have a long talk with Susan as soon as possible.

# Chapter 10

# *Bear Goes Camping*

Susan got a call late the next morning. Miranda hadn't been able to reach Merawl, so she phoned Susan to unload all the worries and questions that had grown in her mind during the night.

As Susan flipped her phone closed, she shook her head, trying to rid herself of the images of predatory gremlins that Miranda had just shared. She had no desire to think about gremlins, disembodied bear heads were enough for her. She looked up at her bear head, which had found a permanent position on top of her bookcase. It had taken three of her friends to secure it there, but it felt good to have it up and away, off her desk.

Susan placed her hands on her hips and addressed the head. "So what do you have to say about monsters showing up in the N-World?" The bear was silent. "Good, I don't want to talk about them anyway."

She turned and plucked a folder off her desk, waving it at the head. "What do you think about this amendment to the stream bill that I toiled over so long? It passed the legislature! That means not only will the waterways in Fresno County be protected from mining sludge, but you, the California Grizzly Bear, are now a protected species. Even though it's only a symbolic gesture, to honor your being the state animal and on the official seal and all, it's now against the law to harm you. They're going to put up a statue and plaque in Fresno County where the last of your tribe was killed in 1922. Of course they had to add a clause specifying that it only includes California Grizzlies and not any wandering grizzlies that may stray into California, so tell your friends in Canada and Yellowstone not to hitchhike down expecting an enthusiastic reception, but if you come around again, you'll be safe."

The bear head nodded and fell off the bookcase.

Susan jumped back as a shower of books accompanied the head to the floor. "Hey, what happened? I had you securely balanced up there."

Susan walked slowly over to where the head lay partially covered by a scattering of books. She kept away from the bookcase, not wanting to look up at where the head had firmly sat for so long, afraid she would see a green hairy hand groping along the top of the bookcase. She touched the head with the toe of her shoe, feeling sweat dampen her forehead.

"You just fell by accident, right? Nothing weird about it, nothing to worry about." Taking a tight breath through gritted teeth, she stole a quick glance at the top of the bookcase. It was empty. Susan let out a sigh as she knelt down, picking up the books, carefully stacking them in her arms.

Setting the books on her desk, she considered calling Miranda back, recollecting the support she had received when the N-World had felt like an open grave to a teenage girl who heard angels.

Susan's hand started to reach for her cell phone, but she jerked it back. Addressing the head, she stated firmly, "You just happened to topple off when I was talking to you."

The file of papers she'd dropped when the head fell drew her attention. She picked them up, leafing through the legislative bill she had helped author. Nodding her head, she told herself resolutely, "I can handle this. I'm a monstrously mature woman. I'm practically a lawyer. I just have to find an ordinary, supernatural reason for this. That has nothing to do with gremlins sneaking through movie-created gaps into the N-World!"

She replaced the file on the desk, then a smile broke out on her face and she spun around, arms wide. "BB! You did this! Where are you?" She continued spinning around searching for BB's familiar, comic appearance. "BB! Come on, materialize. This is just the sort of thing you love to do. I know you're here somewhere." Slowly she stilled her turning, a tightness pushing her breath out, leaving less room for air, making it harder to think as fears swam around the edges of her awareness. "BB?"

She crossed her arms over her chest, and pulled her shoulders back. "This is silly. BB is just busy, and I'm scaring myself thinking of those monsters. Why did Miranda have to tell me about them anyway? Especially if thinking about them can let them enter the N-World." She stared down at the source of her agitation, which was giving her a toothy sideways grin, its jaw propped up on a couple of thick books Susan had neglected to pick up.

She continued to barrage herself with instructions on how not to be upset, and how not to think about any scary fanged monsters. But instead of calming her, her heart increased its beating and her shoulders pressed tighter in, making it more difficult to breathe as tears threatened her eyes.

A presence began coalescing behind and above her, as though it was pulling light particles from the air, darkening the room as all the brightness was transported to this new being. Susan's head was bent down and through the tears, she didn't notice the changes surrounding her. The being gathered more substance, coming more fully into the N-World, wings stretching out as it floated toward Susan, dropping down, enveloping her, as she began to weep. Her legs bent and she folded onto the floor, the spirit following her down, now showing a slim, ethereal body and a head between the illustrious wings.

"Angel," Susan sighed, recognizing her guide, the angel who had protected her growing up and who had inadvertently caused her family to think she was crazy.

With Miranda's help, she now fully enjoyed her connection with Angel, who helped her negotiate all the nuances of living in the N-World. Angel, appearing as if he had just flown off a Michelangelo painting, sent waves of loving support to Susan.

Ten minutes later Susan rose, feeling stronger and more secure. She struggled to lift the bear head off the floor, looking up at where it had been securely resting the last months. She shook her head in resignation, knowing she was not going to be able to return the bear to where it had been before, out of the way, so she carried it over to the end table by the front door and left it there.

The next day, when TMSC/Thomas stopped by and saw the bear head, he insisted she bring it with them to the dedication of the statue in Fresno. The two interns' contributions to the assembly bill were going to be acknowledged there and since they were going be so near the Sierra Mountains they had decided to spend a couple nights camping out to enjoy a short vacation and recover from the intense work of the spring.

At first, Susan was resistant to Thomas's suggestion of bringing the bear, until she perceived the protective advantages of having a grizzly bear head accompany her on a camping trip with Thomas.

Susan was apprehensive that Thomas might construe the time together as a sign of her being interested in forming a closer relationship. She'd tried asking other friends to come and make it a threesome, but no one was available. Now, she felt more secure, since having a bear head in the center of the tent should provide a proper discouragement for any romantic gestures.

At the ceremony, there was a profusion of political backslapping and self-congratulations on finally protecting California's state animal. They seemed to forget the symbolic nature of the gesture as they boasted about the stiff penalty for anyone harassing or harming the extinct bear.

After the ceremony, Susan and Thomas headed up to Sentinel Campground in Kings Canyon where they hiked Lookout Peak until sunset. They returned to their campsite and heated a one-pot dinner of vegetables and noodles over a propane stove, then set up the tent.

When Susan lugged the bear head out of the back of the truck and toward the tent, Thomas exclaimed, "What are you doing? We don't have room in the tent for that head."

"Well, I can't leave it in the truck, and you're the one who said I should bring it."

"Why can't you leave it in the truck? No one will steal it." He strolled over to where Susan was down by the opening, balancing on her heels, the head in one arm as she attempted to open the tent zipper with the other. "Here, I'll help you." He knelt down, pushing his body against her side as he tried to take the head out of her arms. "I'll put it in the truck, under that extra blanket so no one will see it, and I'll keep you warm during the night."

Susan swung the head away from Thomas as she simultaneously succeeded in getting the zipper open, which overbalanced her and she fell into the tent, pulling the bear head down on top of her. "Oomph!" she exclaimed, then looking up at Thomas added, "There's plenty of room in here. It's big enough for three people. The bear can sit right in the middle."

"But I brought a candle lantern to put there. I even have some scented oils in case you'd like a massage after all that walking today."

"I'm fine." Susan managed to move the sleeping bags apart far enough for the head to be right in the center of the tent. "There. It fits perfectly." She backed out of the tent. "Shall we go over to the ranger talk? They said there would be some hot cocoa by the fire, and it's going to be really dark tonight: no moon and these woods are thick so hanging out at a fire sounds good."

Thomas looked forlornly at the tent, but reluctantly followed Susan down the trail to the campfire. The program was on the ecosystem of the region and the differences before and after the European settlements.

It was nine o'clock as they walked back to their camp, following the beam of Thomas's flashlight. When they arrived at the truck, they both silently grabbed toothbrushes and towels and headed toward the adjoining bathrooms five campsites away. Susan hurried through her nightly routine planning to beat Thomas back to the tent, so that she could crawl into her bag and pretend to be asleep before he returned.

As she left the amber circle of light near the restrooms, she realized she had followed his flashlight over and had forgotten her own. Rather than wait for him, she headed down the road hoping she would be able to figure out where the tent was. She was sure they were the fifth campsite on the left. As she counted down the spaces, she thought she recognized the shape of her truck and there was an outline of a tent where she remembered pitching theirs.

She headed toward it until her foot brushed against a flap of fabric. Bending down and unzipping the opening, she reached inside feeling something large and warm in the middle of the tent.

"Oops, I'm sorry." Susan backed away quickly until she ran into a vehicle. She ran her hands along it trying to tell what it was. When she got to the door, she fumbled for her key, which easily fit into the lock. The glow from the cab light was a dull, fuzzy gray by the time it illuminated the tent, but she could tell it was hers.

"Damn," she muttered to herself, "Thomas got back before me and he's right in the middle waiting for me to crawl in on top of him." She briefly considered sleeping in the back of the truck, then her annoyance built up and she took a heading on the tent, slammed the truck door closed, and walked as noisily as possible in the direction of the tent. She bumped into the edge then felt for the zipper.

"Hi, I'm coming in. I didn't realize you got through before me. Can you move over? And shine the light so I can see." A grunt answered her and she heard some movement but no light. She bit back an angry response and swinging her butt into the tent first, she scooted backwards, pushing against the bulky warmth taking up most of the room inside.

With her legs sticking out of the tent, she reached out and started to untie her boots, being careful not to get dirt into the interior.

She got one boot off and was starting on the second when she noticed a light approaching. The ray swung back and forth until it landed on her then it stopped.

"Hey, don't shine that on me. This isn't your tent, you got off the road. Go back a few steps and you'll find it."

"I'm not lost, Susan. I was waiting for you at the bathroom, since I knew you didn't have your light. Then I realized you'd already left so I headed back here."

"Thomas?" Susan froze, her entire body intimately conscious of the warmth and pressure against her back.

"Of course. Who else did you expect out here?"

"If you're out there then who's in here with me?" Susan was torn between the urge to swing around and look behind her, and the desire to jump out and run away, which meant she was stuck doing neither while Thomas crept closer with the light.

"What do you mean?" Thomas bent down and shone the light around Susan. "Ah . . . Ah . . . you should get out of the tent. NOW! Slowly, don't show any fear."

"Fear of what?" Susan twisted around and stared into the familiar face of the grizzly bear she had known for the last two months. Only now, the mouth was closed and the nose was moving closer to her. "Agh!" Susan sprang out of the tent, landing on top of Thomas.

"Susan, be careful. Don't upset it!" Thomas struggled to get on all fours, then began groping for the flashlight, which had rolled away during Susan's flight out of the tent.

"Upset *it*? What about *it* upsetting me?" She froze as a large paw covered her bare foot, preventing her from backing farther away. Part of her mind was screaming incoherent terrors, while another part noticed how the pad of the bear felt soft and warm, like human flesh on her bare skin.

*:Hello:* The word floated into Susan's mind, along with a sense of calm, causing her to take a much needed deep breath.

"What?" Susan looked around, unclear where the greeting had come from.

"I said be careful, get away from it!" Thomas hissed in a panicky whisper.

"I heard you the first time. Who said hello?"

*:Said hello, I did:*

"I didn't say hello. What's wrong with you? Get away from that bear and help me find the flashlight. I can't see a thing."

"You said hello?" Susan looked at the dark shape, which appeared to be moving closer to her. She was receiving a reassuring, relaxing vibration from the bear, which was completely at odds with the fear she thought she should be feeling.

"No!" Thomas's voice was tight with tension. "I told you, I said be careful. There's a bear in our tent!"

"I know. And she just said hello to me."

"What?"

"Shhh. I'm trying to talk to the bear." Susan focused on the earth beneath her, trying to center so that she could send her thoughts to the bear, who was still keeping what felt like a very real physical paw on her foot.

*:Who are you? What are you doing here?:*

*:Here is place, brought me you did:*

*:You can't be the bear head I was given by that old guy at the powwow:*

"Susan, I found the light!" Thomas yelled from behind her. "I'll shine it on the bear, then you run as fast as you can away from it."

The bear blinked as the light hit her eyes, then she turned back to Susan. *:Why past not possible be? Powwow place meet we did. Take me to your den you did, where up high raised me you did. Then suggest you this time, good time would be, to be born again into this world:*

Thomas continued to scream instructions at her, but Susan just stared numbly at the bear. As she continued to sit frozen in front of the grizzly, Thomas began to cautiously creep up behind her. When he was close enough, he reached forward and yanked on her jacket.

Surprised, Susan jumped, swinging around and seeing Thomas behind her.

Annoyance momentarily confused her as she clenched her teeth and mentally yelled at him, :*Stop that!. Leave me alone:*

:*Sorry I am:* The bear bobbed her head at Susan and moved completely out of the tent, releasing her foot.

Susan turned to follow the bear, but still distracted by Thomas, she spoke out loud to her. "Not you, him!"

"Him, who?" Thomas seized the end of Susan's jacket and pulled hard, rolling her backwards towards him.

Susan yanked out of his grasp and sat back up. "You—who! You're the only one here besides the bear and me. Now be quiet, I'm getting confused with both of you talking at once."

"Don't get upset with me, I'm trying to save you." Thomas made a grab for Susan, but she pushed him away. He sat back hard on the ground, but quickly recovered and shined the flashlight on her legs. "Are you hurt? Can you move? Once I get you to safety, I'll go for help. The ranger should still be nearby."

"Thomas, quit this craziness. I'm fine. The bear is no threat to us. We just need to find out what she wants."

The bear swung back around looking directly at Susan. :*Food place this be? A whole forest full of berries now could I eat:*

"There, see? She just needs something to eat. Use your flashlight and see if you can find that bag of granola we brought. I think it's in the storage bin attached to the picnic table."

"What? You're kidding?" Thomas backed up, inadvertently shining the flashlight on the table, as he stumbled into it. "You're not going to feed it granola are you? That would be really dangerous."

:*Dangerous? Granola dangerous food is? Prefer safe food:* berries. Fish good. Any fish?: The bear lumbered over toward the picnic table her nose sniffing the air.

Thomas crawled on top of the table and huddled there. The bear followed her nose to the end of the picnic table where there was a locked storage area. She pawed at the doors then tried twisting her claw around the latch. It was built specifically to prevent bears and raccoons from opening it, so all she managed to do was entangle her paw in the door.

Susan stood up and hobbled over to the picnic area, being careful of her bare foot and the numerous pinecones scattered over the campground. She glanced at Thomas, who was still on top of the table, arms wrapped around his legs, flashlight pointing upward, giving the picnic area a soft yellow glow. He didn't look like he'd do anything foolish so she continued toward the bear.

"Here, let me help you," she told her.

The flashlight swung down, focusing on the bear, as Thomas said, "Susan, I'm okay. It doesn't seem to be attacking me right now. Just go for the ranger. Don't go near the bear, it could kill you!"

Susan looked at Thomas and shook her head. "I wasn't talking to you!" Seeing the panic in his face, she relented slightly, laying a hand on his trembling leg. "It's okay. The bear hung out with me, with its huge toothy grin, for two months and never hurt me. I don't think she will now." She moved back over to the bear as Thomas tried to shrink into the tabletop. Susan reached out a hand, touching a soft ear. *:Are you BB?:*

*:That term not exact is:*

*:That's true, you don't sound like her. You're more formal. And you haven't made a joke yet:*

*:Joke, what purpose joke is?:*

*:No, you definitely aren't BB. But what did you mean by 'that term is not exact'?:*

*:BB spirit is. Now physical am I. When we both be spirits, we be connected. Then we be one. Now I am in your world. N-World you call it, yes?:*

Susan patted the bear's head. *:Yep, you seem to be fully in the N-World. You're similar to BB in that you both speak in riddles. Though I'm afraid you need an English lesson:*

*:Riddles these not be. As spirits, we are one in spirit world. All spirits one. As physical, I am more in physical world, less connection. I am not one with BB anymore:*

*:Please save the metaphysics lecture for later. Let me get you some granola:*

Susan reached back and nudged Thomas. "Can you shine your light over here? She's got her claw all tangled in the latch."

Thomas slowly got off the table and inched over toward the bear, shining his flashlight on both the bear and Susan. "That does look a lot like that bear head you've had at your place. But that was . . . I mean this is alive . . . it can't be the same."

Thomas reached out a hand toward Susan, who, hearing the restrained terror trying to pass as rational logic, squeezed his hand, pulling him closer.

"It's okay. This kind of weird stuff has happened to me before. If this was a wild bear it wouldn't have let me move its paw around so I could get it dislodged from the door. And see how politely she's waiting for me to open the granola bag?"

*:Granola, safe it is?:*

Thomas let out a long breath. "I, uh . . . guess you're right. But, I mean . . . this is still all impossible."

Susan ignored Thomas, turning back to the bear. "Yes, it's safe."

Thomas flinched, "I don't know that I'd go that far—calling a full grown grizzly safe. Especially one that came from a hundred-year-old head—if that's what really happened."

"Sorry, I meant the granola was safe. I keep forgetting and talking out loud." She patted Thomas's shoulder. "You can pretend you're dreaming if you want."

"Yeah, that's what this is. A really, really vivid dream." He turned and looked at her sharply. "And it's all your fault for making me sleep next to a bear head." Susan smiled and shrugged. Thomas took his other hand and touched Susan's face. "If this is a dream, then maybe you'll let me kiss you. I've been wanting to for months."

"Since I'm in this dream too, I'm going to tell you as gently as I can that I don't have feelings for you that way." She glanced down at the bear finishing the offering of oats and nuts. "You see I'm really a bear spirit in a human body and that's why I'm not attracted to human males." *That should keep him from trying anything with me again. And if he does, I can just remind him of the grizzly bear. And making him believe he's dreaming all this is easier than trying to explain it to him. Especially since I don't understand it yet.*

Thomas nodded slowly. "Okay, I guess that makes sense. So it's not that you don't like me it's . . ."

"Not at all, you're very nice. I just can't get involved with human males."

"I think I need to go lie down so I can try another dream." Thomas handed her his flashlight, then wandered off toward the tent, his limbs hanging loosely from his body as though he was sleep walking. "I can't wait for the morning so I can fully conclude that this was all a dream. Otherwise," he turned back and looked at Susan who was now feeding their apples to the bear, "this might sound crazy, but that bear head just got herself a body."

"That's okay my TMSC/Thomas. The universe does seem to be expanding in weird directions a bit enthusiastically right now."

Susan watched him crawl into the tent, then she turned to the grizzly bear serenely munching on their fruit. "Okay, so if you aren't BB, what should I call you?"

*:Name me as you wish:*

*:Okay, I'll call you GB for Grizzly Bear. Now how exactly did you change from a bear head to a full bear?:*

*:Head good way for humans move me in N-World. Now fully me I am. Say you did that being here okay it is. So all of me is here now:* GB bent and poked her nose into the storage area at the end of the picnic table. After several thumping and bumping sounds, the bear backed up with a box of macaroni held gently in her jaws. *:Good food this be?:*

*:Sure, help yourself:* Susan waved at the food while her mind tried to digest what the bear had told her. She watched as GB clamped her mouth closed, bursting the package open and scattering pasta all around her.

A mixture of tranquility and incredulity bubbled within her as she watched the bear carefully find and eat every piece. *This has got to be the weirdest camping trip I've ever been on. I can't believe I'm feeding a grizzly bear. No. What I can't believe is that there's a grizzly bear here at all.*

GB finished the food and looked at her expectantly. Susan shrugged. *:Sorry that's all the food I have:* The bear swung her head toward the woods beyond the campsite. *:Wait! Don't leave.*

*You have to explain how you came alive again:*

*:Always alive was I as spirit. Then invited me to be physical again you did. Good time to come alive again you told me:* GB rested her paw on Susan's leg. *:Thank you for opening the N-World so that fully physical I can be. Help others come too. Like this place I do. Food is good. Eating is good. Thank you for food:* GB removed her paw and waited, but Susan just gave her a blank look, slowly shaking her head, her hair swinging from side to side. GB hesitated another minute, then ambled off into the woods.

Susan swayed as she rose from the picnic table and started to follow the bear. She got halfway across the clearing then stopped. *What am I doing? I can't just wander off at night after a grizzly bear, even if she is friendly.* She looked at the opening GB had disappeared through. *Damn, why didn't I ask her more questions? I can't believe I just spaced out like that. What an opportunity I missed!*

After standing in the middle of the campsite for a few more minutes, she sighed and crawled into the tent. Thomas was softly snoring, wrapped tightly in his sleeping bag. *I don't need a bear head to protect me from anything he might try now. I bet sex is the last thing on his mind after having GB show up like that.* Susan snuggled into her sleeping bag, falling to sleep easily and dreaming of bears showing up as grocery store clerks, bank tellers, and furry waitresses.

The next morning they both kept busy taking down the tent and cleaning up. When Susan mentioned they didn't have any food left, Thomas didn't ask any questions, just agreed that it was a good idea to head back to Sacramento.

After she dropped Thomas off at his apartment, she dragged her stuff up to her place. The apartment felt empty and lifeless without the bear's presence, so she tried turning on the TV. The evening news was bursting with accounts of grizzly bear sightings throughout the state. Susan was relieved when the bill was mentioned, emphasizing the coincidental aspect of the recent proliferation of grizzly bears and the ban on harming them.

# Chapter 11

## *Bearly Physics*

Sonya left a message that she was being picked up early on Saturday and would leave the door unlocked so Miranda could get in.

Miranda let herself in, walked into the Blooms' living room, and ducked as a *Newsweek* magazine sailed across the room, almost hitting her.

Peter was sitting on the edge of his recliner, with magazines strewn across the floor. Several magazines were perched precariously on end tables and the back of the sofa.

"They're destroying our home sphere! What are these fools thinking? That God's going to open up the heavens for them and everything will be okay? Don't the imbeciles read their own Bible? God gets mad when they mess things up. He wouldn't let them into the Promised Land until they got it right. Maybe there is a God and he—or she," Peter nodded, acknowledging Miranda for the first time since she'd arrived, "is going to make sure all of us in the older generation who messed up the world are dead.

Make us wander in the wilderness for forty years so only our children will receive the new land. Only, I don't have any children, because some goddamn idiot decided to drink one night and God certainly wasn't there to prevent that."

Miranda glanced at Peter's end table, wondering if he'd had something to drink before she came over, but only Peter's familiar tea mug was perched on it.

"You sound really upset."

"Don't you start with those 'you sound' patronizing platitudes." Peter brandished an *EcoPolitics* magazine at her, before launching it across the room.

Miranda's gut clenched. *What am I doing wrong? He's been ranting about pollution and the destruction of the earth for the last three visits. I should've been able to get him to focus on his feelings of personal loss by now—not keep it so global. I'm not helping him.*

Her self-criticism reminded her of the hospice training she facilitated last week. A volunteer had asked: "How do we know if we're helping someone?" Her stomach relaxed as she remembered assuring the woman that the most important gift to offer a client is to be present and to listen. She sighed and started retrieving the scattered magazines: *Earth Politics*, *EcoReligion*, *Particle Physics*. She placed them back on his end table and righted a picture of Sonya that had gotten knocked over. The gold frame held a black and white photo of a young, dark-haired woman in a flowery dress with an impish smile.

Peter picked up the picture, staring at it briefly. Often he would hold it and tell Miranda the story of how he first won the heart of his fairy princess. But this time he put it down, continuing his lecture on the hopelessness of the world. Miranda nodded, concentrating on the pain and fear beneath the complaints, remembering that at the heart of his sermon was the uncertainty of his approaching death.

After twenty minutes, Peter lapsed into a heavy silence, so Miranda wandered into the kitchen to prepare tea for both of them. She reached for the familiar tea balls, preparing to fill them from the glass container of bulk tea.

As she twisted the first ball, it fell open in her hands, matching halves of what had just been a perfect sphere. Miranda stared at the two pieces, hearing Earthweb's words in her mind. :*Opening approaching. Healing soon. You, who will help must prepare:*

Her mind flew back to the waiting room at Future Pharmaceutical two weeks ago. Susan had successfully gotten an interview with one of their lawyers so that Miranda could have an excuse to go back and talk with the grandmothers. She drove Susan to her appointment, then found a chair in the corner of the waiting room where she crouched, head bent over a book she propped up on her lap. Staring at the pages without seeing them, she sent her spirit up the hill to try to converse with the grandmothers.

Gazing at the divided tea ball, her gut clenched and her shoulders shot toward her ears. *I still don't know what they want! I know they all firmly believe that an Earth-wide healing is approaching, but I wish they'd explained it to me better. What do they want me to do?*

Miranda clenched her hands together, the metal edges of the tea ball bruising her palms, as she remembered Earthweb telling her, :*You, who help, must be careful. Changes to make:* Her stomach spasmed as she remembered how hard she had tried to learn the specific details of the instructions. But every time Earthweb had started to explain to her the crucial role she was to play, her worries had dragged her away from the grandmothers and back to her body, sitting in the waiting room at Future Pharmaceutical. Now, all she had were broken messages and a stronger feeling of foreboding than before she went. *I'm going to mess this up. It's like they're expecting me to run a marathon when I'm missing my left foot and half my brain.*

She mentally shook herself and focused on filling the tea balls and heating the water. *The one clear, hopeful thing I did hear was: You, who will help, will be helped.* Miranda looked around the kitchen, wondering what form that aid would appear in, and wishing Sonya was there so that she could ask her advice.

While the kettle warmed, she put out a telepathic call for help. *:Adnarim! Are you here? I need help:*

A tall black woman, wrapped in a green cloak materialized, hovering near the stove. *:Yes. The water will naturally boil if you can attend long enough:*

Miranda tensed her shoulders, holding back her frustration, as she tried to form her thoughts clearly. *:I don't need your help with the tea! I need help understanding what the grandmothers were telling me. Can you help me with that?:*

*:Yes:*

Miranda waited, working hard not to look too closely at Adnarim, so that she wouldn't disappear. It seemed to her that since Adnarim was the spirit-essence part of her that did not enter the N-World when she was born, she should have an easier time conversing with her.

The teakettle began whistling and Miranda pulled it off the stove, filling the two mugs, then setting it back on a different burner. *:Well, are you going to help me? I don't understand what Earthweb told me:*

*:Yes. No:*

*:Yes, what? No, what?:* Miranda's teeth hurt as she clenched them together.

*:Yes—I will help you. No—you do not understand:*

*:Okay, fine. Then help me. What's Earthweb expecting me to do and why do I have to be so careful choosing?:*

*:The grandmothers are expecting you to help when the opening occurs in the cave. Nothing is set, all is flowing naturally. You must pay attention so that you can choose where your gath will progress when the time comes:*

*:Are you saying there will be an opening? A dividing? And I need to choose where I'll end up?:*

*:Yes. No. All will be original. Yes:*

"Miranda, Sonya left us some cookies." Peter's voice carried in from the living room, startling her. "They should be on the counter there. And there are plates in the cabinet by the refrigerator."

Miranda swung around, spying a package of lemon shortbread cookies. She headed over to them, then twisted back searching for Adnarim.

*Damn. And I was finally getting some useful information from her.* Picking up the package and tearing off the plastic wrapping, she noticed the hot water in the mugs was now a golden amber. She slowly lifted the tea balls out, watching the drips create ripples in the cups.

Miranda considered dumping the tea leaves on the counter, hoping to find some clarity and wisdom in them. But figuring she'd just end up with a physical mess to match her mental confusion, she opened the tea balls over the compost bucket and let them start their transformational journey back to dirt and maybe into a tea plant again. She placed the cups on a tray, added a plate of the shortbread cookies, and headed back to the living room.

"Well, what do you think?" Peter demanded as she placed a mug of Earl Gray beside him.

Miranda pulled her attention back to his anguished ramblings. "About what specifically? You've covered a lot of topics: from physics to religion, to politics and back again."

"About how we've messed up the world and no one seems to notice or care. I won't have to watch. My atoms will soon be re-scattering themselves into the universe, but you're young enough to have to live through the end of humankind."

"I don't know." Miranda seated herself in Sonya's recliner, pulling the blue-and-gold shawl over her legs a moment before Doogie jumped onto her lap. "I still have hope that something might happen to facilitate a healing. That somehow humans can return to the web of all life and live in balance with all other beings on this planet." Miranda saw an image of the Northern Grandmother and heard her saying again how a healing time is approaching.

"Impossible. You read my article; it's too late now."

Miranda desperately wished she had been able to absorb more of Earthweb's revelation, to understand why the grandmothers were so certain that humans could still heal their relationship with the earth. She wanted more assurance, not just for Peter, but for herself. She squirmed in her chair, a small place inside her silently agreed with the grandmothers, but her mind was clogged with lists of impossible problems.

She was distracted by images of floating islands of plastic, clogged freeways, and an acute awareness of each piece of trash she created, including the wrapper for their cookies, for which she had found no way to recycle or reuse.

As she tried to find a response to Peter's statement, an old saying bobbed about in her brain. She grabbed at it, uncertain where it came from, or even its full significance. "What if the healing comes through another source? I've heard that you can't solve a problem using the same tools that created the problem."

He begrudgingly gave her a half-smile "What are you trying to do? Quote Einstein to a physicist?" He wagged a finger at her. "Now don't try to propose any mystical madness about how if we think right we can alter biochemical laws to undo humanity's damage."

Miranda concentrated on stroking Doogie, whose tail beat enthusiastically against the armrest. "I have heard of some things that seem . . . well, beyond normal experiences or expectations."

"Now you're starting to sound like Sonya. I don't believe in all that fanciful nonsense she writes about." Peter grinned at Miranda. "You'd better not tell her I said that." Then he looked at her seriously. "If you could present me with some solid facts, I wouldn't mind believing it's possible to miraculously clean up the world, but if you can't, I can't digest this blind faith business."

BB walked through the wall, balancing on her hind legs, one paw holding a white cane, which she tapped on the floor in front of her, the other paw covering her eyes. Doogie sat up and started whining. Miranda petted him as he swiveled back and forth: first looking at her, then at BB, then back at her. "I think of faith, not as believing *in* something, as much as being open to whatever shows up." BB dropped the cane, placed her paws together high over her head, prayer fashion, then fell to her knees on the rug. "Though whatever shows up might seem a little strange and not relevant at the time." Miranda nodded at BB. "Still there might be some message in it. And if you want solid, extraordinary facts, how about all those extinct grizzly bears showing up in California?"

Peter waved his hand toward the center of the room, unknowingly including the spirit bear in his dismissive gesture. "I heard they solved that mystery. Someone had been illegally raising them on a ranch and then released them all at once throughout the state."

"That's what they say, but they haven't found the person, nor the place, nor how the bears could have been transported. And I haven't heard an explanation of how this theoretical person obtained California grizzlies to breed in the first place since there were none before last month."

Peter shrugged, "I'm sure there's a logical explanation, they just need to find it."

Miranda sighed, keeping her rejoinder to herself. *And if they can't find a rational rationale, they will probably just create one. Something that sounds plausible enough to believe in, for all the people who don't want to consider the alternative of anything mystical occurring.*

She continued petting Doogie, whose agitation continued to increase, until he bounced off Miranda's lap and began circling the spot on the floor where BB was now sprawled in an imitation of a bear rug.

Peter squinted at his dog, then frowned and patted his lap.

"What's got into you, boy? Come here Doogie, come on boy." The poodle ignored him as he sniffed BB's foot. "Stupid dog. At least he'll be good company for Sonya when I'm gone." He turned back to Miranda and took a swallow of tea. "We were talking about faith. If you want to equate faith with being open, don't forget what they say: 'Be careful your mind isn't so open your brains fall out.'" He nodded in satisfaction as though he had just explained the Heisenberg uncertainty principle to a group of college freshman. "It's important to have a rational foundation for your beliefs. That's why I'm an atheist. I've never seen any proof for the existence of God and I'm not going to take on faith something as important as someone controlling *my* life."

BB rose from the floor as though there were strings attached to her legs and began walking zombie-like around the room. Miranda covered a laugh by pretending to sip her tea.

"I'd think that would make you an agnostic. Saying you're an atheist and that there is definitely no guiding force in the universe seems just as extreme as a person having full faith in God. After all, there's never been any proof that there absolutely is no collective energy that could be called God."

"Agnostic or atheist, you won't find me turning to any religion. And no religion would have me." Peter crossed his arms over his chest, daring Miranda to challenge his statement.

Miranda pulled one of Sonya's books, *Listening to Your Wisdom Voice,* from the bookcase next to her, nonchalantly turning it over in her hands.

"You could be a part of Chris's and my religion. There are plenty of agnostics and atheists who are Unitarian Universalists."

Peter raised his hand in protest, but Miranda hurried on. "People often confuse religion with a set of beliefs or answers to the fundamental questions of life. But religion is really about asking the questions: Who am I, how should I live my life, and what will happen after I die? If you go back to the origins of any religion, it starts with an exploration of those questions. Look at Christianity. It began with Jesus questioning the dogmas and traditions of his Jewish heritage. He was asking 'How should I live?' and wondering if there were a more pure path to universal love, peace, and connecting with the divine."

"Yeah, and it turned into the largest bureaucracy of the modern world!" Peter raised up in his chair, preparing to launch into another of his diatribes on the illogic of religion, when he turned to Miranda, his eyes displaying a mixture of confusion and pleading. "Wait, what were you saying about a religion that has atheists in it? Isn't that a contradiction?"

"Not if you focus on religion as exploring the fundamental questions of existence. It's just that most religions try to give answers. Unitarian Universalism encourages people to hang out in the unknown and explore. It acknowledges the universal nature of all faiths. Try thinking of all the different religions as spokes of a wheel, each taking different paths into the center. Universalism would be at the hub, recognizing and valuing every path, yet not requiring adherence to any set of creeds or dogmas.

People who are UU may consider themselves atheists, agnostics, Christians, Buddhists, Pagans, Muslims, or humanists, however their personal beliefs speak to them, but it's the Universalism at the center that holds us all together."

"So you can believe anything and do anything in this faith of yours?"

"There are agreed-upon principles."

"Aha!" Peter raised a fist triumphantly. "So this . . . What did you call it? . . . Utilitarian Universal religion of yours does have a dogma you have to blindly believe in."

Miranda smiled. "It's Unitarian, though I guess its practical nature and inclusion of human reason does make it a utilitarian religion. But it's easier to remember the name if you just focus on Universalism, since that's really the heart of the faith. Concerning our principles, if you want to call belief in the inherent worth and dignity of all people, respect for our connection to the earth, search for inner truth, and pursuit of justice and equality in the world dogmas, then you can. But I see them as guiding principles, helping me to know how to live in the world."

Peter was chewing on his lower lip and appeared to be battling within himself.

BB slowly nodded her head at Peter, then curled up in the center of the floor. Doogie finally quieted down and sat attentively beside BB.

Miranda followed their cue and waited silently while emotions flashed across Peter's face. Tears started to form in the corners of his eyes, then his face flushed with anger and he started to move forward to speak, but he pushed himself back in his chair, his hands and jaw clenched in anxiety.

Emotions continued to cycle through him, as his personal struggle was displayed on his face and body. Miranda began to feel uncomfortable with the intimate nature of the quietness, as though his deepest feelings were being projected unconsciously for her to see.

After a few more minutes, she stood up, retrieved their mugs, and went to get more tea, rationalizing that she was giving him space to digest all that she had shared.

When she returned Peter seemed calmer, but was leaning
forward in his chair. He nodded his thanks for the tea and
waited for Miranda to settle back in Sonya's chair. "So what
does Universalism say happens after you die?"

Miranda smiled and felt her heart opening in response to
Peter's courage in asking the question. "As a religion, we don't
have *the* answer about death. What we offer is a supportive
environment to search for understanding and wisdom, yourself."

"And what exactly does that mean?"

"Hanging out in the unknown can be hard, especially when
you try to do it alone. The extremes can have the illusion of
being easy, because they seem to have absolute answers: God
will be there when you die, or there is no God and no afterlife.
But life and death has a way of being more complex than
simple answers can account for. By proclaiming that you're
an atheist, you don't give yourself much room to explore the
question of death as you approach the end of your life. I know
you don't want to explore it with someone who will try to
persuade you there is absolutely an afterlife and that you need
to believe in a certain type of God to get there."

Peter nodded vigorously and said, "Even with Sonya as
sweet as she is and as close as we are, I can't share my fears or
feelings with her. She doesn't believe in God the way most
people do, but she's absolutely certain there is something
mystical holding the universe together, and she just doesn't
understand my dilemma."

Miranda smiled to lighten her words. "Do you think that
might be because you try to pretend you don't have any
dilemmas, any doubts?"

"Okay, you got me there." Peter looked at Miranda, his face
the most open and vulnerable she'd seen since they began
visiting four months ago.

Miranda reached over and held his hand. "When I talk
about faith, it's not that you have to believe in something,
only that you're open to possibilities. Like the possibility
that maybe after you die, your atoms might hang out in
another form, that death is really a great transformation, not
an end."

"I guess as a good scientist I have to explore all options, including that hypothesis. You're right, I can't absolutely prove death will be the end of me, any more than I can prove there is no God. "

BB sent a halo, spinning like a Frisbee, across the room to float over Peter's head. When Miranda turned to look at her, she was holding a feather duster in her paw, intently cleaning a small Earth that was spinning a few feet off the floor. It reminded Miranda of the start of her conversation with Peter. She tried to piece together all the topics they'd covered so that she could return to where they started. "If you can contemplate the possibility that your atoms might transform after you die, into something you can't currently conceive of, then maybe there's a chance that the atoms in pollution can be changed also."

Miranda allowed a silence to float in the room as BB reached down and shooed Doogie toward Peter, who bent down and pulled the dog onto his lap. Peter started stroking Doogie then looked toward Miranda. "If there can be a religion with no creeds, maybe there could be a world with no pollution. Are you suggesting a way it could happen?"

"I'm not sure myself . . ." Miranda thought back to the disjointed bits of wisdom she had been able to snatch from Earthweb's explanation and Adnarim's brief, enigmatic comments. "I think it must be totally original, something we've never experienced before—an opening of some kind. Maybe we'll be able to go beyond chemistry."

Tilting his head to one side, Peter stared at her, eyes slanting across his pale wrinkled cheeks. "Beyond chemistry?" he echoed.

"You're always saying it's all the chemicals we've added and altered in the world that are causing the irreversible damage. But what if there can be a healing in the physical world that isn't a chemical solution, but something else?" Miranda glanced back at BB. The earth was now a ball of light that BB was staring at intently. BB flicked a paw at the light and it turned into a wave of light oscillating around the room.

Memories of high school physics appeared in her mind. "Maybe we need to manipulate light."

Peter leaned forward, pushing himself halfway out of his chair. "Wait, what're you—"

"No, you wait," Miranda interrupted, more forcefully then she had intended, but BB was distracting her. Sitting in the middle of the floor, the bear was waving her paws, making the sphere of light, now the size of a golf ball, change into a stream of light, which danced circles around her. She flipped her paws, turning it back into a ball, then again into the stream, the ball, the stream, gaining speed with each change. The alternating rhythm reminded Miranda of Earthweb's demonstration of how to move energy within the deep cavernous sphere. Earthweb had waved her arms making a stream of energy sweep back and forth across the cave. It had grown, gaining force and size with each passing. It had begun to separate the cave along the line Waterweb had pointed out to her when she had first entered the cave. Earthweb, her voice resonating with the rocks surrounding them had proclaimed, "You, who will move. Worlds part. Original. You, who will allow opening" Miranda scolded herself again for having allowed her anxiety to escalate to the point that she'd lost contact with the grandmothers, and lost valuable information.

"Well?" Peter was scrunching his forehead in concern as Miranda's head swung back and forth watching BB's performance.

"Shhh . . . hang on. I think I'm getting it."

"Getting what? A neck ache? What're you watching? I don't see anything." Doogie started whining, then jumped off Peter's lap and began racing around trying to grab the ball of light that was dancing in the middle of the room. When Doogie came close to catching the light, BB would wave a claw at it, turning the ball into a stream of light and making it chase Doogie, dipping down, passing through the dog's tail, causing him to yelp and run faster. After a few circles, BB would point a claw and the light would become a ball again hanging in the air, and Doogie would swivel around trying to grab it. Then the chase would begin again.

Miranda perched on the edge of her recliner, peering intently at BB's antics. She clenched her hands, nails digging into her palms until the pain brought her back to the discussion with Peter, who she noticed was looking at her with a concerned, puzzled look. She stared at him for a moment, then the fact he was a physicist exploded in her mind and she let her words tumble out. "You can help me figure this out. What is it about light that allows it to change between a particle and a wave, depending on the observer?"

Peter raised his eyebrows. "That's not quite how it works. You're making it sound as though the observer affects the substance of the light. Light appears as particles, photons, and it also moves as a wave. There appears to be a dual nature to light that we haven't fully analyzed."

"What if it isn't a dual nature?" BB dropped her arms, the light disappearing entirely, as she stared at Miranda, ears pointed straight up, eyes wide, which Miranda took for a positive sign. "What if it's always both?" BB lifted her paws, shaking her head, looking first at one paw and then the other. Miranda chewed on her lip, trying harder. "No, wait. Not both. That still implies a dual nature. What if it's all about the interconnectedness? Don't you physicists have something called the butterfly effect? Where the flapping of a butterfly's wings in Brazil affects the weather in Texas?"

"That's not exactly what . . ."

". . . but the point is that physics is beginning to show how factors we never fully took into consideration before may actually be having a major effect in the world. Maybe relationships are actually the dominant determinates in the world. Maybe we've been focusing on objects too much. What if it's the space between objects, like between light and the observer, where we could find the answers to our needs right now?" Miranda felt an excitement climbing up her body. "What if somehow we put ourselves into the equation? What if light does change from a wave to a particle because of the way the observer relates to it? We know the world through relationships, but we don't usually understand or acknowledge them."

Peter raised his hand, leaning forward, but not saying anything in words. Miranda glanced at him, then continued, following what she assumed was BB's suggestion, since the bear was now lying on her back on the floor, eyes closed, holding a lily in her paws. "What is it you really want to continue after your death? Is it your books and accomplishments? Or is it the relationship people will have to them? Is it the objects themselves? Or is it the experience you had creating those objects that is important? If there was a monument built to you and your achievements that would exist after your death, would it have meaning if no one ever saw it?"

Peter sighed, sinking back into his chair. "That makes me think of Sam."

Miranda felt tears dampen her eyes. Whenever they talked about death, it always seemed to weave its way back to Sam, and the tremendous loss Peter experienced when his son was killed. She reached out, touching his arm and silently encouraging him to continue sharing.

"What I really miss about him is all the potential wasted. He never got to have kids to raise, never got to travel the world. When I received that life achievement award from the University at my retirement, I didn't miss him seeing how successful his Dad was, but that we couldn't share that moment together. I've hung onto his baseball cap all these years, not because that ratty old thing is worth anything, but it reminds me of throwing him the ball all those sunny Sunday afternoons when he was young. I bought him the cap so he couldn't complain that the sun got in his eyes. But he would anyway. Every time he missed a throw, it was always the sun's fault. It got so anytime one of us made a mistake, from baseball, to breaking a dish, to busting a window, we'd just say 'sun's up' and laugh."

"That's what I mean. Science isn't taking love into account. We're looking at how to chemically clean up the pollution. But what if we factor in love?"

Peter continued to stare at the old baseball cap perched on the top of the bookcase, while asking, "How would you do that?"

"Maybe love is too general. Caring might be better." BB rolled over, placing the lily into the carpet where it became a bouquet of lilies. As she sniffed each one it grew bigger and brighter. Miranda remembered an article Chris had shown her when they'd set up their house together and brought in some greenery. "Weren't there studies that showed the more people cared for plants, talked to them, paid attention to them—beyond watering and sunlight—that those plants did better than the control studies where no one gave them attention?"

"Yes, those were very reputable studies. Some of my students were involved in ones that showed a similar effect on humans. They had groups of people pray or hold positive thoughts for people who were having surgery. The group who received the thoughts recovered faster than the control group."

"So maybe there is an untapped power we can use for healing the earth? The power of caring."

Peter shook his head. "People have been caring for a long time and it hasn't stopped the degradation of the earth."

Miranda smiled as she watched BB swatting at tiny clear bubbles, each holding miniature scenes of nuclear power plants, landfills, smokestacks, whaleboats, and other examples of Earth-harming human practices. They were swarming around her like a cloud of mosquitoes, and for each one that BB hit, ten more appeared until she was covered by a bubbly foam of gray images.

"Yes," Miranda agreed, "we have been caring, but not enough of us. And there are too many separate issues. We take care of one species and ten more go on the endangered list. We try to stop one strip mine and twenty more are built. We need to be more . . . more . . ." Miranda paused as she watched BB brush off all the sticky images, roll them into a ball, blow on it, then hold it up as it became a perfect blue-green sphere of Earth floating in the living room. Miranda nodded as she finished her thought. ". . . more connected. We need to pull all our caring efforts together—a world-wide healing."

"And you think we can save the planet just by caring about it?"

Miranda was half in the cave with Earthweb, piecing together fragments of her instructions and half in the room with Peter. "That and maybe a bit more. Maybe some of us will have to nudge the change, guide it a bit to help it occur."

"What do you mean? What are you getting at?"

Miranda was again seeing Earthweb moving her hands together and apart, apart and together.

Peter's voice came through anxious and concerned. "Miranda, what's going on? You seem to be off in another world."

"That's it!" Miranda turned her full attention to Peter. "Another world. Don't you have theories in physics about parallel universes? Ones that are similar to this one?"

"The Multiverse hypotheses. Yes, there are many theories by different scientists, though it gets totally distorted by the media into science fiction and fantasy. I personally find the idea intriguing. I think it is more plausible that they do exist than that this world exists uniquely, unaccompanied by any other dimensional worlds."

"How are they created?"

"The theories really just talk about them existing. I think the idea is that they have always existed."

"But how are new ones born?"

Peter was peering at Miranda, lips scrunched together. He looked as though he was trying to follow her into a realm that he desperately wanted to enter, but wasn't sure there was a visible door for him to walk through. "Are you suggesting that maybe as we die we enter another parallel universe?"

Images of Don's cremation flashed through Miranda's mind, as she again felt the energy transference, as the body Don had used was transformed in the furnace.

"No, I'm thinking about the whole world and how new ones are born and how they die. We know this planet on one level is dying; we humans are killing one form of it, but what if that's what's needed for another world to be born? Maybe humans need to exist in parallel universes because our lives are so much about choices and different paths. That's how we're different than animals. They have a one-path life. They don't change their careers, or go back to school to become something else.

They might decide on a mate, but then they don't have divorces and all. But humans have so many choices with their focus on free will. Only namens don't have that. They follow their path. Or at least try to. So maybe it's that most humans don't follow a path, but make choices as if their decisions affect only themselves . . ." Miranda's words trailed off as her thoughts became a logjam, preventing any coherent concept from coming out of her mouth.

Peter leaned forward peering at her, a mixture of confusion and curiosity displayed on his face. "I think I'm following you there. About the difference between humans and animals, but what's a namen? I don't recognize that word."

"Chris came up with that word: it means a human who is intimately tied in with nature. *Natural human*. They follow their gaths, which means 'guided on one's path'. So instead of making decisions based on power, money, prestige, or fear, they gath their way through life by staying focused on where it is most right for them to be at that moment as it relates to the great tapestry of the whole world. Gathing is a sense of doing and being what you're supposed to do and be, from an internal sense of rightness, not from external expectations."

"Gath. I like that. Namen too. Words help me in understanding the new concepts you're proposing. We're evolving faster than our language." He sat back, staring at the ceiling for a minute. "I think I'm beginning to *aware* it."

"What?"

"*Awaring*. How about making *aware* a verb? Then gathing means awaring what you're supposed to do." Peter smiled and sat up straighter, as though he was addressing a class of students. "We need a new word for *supposed to*, because that implies doing things through guilt, and gathing isn't about guilt, right?"

Miranda smiled back, pleased Peter was joining her in creating new concepts. "Yeah, no way is gathing about *guilt-supposed-to-ing*. Gath is a way of being in synch with the natural world around us."

"Then how about calling it 'following your *be-ness*'? Then it can be a pun on business. Only the business of *be-ness* is to increase your connection to the natural world, not your material possessions."

"I like that. There're a lot of words that could be larger and more inclusive with a *ness* after it. And more concepts need to be verbs rather than objects. I bet you would be more comfortable with spirit or soul if they were verbs." She glanced at BB who was now holding a sign between her paws proclaiming: "Miranda-ness" with a happy face next to it. Miranda turned back to Peter. "So how does your Peter-ness feel now?"

"Better." He bobbed his head at her. "I like the idea of exploring what my Peter-ness will do after my body-ness ends."

Miranda stood up and picked up the teacups. "Good, I'll look forward to awaring with you again next week."

# Chapter 12

## *Sacrifices*

Miranda hugged Peter goodbye, then leaving him securely seated in his recliner, let herself out the front door. Striding down the Blooms' walkway, she flipped her phone open. Her contact screen kept flipping sideways when she tried to hit Susan's picture, so she gave up and started punching in the numbers: the tapping synchronizing with her rapid footfalls. Instead of heading for her car, she took a left at the street, as her phone impatiently rapped on Susan's electronic door.

"Hello?" A sleepy response finally drifted through the airways.

"Did I wake you? It's after two o'clock in the afternoon."

"I'm just doing my student impersonation. You know, staying up until four a.m., then sleeping through the day. Don't want to forget all those useful skills I learned at Berkeley."

"I think it's because you piled that queen-size waterbed of yours full of fluffy pillows and comforters and now you never want to leave it."

"I'm sure you didn't call just to comment on my sleeping arrangements, so what's the massive missive you have for me?"

Miranda veered around a corner, her excitement propelling her down the sidewalk and through the neighborhood. "I think I know why the grandmothers are always saying 'you, who.'"

"Yoo-hoo?"

"No. You who."

"Isn't that what I said? Yoo-hoo. Who-you? You-you, who-who."

"They aren't owls! It's you . . . who. As in 'you, who are the one to help the world divide.'"

"Whoa, send me a boat. I am not on your island."

"Okay. I was just talking with Peter about parallel worlds. I realized it's all about the extreme differences we are experiencing right now. This world is split. People are on opposing sides: some loving trees, others destroying them; some working for peace, others staging wars. Not only is the world divided, but some people are creating a wider gap between the haves and have-nots. The separation between groups of people is getting so huge it's time for the world to split and a new parallel world to be born."

"Parallel whats? Splitting where? Dividing Worlds? What are you jabbering about?" Susan's voice came through confused and jumbled.

"Earthweb was talking about the opening coming. I think she means that I need to help create an opening between the worlds so that they can divide. That's what the line in the cavern must be for."

Susan's tone was now louder and more insistent. "I don't understand. What are you saying? And what's that noise?"

"I was just passing a guy with one of those idiotic leaf blowers! You know, the kind that screeches enough to annoy rocks and then all it does is move leaves from one place to another so that the wind can naturally re-scatter them again. Is this better now?"

"Yeah. So are you saying that Earthweb wants you to help separate the world?"

"The world is already so divided; all it needs is a little push.

The grandmothers were reassuring me that the task wasn't hard. I just need to be clear which side I end up on. I sure don't want to end up on the wrong one."

"That's calling a mountain a molehill. Wait, let me see if I can envision this. We're going to have two different worlds? Will they get the same basic stuff as us?"

"I wouldn't think so. This is supposed to be about dividing. The grandmothers were talking about it all being a choice—including where I ended up. So I imagine there'd be the basic rocks and mountains in each world, then it would be populated according to who belongs where. Or who chooses to be where." Miranda came to a stop, as the street she was walking on dead-ended at an intersection. She paused, glancing left then right, considering which way to go.

Susan's voice came through loud and excited, "Hang out with me here, I just woke up to what you're saying. Are you really telling me that the earth is going to divide so that the people who want to destroy the earth will all end up on a different world and we'd be free of them?"

"That's the sense I'm getting."

"That'd be incredible! Without the consumerist cockroaches, we could work together to heal this world. Humans might even be able to stay on it. If those mysterious grandmothers are right, I might even have a chance to be a grandmother myself."

Both women paused, pondering a promising future. Then Susan's voice continued with a mischievous tone. "Maybe actual cockroaches could go with them to their world. And mosquitoes and flies. Do you think they'll take stuff like prejudice and shame too? And they should take all the autoimmune diseases their chemicals have caused and also they deserve . . ."

The phone blared static as Miranda crossed the street, heading for what appeared to be a path between two houses. She walked briskly along the narrow path, hoping the reception would clear once she was past the houses. She emerged into a patch of green, surrounded by backyard fences. It was a small park with clusters of trees, picnic tables and benches scattered through it.

An older couple sat on one of the benches feeding a flock of pigeons. She paused, releasing some of her hurried energy as she surveyed the peaceful area, then she headed toward a table as her phone emitted Susan's faint voice.

"Do you really think that it's possible?"

Miranda sat down on the table, looking up at a transplanted New England maple tree, its leaves beginning to lighten in the lengthening nights. *So if I actually help divide this world, will all the plants return to where they originally came from? And what about people?* Her heart jumped as she tried to consider all the infinite possibilities her idea was creating. She brought the phone closer to her mouth, speaking softly. "I don't know. I want to believe it. It feels right, but it's so . . . incredible." Miranda sat down on a picnic bench, wishing she could actually be with Susan and not have to rely on a machine to connect them. "Keep in mind, this is all coming through my very disjointed mystical meetings with them. Maybe I'm reading something into Earthweb's words because of some misguided egotistical need to feel special or important. I mean, why me? They seem to think I'm necessary for this dividing to happen. But I could be misunderstanding it all."

"Don't start that again! If you start questioning yourself we're going to get nowhere."

"But I have to analyze it now, and you're the only one I can discuss it with. Chris just gets nervous that I'm going to do something dangerous, so I try not to say anything about the grandmothers at home. And when I'm with them at the top of the hill or in the cavern it's hard to question what they're saying because in some ways it just feels right."

Susan sighed, "Isn't that what you told me was a good indication that something is right? That it feels right? When I'm with Angel it feels like such a special event – everything just makes sense."

"I know, that's the hard part. When I'm there listening to the grandmothers, there is a sense of being held and connected to the whole, so that one piece of me stops questioning."

"Until you come back."

"Well, yeah."

Susan's voice was firm. "You can't play games with me. You taught me. If you're having a special connection, an Event with a mystical spirit, the best guide is how you feel in your gut, not what your mind says later. When an Event happens, listen! An Event happening is an . . . an *Evappening* and you have to follow it."

"What are you talking about? Did you just create another Susan-ism?"

"Yeah. Evappening. It means the feeling you get when an Event is happening. You know, that sense when things feel right, even if you can't rationally substantiate it afterwards."

"Still, why did they choose me? Sonya was at that meeting and she's the one who wrote all the books on spirits."

"Don't go merry-go-rounding again. We've been through that. Besides you believe in gathing, right?"

"Of course."

"Then just focus on it being your gath, and that's the reason they're talking to you. Sonya has her own gath to follow. Isn't that what you taught me is the difference between following one's own gath and admiring what someone else is doing and thinking you have to be the same as them—when in reality everyone is a unique person with a unique gath."

"Yes, but, how do I know it's really my gath and not my ego wanting it to be my gath?" The phone was silent. Miranda imaged Susan shaking her head and rolling her eyes. She was probably still in bed, propped up on all those pillows like a queen in her bedchamber. "Susan, are you still there?"

Susan arched her back against the pillows, switching the cell phone to her other ear as she tried to get the sleep kinks out of her neck. "Yeah, I'm here. Are you going to listen to what you taught me or not? Are you feeling pulled to do it? Or are you focusing on some kind of personal gain from doing it?"

Miranda's sigh came through the phone loudly. "Okay, you got me, teacher. Using my own questions against me. It's a pull. I'd avoid it if I could, but I can't, so it's my gath." There was a pause, then Miranda continued. "But are you just trying to convince me of this because you want to believe the worlds will divide and all the problem people will go off onto a different one and leave us alone here?"

"Alone to clean up their mess, don't forget. It won't be easy. But yeah, I do want to believe it. And it feels right to me. I'm always thinking that so many people feel like they're from another world, starting with my family." Susan glanced at her wall where a small picture displayed a seemingly perfect family of two parents and five adult children, all nicely smiling for the camera.

Miranda's voice softened. "Wouldn't it be nice if it did happen? Then those neighbors of Peter and Sonya's would be gone and no one would be hurt by their self-centeredness again. Hang on, I'm heading back to the car, and I might go through a dead zone again."

Susan turned over in bed, flopping onto her side. Her voice lightened as her humor woke up. "I like the sound of all this. Get rid of those evil neighbors. And maybe poison ivy, sand spurs, and bedbugs will all go with them to the other world – and ticks and tarantulas too. And they'd better take all their toxic dumps with them, 'specially the nuclear ones. They can have all the smelly stockyards too; we'll take the free-ranging, happy cows. Or do you think we'll all be vegetarians in this new world?"

"That would make Chris happy, as long as I make it to this new world. We had another 'discussion' about my doing anything dangerous. But Chris knows I have to follow my gath. I can't be holding back when the time comes, trying to play it safe. I have to be willing to give everything I can for it."

"What are you talking about?" Miranda's answer was overrun by street noise. Susan waited until the noise died down before pressing the phone close to her mouth and asking, "Shouldn't it be easy to choose? It's not like we have anything in common with the ones who believe killing people who kill people will stop people from killing. Or the ones who believe it's okay in the pursuit of life, liberty, and money to sell harmful products to kids. It can't be that hard to make the right decision."

Susan glanced over at the thermostat control on the far wall, then down at the cold wood floor and settled on pulling the comforter over her head, shifting deeper into the pillows.

Miranda's voice came through muffled. "It's not going to be easy for me to tell the difference between the two sides inside that rock-like tomb. From in there it all looks the same. That must be what Earthweb was warning me about when she said, 'Choose well. No return.' There must be a possibility that I could end up in the wrong world. But it would be worth the risk to divide the worlds, and be able to save our side—even if I weren't able to live on it."

"No way! We gotta straighten this out. You're not going to do something that dangerous. Hang on, I gotta sit up and think this out."

Susan struggled to sit upright in her waterbed, but only succeeded in thrashing about in her pile of pillows, comforters, and sheets. She reached for the edge of the bed, trying to leverage herself up, but instead of wood, her hand connected with a soft furry ear. She hesitated as she realized she'd just grabbed a piece of the large wolf head she'd left balanced on the edge of her bed before going to sleep. Her fingers started to slip off the sleek hairs so she swung her other hand around, losing the phone, but connecting with the other ear. She began to emerge from the bedding, until she pulled the animal head off the edge and it crashed on top of her, driving her deeper into the sloshing bed. She could hear a muffled, "Susan?" echoing urgently from under the covers.

Swearing, she scrunched into the corner of her bed, pushing aside the furry head, and digging out the phone. "I'm here, sorry. I was just struggling with a new 'friend' I inherited."

"New friend? What are you talking about?"

"Never mind." Susan stared down at the wolf's head tipped sideways in her bed, mouth open, showing yellow teeth against the black muzzle. She poked at the reason she had been up late the night before, wishing she could switch the conversation to her proclivity for attracting extinct animal heads, but she was too concerned about Miranda and what the grandmothers were asking her to do.

Susan closed her eyes, so she wouldn't have to see the black, glowing glass eyes staring at her from the wolf's head.

"We have to figure out a way that you can be sure to tell the difference between the worlds, so you end up in the right one. I don't want to lose you to a world that would rather rip you apart than respect your wisdom."

"The good of the many would outweigh the good of the few, or the one."

"Don't go Spock on me! After he sacrificed himself to save the ship, Star Trek was able to make another movie and have him come back to life. How am I supposed to write a script the universe will follow?" Susan swung her legs over the side of the bed, toes jumping at the touch of the cool wood beneath her feet.

Pushing her knees together, she gritted her teeth, "Miranda, can I call you back? I gotta go to the bathroom bad. I'll just be a minute."

"Oh, that's right, I woke you up. I'm almost at my car right now. Why don't you take your time and give me a call in half an hour?"

"Okay, bye." Susan rushed to the bathroom, pulling a robe around herself as she sat on the toilet.

Relief flooded through her body, which then released a torrent of tears. She sobbed, imagining Miranda stuck in a world filled with eco-hating tree-murderers, separated from her guides and her friends, tortured by a mob who misunderstood her, dying alone in misery.

Susan felt Angel trying to contact her and comfort her but she pushed him away. "You guides demand too much! It's not fair!"

Part of Susan wondered if she was referring to Miranda, or to herself and her new task, given to her by the same mysterious man in the beaded jacket and cowboy hat.

She glanced at her bed, seeing a gray furry ear sticking up from the middle of her comforters and pillows. She should have known when Thomas insisted that she go to the craft fair with him that something crazy would happen. He'd gone to check on food while she walked down the rows of ceramics, silken flowers, and painted jewelry.

She spied a carved, wooden wolf's head amidst the clutter of a very eclectic booth, so she stopped and picked it up. It felt more like silk than wood as she turned it over and over in her hand, admiring the realistic craftsmanship.

She looked up, wanting to ask the price from the vendor. Her stomach plunged into a deep well as she realized she was staring into the eyes of the same man who had given her the bear head three months ago.

Before she could move, he slipped around the booth, grabbed her hand, dragging her back to a familiar pickup truck. The fearful part of her wanted to run away, but her rational mind was in a daze as too many questions collided together, the primary one being: "Why does this man keep showing up in my life?"

He spoke in the same incomprehensible language as before. The only words she recognized were Colorado, south and Rocky Mountains, which was where she and Thomas were heading for a seminar in two weeks.

Now, sitting on the toilet, she had a sinking feeling she was inexplicably involved in returning the extinct Southern Rocky Mountains Wolf to Colorado.

Pushing her own dilemma away and refocusing on Miranda, Susan stood up, shuffled over to the mirror, and washed both sleep dust and tears from her eyes.

As she stared at the mirror, a sickening feeling beginning in her stomach started to overwhelm her.

"The grandmothers are setting it up so Miranda will have to sacrifice herself to help this world divide and heal." Susan told her horrified reflection. "They aren't telling her directly so she won't be able to back out. But that's what they're going to do. I just feel it!"

She hurried back to her bed, grabbed the phone, and dialed Miranda's number

"Hi, Susan, I'm driving right now and—"

"Miranda, you can't do it. The grandmothers have to find someone else."

"What are you talking about? I finally figured out what they want me to do."

"It's not fair. I don't want to lose you."

"Hang on, let me pull over and I'll call you back."

Susan paced her apartment, waiting for Miranda to call. She glared at the wolf's head every time she passed it.


Miranda turned into a residential street and parked by a house with kids playing ball in the front yard. She dialed Susan who answered immediately. "Ok, Susan, I found a place to park so I can talk again. What're you so upset about?"

The phone was silent, then Susan's voice came through in a hesitant whisper. "I . . . I just never thought . . . I mean, I knew you were important but I never considered you having to make the big S. I just don't know what I'll do without you. I know I—"

"What big S?"

"Sacrifice! What the grandmothers are asking of you. Just like Jesus had to sacrifice himself to save the world."

"Don't go comparing me to Jesus! Especially not in that way!"

"That's what the grandmothers were talking about when they kept referring to 'you, who are the one.' That's what the 'you, who' meant."

Miranda was pulled away from her conversation with Susan, back to the cave with the grandmothers. She heard Fireweb saying: "You, who are the one. You, who will make the way for the many."

"Miranda, are you okay? Say something. What's happening?"

Miranda's chest clenched as she remembered the rest of the conversation in the cave. She had trouble answering Susan's pleas for reassurance.

"Yeah, yeah. I'm okay. I just . . . I just was thinking of what one of the grandmothers said."

"What? What'd she say?"

"I'm sure it doesn't mean anything . . ."

"What? Tell me. What'd she say?"

"They asked me how committed I am. I just figured she was referring to how I get distracted by my anxieties, and jump back into the N-World and miss what they're saying. But now you're making me think of it differently."

"That's what I'm talking about. See, God asked that same commitment of Jesus."

"Will you quit comparing me to him!" Miranda clenched the phone, wanting to throw it out the car window. *Why can't you listen to me! I just figured out what I'm supposed to do and now you're turning it into a nightmare. Maybe Peter was right. Religion is totally irrational.*

Susan sounded on the verge of tears. "I don't want to lose you. Things are getting crazy. Grizzly bears returning, who knows what's next. I can't live in this world if you're not in it. You taught me to how to soar above all the N-World crap. If you go, I'll be plunged back into it."

Miranda held back her initial response. *You're supposed to be stronger than this. What happened to all you learned from Angel?* Out loud, she said: "Susan, you can do it on your own. Look at all you've accomplished. You're almost a lawyer now and already with political connections, not to mention the spiritual advisers you've learned to connect with. Look at how well you and Angel communicate now."

The phone was silent for a moment, then Susan's voice came through quieter. "I'm sorry. I don't mean to whine at you. Please promise me you'll bring it up with the grandmothers – find out what they're really expecting you to do. Or check with Adnarim. I'm sure she doesn't want you sacrificing yourself. She'll find some way out of it."

"I will, I promise. Now go back to bed and try waking up again and don't worry about sacrifices. That was back in ancient times. Human sacrifices aren't in vogue anymore. We're such a messed up species we're just not worth much as sacrifices. I'm sure the gods are back to preferring goats and oxen."

Susan attempted to laugh at Miranda's weak joke. "Just promise me you'll take care of yourself."

"I will Susan; don't worry so much." Miranda closed her phone, shutting off her conversation with Susan.

*I hope that makes her feel better, because I don't know how I'm going to stay present long enough with the grandmothers to figure out how to tell the difference between the two sides of that cavern.*

*I can't even figure out a way to get back to Future Pharmaceutical to talk with them again.*

Miranda sat in her car, not ready to head home yet. *What am I going to tell Chris about all this? I can't mention anything that even hints at my leaving the N-World. Damn Susan, why'd she have to bring up that sacrificing nonsense? That's all I need is for her to start worrying. On top of Chris's anxiety, work's going crazy, and Merawl is having trouble showing up again!*

An insistent voice in her head, one that had been quiescent for the last eight years, started sympathizing with her, encouraging her to take some time for herself. It reminded her how satisfying a cool drink of Stormer's beer would be right now, and pointed out how she was obviously beyond being an alcoholic since she'd had many drinks lately, with no bad effects.

Miranda started the car and headed for the closest grocery store. After she'd picked up a six pack of Stormer's, she headed for a local park that boasted some secluded picnic tables near a grove of pines. As she drank the beers in blessed silence, she stared at the ground, unaware of the tall, slender spirit that materialized behind her. She felt her mind growing numb.

The whole idea of sacrificing seemed amusing now and she promised herself she wouldn't share so much with Susan and Chris, since they kept getting so anxious about it.

*I can handle it myself. I feel better now than when I was confiding in Susan. I just need more time by myself.* She finished off the beers, then took a walk before carefully driving home.

# Chapter 13

## *Adnarim's Advice*

Miranda came home after the park to a solitary house. She stood outside by the mailbox, swaying slightly as she observed the clouds fluttering across the sapphire sky. They looked like maps of an ethereal realm, revealing shifting pathways that were navigated by ravens, who called urgently to each other across the expanse. The birds and clouds felt like her thoughts. Some flitted across her mind, cawing dramatically while others drifted slowly, dissipating when she tried to grasp them.

She opened the door, placed her bag on the sofa, dropped her jacket on the floor, and kicked her shoes towards the living room. Tasting beer in her mouth, she frowned and went to the bathroom to brush her teeth. When she returned, she dropped onto the couch with a box of crackers and a glass of water.

Struggling to force her thoughts into a coherent telepathic message, she tried to send an appeal for Adnarim to visit. But it was like trying to guide a gaggle of balloons in a wind storm. Stray worries kept flying free and distracting her.

Finally, she settled on just concentrating on Adnarim's name, hoping she would show up so that she could share all her concerns with her guide. Eventually she was rewarded with an olive-skinned, red haired woman in a peach shawl who appeared next to her. Miranda closed her eyes to dismiss the temptation to stare at Adnarim's provocative appearance.

She tried to prioritize her anxieties, afraid Adnarim would disappear before she could fully articulate her dilemma about what the grandmothers were asking her to do. Speaking out loud, she asked, "Is Susan right that I'm going to have to sacrifice myself to help the worlds divide?"

*:No:*

Miranda relaxed, breathing freely for the first time since talking with Susan. "So I don't need to worry about choosing right?"

*:Yes:*

"Yes?"

*:Yes, you need to choose right:*

"But I can't tell inside that egg-like cavern which side is which. And I can't get back to Future Pharmaceutical to talk with the grandmothers. And even if I could, most of the time I keep jumping back into my body and missing what they're saying." Miranda stopped talking and started to chew her fingernails.

*:It is crucial that you be present at the moment you are needed. Choosing well is important:*

"But that choice doesn't just involve me. Susan's really upset thinking I'm going to die. And I probably wouldn't die right away. Is that why you said I wouldn't sacrifice myself at the dividing? Because I'd be alive until some fascist in the messed-up world discovers who I am? But I'll be alone. It would be worse than death. I'd lose Chris and everyone I care about here!" Miranda turned imploringly toward Adnarim who disappeared. "Don't do that! I need you now."

There was the sound of clinking keys at the door and Miranda stood up to let Chris in. After a long embrace, Chris looked into Miranda's dark eyes. "What's wrong? You look like you've been crying."

"I'm just loving you like crazy." Miranda answered pulling her lover back into a bear hug. "I don't know what I'd do without you; the world would be too shallow."

"I'm not going anywhere . . . unless one of your guides is predicting something and then I'm not sure I want to hear about it." Chris's eyes darted around, scanning for any hazy area that might indicate a guide was lurking around the living room. "Are they saying something is going to happen to me?"

"No. Nothing like that. I was just talking with Susan before I came home. She was reminding me of how precious this world is and how blessed I am to enjoy such a wonderful life here."

Chris stepped back, picking up the bags dropped at the beginning of the enthusiastic embrace, and headed toward the kitchen. "You can keep me company and tell me how wonderful the world is while I start dinner. I'm famished."

Miranda hesitated, glancing at the empty couch. "I want to check in with Adnarim again, you go ahead and I'll be there in a little bit."

"You've had all day to talk with them. How long did you stay at the Blooms?"

"Usual few hours. Then I talked with Susan for awhile . . ."

"Then what'd you do?"

"Oh, nothing really." *Damn, how long was I at the park drinking?*

"Then why didn't you talk with them after talking with Susan. Why do you always need to do it when we could have time together?"

"I don't! Just to let you know, I was talking with Adnarim before you got home. In fact, she disappeared right when you arrived. So you interrupted our conversation."

"Well, I'm so sorry." Chris threw the words at her, then turned and marched into the kitchen. Miranda heard the refrigerator door being opened, then forcefully slammed. Sounds of thumping and banging continued.

*How did I end up living with someone who's so unreasonable? And I'm doing all this to help our relationship!* She ground her teeth then bit back a burp as she tasted beer in her mouth again.

*Well, this certainly isn't the evening to share that I'm able to drink socially again. If this kind of bad attitude continues every time I mention talking with guides, I don't know what I'm going to do. With all that noise and bad emotion there's no way I'll be able to get settled enough here to talk with Adnarim.*

She turned away from the living room and headed into the bedroom. She closed the door, put on some soothing music, then sat down on the bed, hoping Adnarim would return. As she waited anger, regrets, and fears darted through her mind, piercing any calm she tried to piece together. When Adnarim did appear, she wore rags of different colors, and what appeared to be multiple long jackets all patched and torn.

Not wanting to risk being overheard, she focused on speaking telepathically, trying to form coherent thoughts, while her mind pitched and tumbled. *:Do you think I should tell Chris anything? What should I say if I did? How much of what Susan thinks should I mention—if I mention any of it? Should I admit that I might end up in the wrong parallel world after they divide?:*

*:Yes. Words. An original conversation; the one you had with Susan is now past. Have a new one with Chris. No:* Adnarim's response came back like a soothing breeze compared to Miranda's turbulent storm of questions.

*:Wait, what did the yes and no refer to?:*

*:Your questions:*

*:But which ones?:* Miranda tried frantically to remember exactly what she had asked Adnarim.

*:The questions you asked me were the ones I answered:* Her voice was soft and calming, though her words did nothing to satisfy Miranda's mental anguish. Adnarim shimmered then appeared dressed all in somber black, with a hood pulled over her head. *:Why do you think you might die then? Why are you conceiving that parallel worlds are not similar?:*

*:What would be the point in dividing the worlds if they were the same? Parallel worlds just mean they exist simultaneously. BB showed me that at the Blooms'—at least that's what I thought she was trying to do. And those stupid, mean neighbors.*

*Can't you feel how divided the world is even now? People are so weird they make no sense:* Miranda felt her frustration increase as her ability to project her thoughts decreased. She bent over, putting her head in her hands.

Out of the corner of her eye she noticed that Adnarim's skin now displayed very thin, even lines of alternating dark and light colors, starting from her toes, and climbing her bare legs.

Miranda closed her eyes before she gave in to the temptation of turning to verify if Adnarim was as naked as she seemed to be.

She felt her guide's attempts to communicate bouncing off her. Miranda tried to grab at the telepathic messages, catching one where Adnarim seemed to still be asking:

*:Why do you believe you have to die?:*

Miranda's mind stumbled in response. *:Why do you keep asking me that? Can't you tell? You should know when I'll die, but then that's really the problem isn't it? It isn't a real death? I'll just be in the wrong world. What will happen to Chris? And it isn't fair, first putting up with a partner who's always flitting back and forth between different worlds, and then to lose that partner when she permanently gets placed into a another world—it's too much:*

Miranda heard in her mind the usual confusing mix of yes's and no's from Adnarim, realizing once again she had let her mind ramble and ask too many questions all at once. She cracked her eyes slightly and focusing straight ahead, noticed that the vision next to her was now of a man in a jester costume, with a confusing mix of green and yellow dots, alternating on a yellow and green background.

*:Why do you keep changing forms?:*

*:To give you your answer:*

*:Explain what you're saying to me!:*

Adnarim's color scheme reversed so that the yellow was now green and the green was now yellow. Then the colors switched again.

Miranda scrunched her eyes closed again, feeling tears threatening.

*:What's all this supposed to mean? Say it in words. I'm sick of all these hints. It all came together when Susan was talking about it—why Earthweb was so insistent on which side to choose. It even makes sense why I was chosen rather than some of the other people who talk with spirits. I'm not that important. The others are all needed to help in the new world. Once we're separate from the craziness they'll all be necessary to form a peaceful, co-existing world:*

Adnarim's form changed again into an old woman wearing a rainbow business suit. *:Meaning is not as important as action. These are words for you to help you choose right. But words can lead and mislead depending on which ones you follow. Being present at the time you are to be present is the most important factor. To follow your gath is for you to do. As others follow their gaths, the world is woven in new patterns:*

*:But that means I have to be prepared to die. I have to be willing to give up my life to be one hundred percent behind the challenge of helping the worlds divide. If I hesitate and am too afraid of dying then I won't be able to be fully present. I'll jump back into my physical body like I always do when I get nervous and then I won't be able to help . . . But if I'm only there spiritually—not physically—does that mean it won't matter which world I think I'm going to, because my physical self will automatically go to the right world?:*

*:Your physical self will not go to a world; it will be where it will be, when it is there:*

*:That doesn't help! You've got to help me make the right choice:*

*:Be present at the time that needs you. Think only that, and you will follow your gath:* Adnarim shrank down to the size of the young boy who had been throwing the ball in Miranda's car months ago. Miranda could see a ball of some type being thrown in the air, then as it descended, Adnarim would hold out both hands, palm open. The ball would momentarily be in both hands at once, then it would be one ball again as it was launched heavenward. She watched the pattern repeat for several minutes starting to feel her anxieties ease. Then the ball became a bird that flew up from Adnarim's hands.

Miranda swung toward her to get a better view, and her guide and the bird both disappeared.

Miranda shook her head slowly, discovering the tension in her neck and shoulders had diminished as she watched the ball going up and down. Miranda rose and started to head out of the bedroom when she noticed her sweatshirt and jeans draped over the arm of a chair. She picked them up and put them in their places. Walking out into the living room she bent down and retrieved the dress shoes wedged under the coffee table. As she returned to the bedroom, she snagged a pair of sneakers from the hallway, placing both pair of shoes in her closet. When Chris came out to tell her dinner was ready, Miranda had emptied the recycling bin and halfway filled it again with papers that had been strewn across the dining room table.

"Hey, what happened in here? Not that I'm complaining mind you . . ."

"Surprise! I thought I'd pick up a bit, to say I'm sorry." She reached over and kissed her lover on the cheek. "I'm even going to set the table for us, and I'll do the dishes afterwards."

"You don't have to do all that. It was my fault too. I know you can't always plan when to talk with your guides. I can clean up the dishes. I ended up making a garbanzo bean curry for you so it's kind of a mess in there."

"My favorite! You're too good to me. And I plan to really do the dishes. The way you like them done, not my usual swipe and dry method, I promise. I'll even clean out the sink, fold the dish towels, and make it so you'd think you'd done it, only you'll be relaxing listening to some romantic jazz, waiting for me on the couch."

"Well, I won't say no to all that." Chris turned back to the kitchen and brought out their dinner while Miranda set the table, swallowing her worries, sending them deep into her belly and promising herself she'd do everything she could to make sure Chris felt her love for all the days she had left until the world divided.

# Chapter 14

## *Bear News*

When Miranda came home Wednesday night, Chris handed her the paper, opened to the third page where a picture of a dead bear stared up at her. A news report detailed the first shooting of a California grizzly since 1922—the first killing since they had repopulated the state and it had become possible to kill them again. The article also described the formation of a lobbying group, HVG: Hunters Versus Grizzlies, whose purpose was to instigate the first open season for bear shooting. Miranda skimmed the message quickly then dug her phone out of her briefcase, touched her friend's picture icon, and was soon rewarded with a human hello.

"Susan, I am so sorry to hear about that hunter murdering the bear. You must be devastated."

"How's that for irony? I'm excited about grizzly bears living; now there's a group excited about killing grizzly bears."

"It feels like we're not from the same planet."

"You got that right. We're from here, they're from wherever. We're attempting to preserve, they're intent on destroying. We're weaving the world together, they're wrenching the world apart. We're endeavoring to live in harmony with nature, they're inflicting the dominion of man over nature. We're inclusive, they're divisive. We're practicing love, they're promoting hate." Susan paused.

There was a long silence between the two women, until Miranda took up the chant, "It's us namens versus the greemens. Humans connected to nature versus the humans attached to greed. The ones open to wonder and the ones inflicting control and domination." Miranda sighed and looked at BB who was curled in the corner with her head between her paws. "I was afraid this would happen, but until I saw it in black and white, I couldn't believe someone would actually intentionally kill one of the repopulated grizzly bears. What's going to be done about it?"

"It'll go to court. Since he was bragging in a bar about killing the bear there isn't a question of guilt, just a question of applying a law that was created to be symbolic, to an actual case."

"I didn't follow the particulars before, but didn't it make murdering a grizzly equivalent to killing a human?"

"Yes, that's exactly what the law specifies. They let us symbolically treat animals with equal respect, now we'll see where the river flows."

"Well, we'll be thinking of you. I'll send BB down to help."

"Sounds good."

Miranda closed the phone and turned toward the corner, but there was no longer a bear standing there.

# Chapter 15

## *Openings*

Miranda threw an arm out of bed groping for her phone, which was meowing like a cat. She rolled over, pulling the phone to her mouth. "'Ello?"

"Miranda!?" A woman's voice came through high and anxious.

"Yeah?" Miranda squirmed around in bed, groping for the clock on the headboard.

"It's Sonya. I can't—" The words dissolved into a confusion of static.

Miranda sat up, her heart thumping. "Are you okay? Is Peter okay?" She pulled the clock onto her lap and stared at the florescent green numbers announcing it was 2:12 a.m. Miranda hunched over, jamming the phone against her ear in an attempt to decipher the message. "What did you say? What's happening with Peter? I can't hear you."

The sound of a quick inhale, then a broken exhale came through the phone, followed by Sonya's voice, thick but clear.

"I don't know what to do. He's having trouble breathing. He'll be breathing fine, then he'll seem to stop entirely, then it gets very labored before going back to normal. And I can't wake him up."

"Have you called your nurse—Maria, right? Or the hospice night number?"

Sonya's voice was small and contrite. "No, I guess I should've called them before bothering you. And on a Sunday night too. I'm so sorry."

"No, no, that's fine. Why don't you stay with Peter? I'll call Maria, or whoever is on call, and then I'll be right over." Chris peered up at her from the covers, eyebrows raised in a question. Miranda whispered, "It's Sonya," and was rewarded with an understanding nod.

She rolled out of bed and scooped up her jeans, t-shirt, and sweater left beside the bed less than four hours earlier. When she came out of the bathroom, Chris handed her a travel mug with a teabag tag hanging out of it. Miranda traded it for a kiss. "Thanks, lover. I don't know how long I'll be. What Sonya was describing sounded like it could be Cheyne-Stokes." Chris gave her a puzzled look. "You know, labored breaths then long pauses between breaths, usually right at . . . well, it shows . . . there isn't much time . . ." She swallowed hard. "I was sure . . . at least I thought he had a few more weeks." Miranda turned abruptly and marched toward the front door. "I'd better get over there. Sonya's going to need a lot of support. I wonder who else I should call, maybe . . ."

"Hey, you." Chris caught up with her, grabbing her shoulders and gently shaking them. "Remember you're not just the hospice helper here. It's okay to have your own feelings. I know how much you care about Peter. Would it help if I came with you?"

Miranda leaned against her lover. "Would you mind?"

"No, not at all. Just give me a chance to get dressed." Chris started to move back toward their bedroom.

"Wait." Miranda ground her teeth and stared out the window. It reflected an image of a woman standing straight and still, like a tree pretending there were no winds in the world that could ever bend it.

"No . . . you'd better stay here. I shouldn't bring someone new over right now." She turned to Chris, her mouth set in a firm line, her shoulders pressing all breath and feelings out of her body. "Thanks for the offer." She forced her mouth into a weak smile. "If I'm there really long, maybe I'll call and have you bring over some breakfast."

"Your wish is my culinary command. But here, at least take these permission slips. You might need them." Her partner handed her a box of tissues, then gave her a hug and whispered, "Don't forget to care for yourself. It really is okay if you cry."

Miranda sighed as she walked out to the car. She opened the door and tossed the tissue box in the backseat. *I wish Chris could've come with me. But it wouldn't be fair to Sonya and Peter. At least there wasn't an argument about my going. I guess ten years has finally taught us to deal with the weirdness of each other's careers. If only Chris could be this understanding and supportive when guides call at odd hours.* She took a sip of the tea Chris had prepared for her. *That's not nice. I'm being ungrateful. I should be more patient when Chris gets scared or jealous of my being with my guides.*

Placing the tea mug in the cup holder between the seats, Miranda backed her car out of the garage. Setting her body on automatic for the familiar drive to the Blooms' house, she set her mind to rehearsing supportive phrases to help ease Sonya's grief.

Miranda parked and walked slowly up the flagstone path to Sonya and Peter's front door. She put her hand on the bronze door knob. It was cold to her touch and she rubbed her clammy hands against her jeans before reaching for it again. It turned easily, allowing her passage into the house, and removing any good reasons for further hesitation. She called softly. "Sonya, it's Miranda. I'm here." No response. She called louder, reminding herself of Sonya's hearing loss, and Peter's current condition, but still no response. The house was unnaturally silent, as though it was holding its breath, perhaps to allow Peter as much room to breathe as possible.

As Miranda walked down the hallway she realized she was missing Doogie's traditional, enthusiastic greeting. She slipped into the guest room, where Peter's hospital bed had been set up, and spied the silent, petrified dog. He was keeping vigil from the far side of the bed, leaning against Sonya as he stared at Peter.

Sonya turned, reaching out a hand. "I can't wake him. I'm not sure what to do."

Miranda stepped carefully around the bed to gently take Sonya's hand and wrap an arm around her shoulder. "Maria should be here soon. How long has he been like this?"

"I'm not sure. He was his usual ornery self this evening, not wanting to eat. But the pain has been getting worse. I know they have him on a lot of morphine now. It often takes a long time for him to wake up." Miranda squeezed her hand as she continued. "I went to bed early. I was just too tired to stay up with him any longer. When I got up to go to the bathroom, I came in to check on him. I noticed his odd breathing. I thought maybe he was in pain, so I tried to wake him up, but I couldn't get any response. That's when I called you." Sonya swayed slightly, leaning against Miranda.

Miranda guided her to the easy chair near the head of the bed, then pulled up a small chair for herself. She patted Sonya's hand, which she was still holding. "I'm glad you called me. Is there anyone else I should call right now?"

"Do you think . . . I mean . . . is this the end? Is he . . ."

Miranda was distracted by stirrings from the corner of the room that felt like a soft autumn breeze, the kind that swirls both dry leaves and hair. Closing her eyes she asked, *:Is there someone there? Are you here to help Peter?:*

*:Yes. I, who is here:* A scattering of words blew into her mind.

*:Skyweb?:* Miranda's concentration stumbled as she recognized the Southern Grandmother's ethereal alto voice. *:What are you doing . . . no . . . don't answer that. Can you tell me if Peter is ready to leave his body?:*

*:He, who is leaving. He, who would know. He, you should ask:*

*:But . . . ah . . .:* Before Miranda could decide what to do with that suggestion she felt a slight tug at her wrist.

She turned and noticed Sonya looking at her. For a moment, she saw not the usual furrowed skin and white hair, but a young woman in a flowery spring dress, with dark hair and a graceful smile. It was the woman from the picture Peter always kept on his end table, taken when they were first dating, the one he'd always point to when he referred to his fairy princess.

"Miranda? What's happening? What're your guides saying?"

Miranda blinked, her eyes now perceiving only the Sonya she had always known, but her heart still saw the young wife, just starting a life with her new husband that would last more than sixty years. Then Miranda's mind registered that Sonya, the author of *Speaking with Spirits,* had just asked her about her guides. "My guides? I . . ."

Now it was Sonya's turn to pat Miranda's hand. "I've always remembered what you said when we first met at that conference, about talking to guides. I never wanted to bring it up when Peter was around." She paused, glancing at the gaunt figure in the bed. "When he was able to hear me that is . . . I was hoping if I didn't focus on your ability to hear spirits that maybe he'd feel safe talking to you about the spirit world, since he was never open to doing more than tease me about it. If he'd just not been so contrary we could have shared so . . . but I'm not complaining. He was the best husband. *Is*—is the best husband." Sonya stopped talking and started shaking her head from side to side.

Miranda imagined she was switching back and forth from disappointments to love, from past to future, and from hope to fear.

Miranda pushed her own nervousness and sadness away as she focused on reassuring Sonya. "He did talk with me about spirits. He even told me he hoped you'd win the argument about whether other realities existed or not. Your connection with the spirit world did give him a lot of solace—even if he wouldn't admit it to you. So what about *your* guides? What are they telling you about Peter right now?"

"I can't contact them now. I'm too afraid of what they'll say. You probably think that's silly. Here I am an 'expert' on guides and I can't even find the stillness within myself to contact them when he's dying." Her voice caught on the last two words.

"I understand. If this was Chris, I wouldn't have the presence of mind to hear anyone say anything, let alone do it telepathically. What my guide suggested was to ask Peter."

Both women turned to look at Peter, then Doogie started whining. There was a stillness in the air, then a familiar male voice entered Miranda's mind. *:I guess you were right. There is going to be something else:*

"Peter?" Miranda gasped.

*:Seems to be me. Or as close as I can get right now:*

"Are you hearing Peter?" Sonya's voice was thick with anxiety and hope.

"I think I did—no, I did." Miranda berated herself for dropping into her habitual questioning at a crucial time when both Peter and Sonya needed her. "Yes. It sounds just like him. He said I was right about there being something else. Try to open up and see if you can hear him."

Tears were flowing down Sonya's face. "I don't know if I can. I always wanted him to experience the spiritual. But now all I want is for him to wake up and rationalize away everything that's happening. Tell me this dying business was just my over-catastrophizing. That's what he called my fears and anxieties. If only he'd just sit up and tell me everything will be okay."

"I know. I wish it too. But you might feel better if you did connect with him now. Try and just breathe. He's still here." Miranda gestured at the familiar body on the bed. "He can't talk physically right now, so it's coming through psychically. Just open yourself up—like you've done with guides all your life."

*:Are you giving my wife a lecture on speaking with spirits?:* Peter's voice came through tinged with humor. *:Well if I'm going to start doing this mystical stuff, I guess it's only fair that she stops doing it and becomes all rational about it:*

"Sonya, Peter's teasing you about needing my help."

"I think I heard him, saying he's doing the mystical now and I'm shutting down to it."

"Yeah, that's what I'm getting too."

Sonya looked pleadingly at Miranda. "Can you ask him if it's his time? I . . . I can't. And ask him if there's anything we should do . . . or anyone to call . . . who he wants to be here."

Miranda scrunched her forehead in concentration and asked, *:Peter? Did you hear that? Is there anything you want? Anyway we can help?:*

*:I can feel everyone's love from here. They don't need to be in the room. But somehow I know Maria's car broke down—so don't worry about her showing up. I guess it'll just be us:*

"Did you hear any of that?" Miranda asked Sonya.

"Something about Maria and her car? I'd been wondering where she was. Should we call someone to help her? I hate to think of her on the side of the road somewhere, so late at night."

"I'm sure she'll be fine. It's probably just that she wasn't supposed to be here for this."

Sonya wiped her face with a tissue then reached out and picked up Peter's limp hand. "Darling, I know you can hear me. So it's okay to go. You've been in pain long enough. We'll always be connected and I'll be joining you before too long."

*:My love, I know we'll always be together. But I'm leaving you here now. Alone:* Peter moaned and both women jumped as he twitched and thrashed his head.

Sonya leaned over stroking his forehead. "Peter, what's wrong? Did I upset you? I'm sorry."

"No . . . no." Came a hoarse, shaky whisper from the bed. Peter adjusted his head to look at Sonya. "I'm leaving you here. I've been so selfish—thinking only of my fears."

"I'll be fine, dear."

Peter gripped Sonya's hand tightly. "Don't lie to me. There's no darn way you'll be fine. I know grief, it's . . . it's terrible." He rolled his head back and forth, scanning the ceiling. "I can't find Sam. I'd always hoped when my time came that I'd see him. Where's Sam? I can't find Sam."

"Oh, sweetheart, it doesn't always happen that way.

Maybe you'll find him later. But don't upset yourself so much. Just go towards the love. I'll be fi—I'll manage. You just relax. It's okay. You can go. I know you've been in terrible pain. Go toward the love." Sonya kept stroking Peter's forehead as he slowly quieted his twitching.

Miranda cleared her throat. "Aren't you supposed to tell him to go toward the light?"

Sonya turned toward Miranda. "It can be confusing for people to be told to go only toward the light." Sonya straightened her shoulders and spoke in her lecturer voice. "Studies have shown that sometimes when people have a near-death experience they find themselves in a dark, womblike place. So it is better to encourage people to go toward love and peace, that way if they're in a dark, gentle place they know they're okay there."

*:Well I don't see any light or dark. But I don't feel too attached to my body right now either. Seems like I'm still hanging in there though:* Miranda and Sonya stared down at Peter, whose eyes were closed and his face limp, except for his lips, which flapped with his irregular breathing.

"Are you hearing him?" Miranda asked Sonya.

"Yes. He seems to be more at peace now." Sonya was enunciating her words in the stilted manner Miranda herself used when she only wanted to be heard in the N-World. "Thank goodness he's okay. I don't want to upset him. Not now."

Peter's voice came through, sounding like a kid who got caught holding an empty cookie jar. *:Must have been all those pumps of morphine I gave myself. Sent myself right out of my body. Didn't want to bother you with how much pain I was in this evening, but I was using that button pretty good:*

Peter kept rambling, and Sonya seemed to hear him by the way she kept nodding, so Miranda stepped away from the bed. She took a deep breath, reminding herself to be strong and that Sonya was the one who needed support here. Her job was to do everything she could to be there for Sonya and Peter. Stilling her emotions, she took a moment to reconnect with Skyweb. *:Are you still here? Can you tell me anything about Peter that can help Sonya? Can you help Peter?:*

*:Yes. No. Yes. Love is here. Help already is:*

Miranda's frustration bubbled up with Skyweb's enigmatic responses. *:Why are you talking like Adnarim? Why can't you just answer me directly? What are you doing here anyway? I thought all of you grandmothers were attached to the cedar grove. I didn't know you could travel around the N-World. Why haven't you contacted me before? You could have explained about the worlds dividing and told me what's going to happen:*

*:Both similar. Yes, am direct. Help Peter. Other grandmothers, yes. I now go where you go. Always in contact. Explain, yes:*

The words floated around Miranda, as she tried to grasp them, tried to string them together to make sense out of them. *:Are you saying you're always with me everywhere? Why are you only showing yourself now?:*

*:Yes, always present. I am part of you:*

*:You're me?:*

*:I am part of you, who are transitions:*

*:What?:*

*:Words I said were, I am part of you, who are transitions:*

Miranda focused inside, trying to keep her next thoughts to herself. *Why do all my stupid guides have to be so literal in their answers? Why can't they just talk normal? Yeah, right— like this is normal. I should be used to it by now. And I'm wasting time! I need to help Peter and Sonya right now, not puzzle out why Skyweb's never helped me figure out how I'm supposed to make the worlds divide without getting onto the wrong one. Damn guides. She can obviously talk to me here. Why've the grandmothers always made it seem like I had to go to their hill to talk with them? What am I doing complaining? I should be helping Peter!* She took a slow breath, finally returning to Skyweb's message. She focused her thoughts toward Skyweb and asked, *:What did you mean by: you're part of me and I'm transitions?:*

*:It is your gath to help with transitions. We are part of a larger whole. We are connected, you, who are transitions:* Skyweb's words swirled around whispering into her mind.

*:So you're an aspect of me? Like Adnarim?:*

*:Yes. No:*

*:You certainly sound like Adnarim now. If she's the part of me that didn't incarnate in the N-World when I was born, then what part of me are you?:*

*:Hey, who are you talking to?:* Peter's voice broke into their conversation. *:Is this Miranda? But there seems to be two spirit Mirandas here:*

Miranda concentrated, trying to send her thoughts toward Peter, when what she really wanted to do was listen for Skyweb's response. *:I was just checking in with one of my guides. She's the one who suggested I talk with you. How are you doing?:*

*:I'm doing fine, but I can't hear Sonya anymore:*

Miranda drew her attention back to the N-World where Sonya was leaning over Peter's body, her shoulders shaking slightly with each breath.

"Sonya?" Miranda reached over, rubbing the older woman's back. "Peter is still here, but he said he can't hear you anymore."

Sonya straightened up, showing a tear-streaked face. "Funny how I've always told myself it's the spirit that's most important since it's eternal, but I'm just so attached to his old body here— I can't stand to think of it becoming cold and stiff."

"I'm going to miss him, too."

Peter's body rocked with two rapid, heavy breaths, then lay still.

"Is that it?" Sonya asked in a small voice, reminding Miranda of the vision of the young wife she had seen earlier.

Miranda swallowed her trembling and spoke in her most calm and compassionate voice. "No, but his breathing will become very erratic—stopping and starting again. And it . . . it is a sign he'll be letting go of his body soon. Just go ahead and keep talking to him and see if you can hear him again. He's right here with us."

Sonya held Peter's hand, speaking softly, reminding him of their long, astonishing life together. The two of them settled into an uneasy rhythm: his breathing stopping then starting, her voice clogging with tears then coming through clearly.

Miranda wished she could call and ask Chris to come over so she could cry in her lover's arms. Instead she went out to the living room to call Maria. Her car had broken down and Miranda let her know there was no urgency in coming over and that she would stay with Sonya as long as needed. When she returned to the room, Doogie was standing near Peter's face whimpering at him.

Sonya looked up, grief and relief warring across her face. "He said he's ready."

Miranda moved to the opposite side and took Peter's other hand, adding her own encouragement. *:It's okay to leave. Sonya has support here and there's lots of love to guide you on your journey:*

*:I can feel it. My nephew just woke up. He's on the east coast and he's thinking of me. There's an old student of mine who's adding me into her prayers. I guess I did touch a lot of lives. And mine's not ending—just transforming, as you said:* Miranda could feel Peter smiling. *:Sonya won the argument after all. Only thing I can't figure out is that this reality seems very similar to being physical. I'm still thinking and talking like I used to. I didn't expect that:*

"It won't last long." Miranda spoke out loud, glancing at Sonya, who bobbed her head, acknowledging that she had been following Peter's questions. "You're still tied to this physical world. So we're talking like we used to all those days I'd come over and sit with you. But that will fade as you drift further from your body. After all you're still taking breaths every minute or so. Just give yourself time and you know both Sonya and I will be here." As she was reassuring Peter, she was becoming calmer herself.

Peter's voice came through strong and clear. *:Who's that other you? It's like your spirit twin is here:*

*:I'm not sure how I'm connected to that part of me. It feels to you like she's my twin?:* Miranda switched to telepathic talking, hoping Skyweb might join in and add more explanation.

But it was Peter's voice that came through again, sounding amused and self-satisfied. *:You mean there's something I'm aware of that you're unaware of? And here I thought you knew it all when it came to spirit stuff:*

*:I've met this guide before—but I didn't know she was connected to me. She said something about being a part of me related to transitions, so maybe she's here for your transition. And there's another transition I'm helping with that she's connected to:*

*:A big one. I'm getting some sense of it. Something major is happening. There's a healing approaching:*

"Peter," Sonya spoke, though her voice was thick and slow. "I can't hear you anymore. You're finally finding the world I always promised would be there for you."

*:Yes, love. It's here. I feel it. I'm in it:* His spirit voice came through strong and buoyant.

"Go . . . go in peace and . . . and . . ." Sonya struggled to get more words out as her voice got fainter. She bent down and kissed Peter's cheek, then laid her head next to his.

Miranda's chest constricted as she felt the enormity of over sixty years of love filling the bed. Her eyes misted over, creating a blur of images as if she was flipping through pages of the album Peter frequently shared with her. She remembered pictures of a youthful Sonya and Peter traveling, entertaining, smiling, arms often intertwined. There were images of the young woman he called his fairy princess with an equally young, mischievous looking man who had Peter's twinkling eyes. As she watched scenes morphing into older versions of Sonya and Peter she noticed it had been several minutes since his old body had breathed. She wiped her eyes, shutting the album of memories and pulling herself back to the moment. "I think he's completely let go now."

They sat in quiet, submerged under overlapping waves of grief, relief, awe, and pain, each still holding on to one of Peter's hands as though to a lifeline that was slowly drifting away from them.

Miranda lost track of time as she sat, cherishing and remembering her too brief friendship with Peter. Then she noticed a lightness and spaciousness in the room and felt the familiar peace that transcends and momentarily replaces grief as Peter's spirit lifted from the body he'd used for eighty-five years.

Peter was no longer communicating in words, but she felt his joy as he started to explore his beloved universe in a new form. She rose and walked around the bed, sitting down next to Sonya, putting her arms around the older woman. Sonya leaned into her embrace, surrendering to the overwhelming flood of emotions and the exhaustion of the last long months of care-giving.

They heard a knock on the door and Miranda got up to let Maria in, who apologized profusely for all the strange delays that had made her so late. Miranda waved away the guilt surrounding the nurse, insisting the timing was perfect, and now that Maria was here, she was going to leave. She hugged Sonya and promised to continue coming by for visits.

# Chapter 16

## *Wolf goes to Colorado*

"Extinct Species Express, may I help you?" a muffled voice said through Miranda's phone.

"Susan?" Miranda leaned back against the couch, holding her phone out in order to double check the number she'd just dialed.

"This is ESE, do you have an extinct species you want brought back to life?"

"Susan, this isn't a good time for jokes. I called to let you know Peter died yesterday."

"Oh, Miranda, I'm so sorry." Susan's voice came through clearly and contritely.

"It's okay." Miranda felt bad for the abruptness of her announcement and tried to soften it. "Peter would have appreciated the humor. So I take it the wolf came to life when you got to Colorado?"

"Right on cue. It happened an hour after sunset. We were hanging out at the camp site. Just the three of us. Thomas, me, and the wolf head. This time Thomas didn't even say 'This might sound crazy, but I just saw a large black wolf smile and nod at me as it walked into the forest.' He just told me he'd refuse to go camping with me if I brought along a saber-toothed tiger skull. At least we were smart enough this time that we didn't put it in the tent with us."

Miranda idly flipped through the paper. "I haven't seen any reports about the Southern Rocky Mountains Wolf appearing in Colorado again."

"Hopefully they'll be smarter. After all there isn't any legislation to protect them. And I bet after California's experience, no state will want to even symbolically write an enforcement policy to protect extinct species." There was a hiss from the phone. "Hey, in case I fade out—we're driving back right now and we're in the mountains so reception won't be the best. Or to be more specific, I'm driving while Thomas is sleeping in the back. During the best scenery too! Good thing he's let go of this girlfriend idea—we'd be a match made in hell. But enough of my affairs, how are you?"

"Fine." Miranda answered more sharply than she meant to. She was feeling conflicted. She had called Susan to tell her about Peter's death, but now she didn't want to talk about him or how she was feeling. "So I read somewhere about the judge not enforcing the California law against that stupid hunter who shot the bear. What was that all about?"

"N-World craziness and too many greemens—what else?" Susan paused, but when Miranda didn't say anything she continued. "It was a pretty ambiguous verdict the judge gave—fines, jail time, and public service. Of course all the different interpretations of that law will keep animal rights' lawyers paying off their yachts for years." Susan continued with interesting legal stories then slipped in a seemingly casual question. "So did Peter get a sense of other worlds by the end?"

"Yes, in fact he did. He got very talkative once his body started shutting down."

"Talkative?"

"Yep, he discovered there is something beyond the N-World. He was able to converse with us telepathically before his body died."

"I'm so glad. And how's Sonya doing?"

"Missing him terribly. So do I. I haven't been able to contact him again. But when I called Sonya this afternoon she said she's felt him several times, though he's not coming through as clearly as he did when he was dying."

The line was silent. "Susan? Susan? Can you hear me?" Miranda waited a few more seconds then closed her phone, laying it beside her as she stared out the window at the evening drizzle.

# Chapter 17

## *A Dinner Interrupted*

Chris had just spread a white linen tablecloth over their dining room table when the phone rang. Miranda looked at the caller ID. "It's Sonya." Chris nodded reluctantly and Miranda picked up the phone.

"Hi, Sonya, I'm so sorry I wasn't able to get by yesterday. I just had so many meetings, but I was going to . . ."

"Miranda, I'm sorry to bother you. You're probably in the middle of dinner. I just wasn't sure who to call . . . I . . ."

"We hadn't started eating yet, what's up?" Miranda shoved the phone under her chin and continued helping Chris set the table.

"It's Doogie. He . . ."

Miranda carefully placed a red tapered candle in a heart-shaped holder in the middle of the table. She started to lay out the plates when she realized she wasn't hearing anything over the phone any more. "Sonya? What's happening? What about Doogie?"

Sonya's voice came through faintly and Miranda had to press the phone against her ear in order not to lose the words Sonya was trying to convey. "He didn't come back after I let him out this afternoon . . . I called and called, but he wouldn't come. Not even for his dinner. I went out to look for him . . ." Miranda started to protest. "I know, I know—I'm not supposed to go outside by myself, but I had to find him. I looked all over and . . . and then there he was, underneath the azalea bush—all stiff—like a wooden dog. My little Doogie. He's . . . he's gone."

Miranda caught the phone as it started slipping through her hand and brought it quickly to her mouth. "I'll be right over. Don't try to go back out. I'll be there in twenty minutes." Miranda turned off the phone, feeling as though the floor had opened up beneath her, but she hadn't started falling yet. She turned to her lover, who was looking at her like a small, sad puppy left home alone too long.

"So what is it *this* time?" Chris's voice was heavy, each word coming out like a rock hitting a shallow pond.

Miranda stared past her partner, her eyes fixed on an empty space on the dining room wall. *No, no. Not Doogie. He's all Sonya had left. Not little Doogie.*

Chris walked between her and the wall. "Are you talking to your guides again?"

Miranda looked away from Chris, images of Doogie jumping up to greet her filling her mind. *My guides—good idea. Maybe Merawl knows something—or can do some magic. Maybe Doogie isn't definitely dead yet.*

"Miranda! Stop talking to those paranormal busybodies and look at me. You promised this meal would be guide-free! What're you doing? We planned this dinner weeks ago and I just heard you promise Sonya you'd be right over. I don't care if she did write *Speaking with Spirits*, she can deal with her own grief for one night this week." Chris glared at Miranda, who was still staring blankly at the wall, then walked back to the table and started slamming silverware down by the plates.

Miranda wandered over to the living room and sat down on the couch. *I've got to do something. Sonya's counting on me.*

She closed her eyes and pressed her lips together, thinking as clearly as she could. *:Merawl? Are you there?:*

A fuzzy cloud of fur appeared next to her. Miranda peered at it cautiously. *:Merawl is that you?:*

*:As good as I'm going to get in the N-World right now. You needed me?:*

*:Actually Sonya does. She found Doogie lying under the azalea bush and she thinks he's dead. But he can't be. He wasn't much more than a puppy:*

A tail rose out of the gray cloud, swishing like an angry fish out of water. *:She's probably right. Cutting those trees was a bad idea:*

*:They didn't have a choice—those idiot neighbors of theirs forced them to:*

*:Everyone has choices; people just say they don't when they don't like the options:*

"Merawl's there isn't he? I can see a furry haze beside you." An angry-sounding voice broke into Miranda's consciousness. "What does he want? Can't you tell him to go away?"

*I'd rather tell you to go away.* Miranda scrunched her thoughts deep inside her mind, afraid they would leak out. *You're mad at me again. Why can't you just be nice about this once in a while? I didn't want to get that phone call right before our dinner.* Miranda closed her eyes again, forcing down the tears. *What should I do? Doogie was supposed to be Sonya's support after Peter died. Ah, man . . . I can't fall apart now. I need to be strong for Sonya. And I'm not being fair; Chris doesn't know what's going on—as usual.* She looked up at Chris. "It's Doogie. He's . . . he. . . . Sonya couldn't find him. She went out and . . . she thinks he's dead."

"Oh, no! Poor Sonya." Chris was immediately contrite, collapsing next to Miranda, hugging her and assuring her that dinner could wait, they could have it the next night, or why don't they go together and bring the dinner for Sonya to share so she won't have to be alone. Still feeling like she was teetering on the edge of an abyss, Miranda agreed. Her logical mind instructed her body to pick up coats and help Chris wrap up the food, and the rest of her just went along, too numb to comment.

As they were walking out the door, Miranda stopped, blocking their way. *Oh, my God, Chris can't go with me to Sonya's. What if she offers me some wine? Sonya'll expect me to drink and Chris'll expect me not to. There hasn't been a good time to explain my social drinking yet—and this certainly wouldn't be it.* "Chris, I just realized it's not a good idea for you to come with me. You've never met Sonya before and it would be better if I went alone."

"I met her at Peter's service—don't you remember? She expressly said for me to come with you sometime. I admit this isn't the best time for a first visit, but there shouldn't be any problem with my going. Or don't *you* want me coming along?" Chris waited, frowning at Miranda.

*I can't say no, now—what reason could I give? Damn, she always offers me something to drink. Maybe if I suggest tea right away. I could even go make some for us. It's either tea or wine. If she does offer me brandy in the tea, I can refuse that 'cause I've done that before. I'm not drinking hard liquor—just wine and beer.* She turned back to Chris. "You're right. I forgot. But are you really sure you want to come?" Chris nodded. "Okay, just checking." They continued their walk to the car, loaded it up with the food, and were at Sonya's house in less than twenty minutes.

Miranda went into the house ahead of Chris, like a scout into a mine field. "Sonya, we're here. Don't bother getting up, I'll get us all some tea." She walked into the living room. There was a pot of tea waiting for them on the coffee table. Miranda stumbled as her body let loose its panic-induced rigidity. *Thank God! I won't have to explain anything to either of them.* She gave Sonya a quick hug, then helped Chris put their dinner in the kitchen. She came back with Sonya's coat and they both assisted her as she maneuvered her walker outside and along the earthen path that ended at the azalea bush. Miranda kept the flashlight beam hovering in front of Sonya to assist her walking, and to avoid exposing anything she didn't want to see, like the body of a dead dog. When they reached the end of the path, a patch of white daisies shone back the light as though they knew the humans needed light and warmth.

Sonya nudged Miranda's arm. "I found him to the right where the branches almost reach the ground." Miranda slowly swung the beam, jumping when it fell on a small tan poodle. The light accentuated the brittle angles Doogie's legs made sticking straight out from his body. Even his fur looked hard and frozen, as though he'd died of fright.

Miranda knelt down next to him. "How can this be? He was such a sweet dog . . . always so friendly, so . . ." She started to reach out to him, then felt the earth fall away as she realized he really was dead. She hugged herself and began to sob. Chris laid a hand on her shoulder, while the other arm supported Sonya, who had begun to shake. After a few minutes they insisted the grieving widow return inside.

They wrapped her in an afghan and warmed her tea, as she melted into her chair, looking lost and helpless. Miranda brought the tissue box over waiting for the reality of Doogie's death to start crashing in.

Sonya looked up once at each of them, saw sad confirmation in their wet eyes and started to whimper. Miranda crouched down and put her arm around her as the sobs began rolling through her body. Chris pulled up a chair for her to perch on, then went and sat alone on the sofa, staring out toward the azalea bush.

Miranda kept an arm around Sonya as her mind swam in circles. *This can't be happening to Sonya. She's lost too much. It isn't fair! What happened to Doogie? He looked terrible. Did the gremlins get through? Wasn't that where Merawl jumped into the alley and got attacked by them? Where's Merawl now? He said it was wrong to cut down the trees. I should've used Cat Vision back there. Why wasn't I thinking! I don't want to go back now. Besides, Sonya needs me here.*

After many long minutes, Sonya inhaled quickly several times. Miranda recognized it as a way people breathe when trying to cut off fear or crying. Her friend's forced breathing interrupted Miranda's twisted thoughts. She turned to look at the older woman as Sonya began, "Do you think . . ." She paused to wipe at her eyes and nose, ". . . since he chose that place to die, should we bury him there?"

Chris jumped up from the couch, as if the idea was a lifeline in a sea of heaviness. "I'll look for a shovel in the garage, and see if there's room under the bush to dig a hole without disturbing its roots. I'll come get you when I've got a spot dug."

After Chris left, Miranda knelt by Doogie's bed, picking up the small blanket Sonya had crocheted for him, but which was seldom used, since he preferred laps. "Shall we use this to wrap him in?"

Sonya nodded. "I just don't understand what could have happened to him. He was running around this morning, following me everywhere. Yapping at the delivery person when she came to the door. Trying to climb on the table to see what was in the package. I let him out after lunch, then I took a nap." She paused, swallowing painfully, tears flowing down her cheeks. "I slept longer than I meant to. I don't usually leave him out so long. Peter would always let him in just as soon as he'd bark. When he wasn't able to do it himself anymore, he'd always be calling after me not to leave Doogie outside by himself too long. I didn't mean to leave him out that long." Sonya looked over at Miranda, like a traveler in a snowstorm searching for a familiar landmark.

Miranda knelt in front of her reaching for her hands. "Oh, Sonya, it wasn't your fault. Animals just die sometimes. He looked like he'd just lain down in that spot and known it was his end. There wasn't anything you could've done. It doesn't look like he was struggling or anything. It's not like he died at the back door trying to get back in."

Sonya kept nodding throughout Miranda's explanation. "I suppose you're right," Sonya said, sighing. Miranda couldn't decide if she should say anything else or not, so she kept herself distracted by analyzing all the possible consolatory platitudes she could imagine. They sat in silence, both wiping eyes and noses as needed, until Chris came in to announce that there was room under the azalea bush and the hole was ready. Sonya struggled to rise, grimacing as she shifted her weight forward.

"Why don't you remain in the house?" Chris suggested quickly. "Miranda can come help me bury Doogie now.

Tomorrow is Sunday, so we can come back when it's light and have a ceremony."

Sonya sank back into her chair. "My heart wants to be with Doogie, but my knees say I should stay here." She sighed. "I'm not sure what I should do."

Miranda scanned the living room. Her mind searched for a helpful suggestion for Sonya while her gut wished she could stay inside and not look at Doogie's stiff corpse again. She noticed a small notepad and a pen and handed them to Sonya. "Why don't you start writing what you want to say tomorrow for the ceremony?"

Sonya nodded acceptance, but just let the paper fall onto her lap while she watched the two younger ones go outside to place her darling companion into the unsympathetic Earth.

Once they were a few steps away from the house, Chris turned to Miranda and whispered, "I'm glad Sonya was willing to stay inside. I found something and I wanted to show it to you first."

Chris led the way to the fence, flashlight stabbing through the darkness until it landed on a half-eaten piece of steak.

Miranda reached to touch the meat, but Chris put a restraining hand on her arm. "Don't touch it. I think might be poisoned."

"Poisoned?"

"I've heard of people using poisoned meat when they want to kill an animal. It leaves them all stiff and unnatural." They both turned and stared up at the fence and beyond to the towering house perched on top of the decaying garage.

Miranda clenched her hands until her nails bit into her skin. "Damn them!" She swooped down and grabbed the offending piece of meat, hurling it at the house where it landed with a satisfying thud.

"Why did you do that?" Chris demanded.

Miranda shrugged. "What difference does it make? They got their way. Again. First killing the trees, now Doogie. If Peter hadn't already had cancer, I'd accuse them of poisoning him too."

"But now we can't prove anything. We could have taken that piece of meat to a vet and gotten it tested. Then if it was poisoned, we could have called the police. Now we won't know for sure if Doogie just choked on a piece of the meat, if he was poisoned, or if he died for some other reason."

"Oh." Miranda chastised herself for another rash action. Not that she did them often, but they always seemed to be the wrong choice, which led to her more customary, hesitant responses. "Can't we take Doogie in to see if he was poisoned? We could tell that way."

"Sure, we could do that. But then we couldn't show *how* he was poisoned. Without the meat we have no proof."

"I guess I'd better go over and see if I can find that piece of meat."

"And get arrested for trespassing? Wandering around at night—what are you thinking? That will just cause more problems."

"So just what do *you* suggest then?" Miranda's tone dripped of implied sarcasm and repressed anger. The anger was actually directed at herself but it leaked out all over Chris, who backed away.

"Look, I'm just trying to help. I could've stayed home, or insisted you not come running over here again and we'd be eating that romantic meal I spent all day making."

"Oh, good. Guilt. That always helps a lot. I'm so glad you remembered to bring it along. It's your favorite spice—goes with every meal."

"Miranda? Chris?" Sonya's voice called from behind them. "What's wrong?"

They both swung around, the flashlight showing Sonya hobbling across the yard toward them, her walker tilting precariously on the uneven path. "Sonya," Chris called, sprinting back to her and steadying her. "What're you doing out here? I thought you were going to wait until we finished taking care of Doogie."

"I couldn't wait alone. I opened the door just to listen and I heard you arguing so I came out to see what was wrong."

Chris and Miranda shared guilty looks until Chris continued.

"We weren't arguing. We were just trying to figure out what to do."

"What to do about what?"

Sonya, with Chris's assistance, came up to where Miranda was staring at the ground. "I'm . . . I'm not sure we should burden you with this . . ."

Sonya leaned on her walker. "Well, you might as well go ahead, I'm here now."

Miranda looked at Chris who reached out and touched Sonya's arm. "I found a piece of meat. A nice piece of steak was lying here by the fence. I'm not sure, but there's a possibility that Doogie could have been poisoned."

"Oh, my." Sonya wobbled as Chris kept her from falling. "Where's the piece of meat?"

"I'm really sorry. I threw it over the fence. I . . . I just got mad thinking about what the neighbors did and I didn't stop to think. I just wanted it out of here and away from Doogie. But now we can't prove they did it. I'm so sorry." Miranda looked down at the earth again.

"Thank you."

"What?" Miranda jerked her head up and stared at Sonya.

"Thank you. I'm glad that meat is gone. I would have felt obligated to have it checked, but now it's gone and I don't need to worry about it."

"But you won't be able to prove the neighbors did it."

"I don't like thinking about that possibility."

"But they can't be allowed to get away with it. They've done so much to harm you and Peter . . . and . . . and now Doogie."

"Is this the hole you dug, Chris?" Sonya peered under the bush next to Doogie's body. "It looks very nice. And you were so careful not to hurt the plants around it."

Chris helped position her next to the small dog-sized plot. "Thanks, and I made sure it was the right size. We can bury him now if you want."

Miranda approached the other two. "But . . . but shouldn't we take him to the vet to have him tested?"

Sonya laid a hand on Miranda's arm. "No dear, there's no point now. He's dead. Let him be at peace. He was a very good dog. Though he could bark up a storm. But he was always there bouncing after me wherever I went." She pulled a tissue from her pocket and blew her nose.

Miranda started to protest again, still fighting the guilt from the consequence of her angry hurling of the meat, but it only came out as unintelligible monosyllables. "Uh . . . but . . . um."

Finally, Miranda knelt down next to Doogie and picked him up. *Poor puppy, I can't wait until those nasty neighbors get kicked off this world. They don't deserve to live near someone like Sonya. Not only did she lose Peter—now you're gone too.* She tried cradling him in her arms, but instead of the usual squirming, fluffy bundle of licks and love, it was like holding a prickly log, with four branches sticking out for legs. Chris helped her wrap Doogie's body in the soft, hand-made blanket, and lower it into the hole.

They looked up at Sonya, to see if she wanted to say anything but she shook her head, her lips making a thin jagged line across her face.

Miranda stood up and wrapped an arm around the older woman. "We'll come back tomorrow and do a real ceremony for him." Sonya nodded, looking very fragile and unsteady. Chris quickly filled the hole with dirt, then they both helped Sonya traverse the empty yard back to the house.

No one expressed any desire for food, but when Chris brought it out they picked at it in silence, broken only by flickering attempts to start a conversation. Like making a fire with wet wood, the words would start to catch, then quickly die.

# Chapter 18

## *Fire and Cookies*

On Thursday evening Chris was teaching an Italian pasta class, so after work, instead of driving home, Miranda headed for Sonya's house. She was feeling guilty for not having gone back since Sunday, when they'd had the ceremony for Doogie. She'd been reluctant to suggest another visit to Chris, after they'd spent most of the weekend with Sonya, but when Chris told her about the class she decided to take the opportunity and spend the evening with her author idol.

The drive between hospice and the Blooms' house took her past a liquor store. Miranda decided to stop and pick up a bottle of brandy, since she knew Sonya was almost out and it was hard for her to do the shopping with her painful knees. Sticking the bottle in her backpack, she strode back to the car. When she opened the door there was a translucent figure in the driver's seat wearing suspenders and knickers. A cap was floating above where a head should be.

"Aghh! Rand! You scared me!" *Damn, did anyone see me yelling at the car?* She swung around but no one was there, so she told her heart to stop racing as she concentrated on dividing her thoughts into quiet private ones and clear telepathic ones. *:Move over, please. I need to get in the car:* She flung her backpack through Rand, trying to push the insubstantial interloper into the passenger's seat.

Instead of moving, Rand materialized fully, opening his eyes wide as the bag passed through him. *:I see yer takin' to carryin' liquid spirits around with ya again:*

*:That bottle's for Sonya, so she can have her hot toddies:*

*:Ah. I remember me hot brandies. It would warm me straight through. When I was carryin' around a body that is. Why don't ya crack it open now and I'll share a wee drop of that bottle wit' ya:*

*:You can't drink. You're a ghost. You just said so:*

*:I ain't talkin' about warmin' me body. I wanna warm me spirit. Ya can do that fer me if'n ye drink:*

*:What do you mean?:* Miranda felt her gut twist and she was acutely aware that she was still standing in the liquor store's parking lot. She glanced at the passing cars, praying that no one who knew Chris would recognize her.

Rand drifted over to the other seat, allowing her to slip in and close the door. *:There's nothin' easier for a spirit to partake in than spirits. Ya just drink up and I'll be feelin' it wit' ya:*

*:I told you, this is for Sonya. And I didn't know you could feel alcohol when someone else drank:*

*:Not any som-uns. Jes' the ones the alcohol spirits have taken a very special likin' to:*

*:Well I'm not one of them anymore. I'm not an alcoholic. I'm over that. There's nothing wrong with me drinking. I just do it to keep Sonya company:*

*:Aye, and when ya're alone, yer keepin' ta' spirits company. Awful nice a ya to be so considerate. They'd been missin' ya t'ese last eight years:*

*:Those spirits are misleading you. I don't have a problem drinking. I can stop anytime I want. I just like the taste of wine or beer, that's all. And I don't drink anything harder:*

Rand tilted his head, and raised his eyebrows at her. *:Okay, I did have some brandy with Sonya. But that was just 'cause she poured it in my tea before I could tell her not to. Just to prove I don't have a drinking problem, I won't drink anything tonight. How's that for you? Satisfied?:*

Rand looked down at the bag, which was poking through his abdomen. *:Poor little bottle. It looks like she's gonna leave ya high an' dry tonight. And I won't be getting a drink of ya neit'er:* Rand made a dramatic sigh and disappeared. Except for his cap, which hovered over the passenger seat all the way to Sonya's house. Miranda tried to ignore the floating reminder of Rand as she picked up her backpack with the bottle in it and headed toward the house.

Sonya led her into the kitchen where two pieces of cake and two glasses of port waited for them on the table. "I know you're coming right from work and you probably haven't eaten dinner yet—but why not start with dessert?" Sonya indicated the bottle standing on the table. "I was going through a closet, trying to clean out some of the clutter we'd accumulated over the years, when I found this bottle. We bought it in Portugal when we went there for the International Physics conference. That must be twenty years ago. They say aging is beneficial for dessert wines, but if it isn't any good I'll fix us tea."

Miranda stared at the bottle. *Damn, I promised Rand I wouldn't drink tonight. And now Sonya's got it all set up for us.* "You didn't need to fix me anything. And I was thinking of having tea rather than wine tonight, if that's okay with you?"

"It wasn't a bother at all. I don't have anyone to cook for anymore. And it's nice to have the smell of just-baked cake in the house." She started to shuffle over to the stove. "I'll put the water on for tea, but sit down and at least tell me if the wine is worth keeping or not."

Miranda sat down at the table. *This'll be easy. I don't like sweet wines so I'll just take a taste to be polite and then I won't drink any more of it.* She tentatively sipped the wine, preparing to put it down and away from her, but she stopped as the port played along her tongue. "Hey, this is good! It's not too sweet at all. It has a very full-bodied flavor."

Sonya smiled. "Oh good. I was afraid it went bad."

"It's aged really well. I've never had a port wine like this before. Usually it's pretty syrupy. This one's really smooth." Miranda swirled more of it around inside her mouth. "It has a hint of oak and hazelnut with a splash of cherry."

"I'm glad you like it. Have some more." Sonya reached over and refilled Miranda's glass. Miranda played with her cake, finding it too sweet, but the wine was a pleasant surprise, helping her relax from a stressful day at work. She'd finally gotten the courage to fire Stephanie, her gossipy, work-avoidant receptionist. She'd delayed it as long as possible, since Stephanie's father was the vice president of hospice's board of directors.

Now sitting and drinking quietly with Sonya, she felt months of tension seeping away. *I deserve a nice treat after finally getting rid of Stephanie.* She raised the bottle, reaching over to pour Sonya more wine, then realized the older woman's glass was still full. Before Miranda set the bottle down she refilled her own glass, then raised it in a salute. "Here's to taking care of business—getting rid of difficulties and cleaning out old closets." She tipped her glass to Sonya. "May you find many more treasures." Bringing the glass to her lips she let the liquid flow into her, tilting her head back to savor the last drops.

"Oh, I'm sure I will. There are just boxes and boxes of things I need to go through. We'd saved them all, anticipating a time we'd go through them together, but life just kept happening." Sonya gave Miranda a forced I'm-doing-fine smile. "It gives me something to do. And I don't want to leave it for friends to go through." Miranda nodded, hiding behind the need to fill her glass again.

After finally accepting Miranda's excuse of no dinner as reason enough to not eat her cake, Sonya finished her own piece, then rose and started clearing the table. "I'll wrap up your piece and add an extra one for Chris and you can have it tonight after your dinner." Sonya placed the package next to Miranda, then started shuffling into the living room. Miranda emptied the last of the bottle of port into her glass, then followed after her widowed friend.

As Sonya settled into her recliner, she started to pull a quilt onto her lap, but stopped as her gaze was drawn to the empty place where Doogie's bed used to be. She tossed the coverlet onto the couch, letting her hands tumble back into her lap. "I just can't get used to him being gone. Sometimes during the day I think I hear him whining for me. I just try to imagine that he's telling me both he and Peter are fine. It's the nights that are the hardest. I keep waking up, thinking I need to go let him in. Then I remember and can't get back to sleep."

"He was a good dog." Miranda winced at her words. *Wow, that was lame. Why can't I think of something better? How many years have I worked at hospice and all I can think of is 'he was a good dog?'*

Those simple words released a flood of tears as Sonya sobbed into the tissues Miranda started handing her. After many minutes of crying, Sonya sat back and sighed, closing her eyes as the tension washed off her face.

Miranda sat in awed silence, watching Sonya's chest rise and fall with her slow breaths. *Sonya's so amazing. So wise about spirits, yet so completely in the N-World too. And I can't believe I actually know her and am sitting here with her.* Sonya's head slowly dropped onto her chest and her breathing became noisy.

Miranda looked at her watch. It was only six o'clock. She didn't want to disturb Sonya by leaving, and Chris wouldn't be home for another couple hours so she glanced around for something to read.

Picking up a book called *Are there Spirits in Your Life?* she made herself comfortable on the couch, unconsciously pulling the quilt over her lap in anticipation of Doogie jumping up. She looked around when there was no squirming ball of fur running toward her. *Damn, now I'm forgetting he's gone. It sure feels empty without him. I don't know how Sonya manages with both Peter and Doogie dead.*

Her gaze was drawn to the window. There was just enough light to identify the azalea bush where Doogie was buried.

Miranda slipped off the couch and wandered over to the sliding door that led to the backyard.

*I should go out and check and make sure no animal has disturbed his grave.* She swung the door open putting a hand against the railing to steady herself as she walked outside. Stepping carefully to keep her balance, she inched toward the azalea bush. The mound was undisturbed, except for a dog biscuit placed just below the wooden plaque proclaiming, "Doogie: best friend to Peter and Sonya Bloom. R.I.P." *Sonya must have been out here today to put that biscuit down, otherwise I'm sure the neighborhood cats would have at least tried to eat it.*

She crouched next to Doogie's grave, reaching out and running her fingers along the fake diamonds on his old collar, which they had placed next to the wooden marker. She glanced to the left of the mound, where three unweathered stumps stood. Furious thoughts pounded in her head. *It's not fair. Sonya's lost too much already. How could they do this? They're despicable imitations of humans. No, they're typical humans, that's why this world is so fucked up. Greemens! Human gremlins—that's what they are.* Miranda felt proud of her clever pairing of the two words.

She bent forward, feeling a movement across her back, and realized she had unconsciously slung her backpack on before leaving the house.

As she shifted her shoulders, the bottle of brandy slid back and forth across her back. Annoyed, she yanked the pack off and pulled out the offending nuisance. With a quick twist she unscrewed the cap and gasped as a yellow haze emerged. She rubbed her eyes and stared until she convinced herself she had seen nothing escape from the bottle.

"If there was a genie inside you," she told the bottle of brandy, which she placed on the nearest stump, "I certainly know what I'd wish for. I'd wish Doogie alive. Hell, I'd wish Peter alive as well. Maybe I'd even wish their son alive." Miranda shook her head, feeling a slight dizziness from the many glasses of port she'd drunk with Sonya. "Well, since I can't wish for that, what about wishing the neighbors gone? Or that their three-story monstrosity had never been built. Then at least the trees would still be here."

*:Wish for whatever you want:* whispered a penetratingly seductive voice.

"What?" Miranda looked around the yard. Seeing nothing, she switched to Cat Vision, which showed her a filmy yellowish-green haze hovering near the bottle.

*:The power is yours. Do as you wish,:* the voice continued.

Miranda grabbed the bottle, waving it at the mist. "Go away!" she hissed. "Whatever you are, leave!"

*:You know me. You have provided me with energy many times in the past. Now you are freely giving it to me again. In addition to taking your life essence in the form of energy, I also offer you power so that you can do what you want to the neighbors:*

"I don't want to do anything to those filthy . . ." Her voice trailed off as the lie stuck in her throat. She gripped the bottle harder. "You're no wish-fulfilling genie. You're the alcohol speaking." The wine in her blood felt like a magnet drawing her toward the bottle and its promises. *Why'd I ever start drinking again? Sonya wouldn't have minded if I'd have told her I was an alcoholic. She's so sweet. But once I started to drink, I definitely couldn't tell her. I had to just keep drinking.* Miranda's hand started to raise the bottle to her face.

An almost-sober part of her called out inside her, *No. Don't drink now.*

*:Pour the alcohol on the ground if you wish:* The spirit spoke in a most reasonably sounding voice.

Using Cat Vision again, Miranda looked directly at the murky mist surrounding the bottle. "I can do that? If I pour you out, you'll go away?"

*:Stop giving me energy and I will go away. I have never forced you. I simply come whenever you offer me your life essence:*

Miranda nodded and tried to tilt her hand, still clutched tightly around the neck of the bottle. Her fingers quivered slightly then lay still. She tried again to get her arm to rotate but it felt as though it wasn't attached to her hand any more. Still upright in her grip, the bottle felt smooth and inviting. There was a slight warmth emanating from it, encouraging Miranda to release a few of the knots of tension in her shoulders.

*:That's right, relax, feel how safe you are with me. I'm here to help you. I know you as no one else will ever know you:*

Miranda swallowed then felt her stomach churning as she stared at the yellow-green mist. "Will you please get back in the bottle?"

*:I am not in the bottle. I have never been in the bottle. But I am inside you when you drink from the bottle:*

Miranda started to turn toward the voice, which was coming from beside her, but she was distracted when the mist started to move. It floated toward the mouth of the bottle, then slithered down the outside and oozed around Miranda's arm. Miranda felt a familiar comfort from the touch, her arm and shoulder relaxing as the bottle inched its way closer to her mouth. *It won't hurt to warm myself up a little. It's cold out here. I won't take but a sip. My throat's dry.* The first sip went down easily, heating her belly and thawing the last of the hesitation. Her resistance melted away completely as she poured more liquid down her throat.

Ten minutes later, Miranda set the half empty bottle down on a stump. *There used to be a beautiful tree here. Was this the one Sam used to swing on? I can't remember.* She swayed slightly, her head buzzing as she reached out a hand, touching the fence separating the two yards. Her mind drifted back to the night she had sat by the stumps when Doogie had come yelping out, running around the stump Merawl was sitting on. She remembered the neighbor shouting how he'd kill the dog if it didn't shut up.

She closed her hands into fists, tightening them until she could feel pressure building in her palms. She stretched out her right hand. Looking at it with Cat Vision, she could see the energy swirling around it that had come from the bottle of brandy. Murky reds and oranges obscured her fingers as the thick fog danced around her hand. *I wonder if I could form this into a ball of pure energy.* The twisting stream coalesced into a misshapen ball floating above her palm. *Can I put more energy into it?* The ball grew as more vapor surged from the alcohol, running through her body and into her palm. She reached down with her left hand, hauling the bottle up and taking a deep drink.

Placing it back on the stump she moved her left hand next to her right hand.

More orange-ish fog seeped from her body, running down both arms and into the ball, which was now glowing like a large eye staring out from the darkness.

A small voice inside Miranda whispered, *This is getting creepy. What if the gremlins come through? They might have been the ones who killed Doogie. You should go inside. Go get something to eat. This is all happening because you've been drinking on an empty stomach.*

The spirit's voice came through clear and direct. *:The power is yours to use. Do whatever you wish with it:*

Miranda's gaze was drawn toward the bottle. Then she noticed the stump it was sitting on. *It wasn't any gremlins that killed Doogie. It was those damn neighbors. Rotten greemens. That's what they are.* The fiery, floating ball started to burn brighter as Miranda's hatred of the neighbors intensified. Her body started to shake, and the small part of her that was pleading to go back inside the house was drowned by another drink of brandy. Her fingers curled, like a tiger flexing her claws. The ball responded by dancing higher in the air.

*I bet they were laughing on the other side of the fence while we were burying Doogie. They deserve to know the pain they've created for Sonya.* A spark flew from her palm, twisted in the air and went out. Another followed and then another. *Fire. They deserve fire.*

A miniature blaze ignited above Miranda's palm, burning intensely yet not harming her skin. It pulsed and sang, "Yes, we are fire. Let us out. We will help you. We will avenge you."

Images of the neighbors' house in flames filled Miranda's mind. *They deserve it. They do! I'll make the fire burn that monstrous add-on they created. Then I'll pull it back so they'll only have that dilapidated garage they started with. Damn, stupid greemens!*

Miranda grinned thinking of Susan and how her term fit the neighbors so perfectly. "I can't wait to tell all this to Susan." Miranda spoke aloud to the flame, which climbed higher, stretching toward the top of the fence.

*Susan.* The name echoed in Miranda's mind. *Susan. I can't tell her about this. What would I say? That I used my abilities to burn down a house? What if they're inside? They're such slobs they're probably sitting in their living room right now, a couple of disgusting couch potatoes.*

The flame swelled, making a last attempt for the house, then vanished as Miranda's head fell into her hands and she slumped onto the ground.

*Oh my God. What was I going to do? I could never have told Susan. And what about Chris? Or Sonya? She's right here. She'd have known what I did. She'd never forgive me for calling fire spirits on the neighbors. And the grandmothers! I'd have definitely ended up in the wrong world for burning down a house.*

*:Well, lass, now ya can be tellin' all them good people what's ya done:* Miranda jerked her head up to see a shadowy silhouette of a man sitting on the stump next to the bottle, smoking a pipe. Instead of the smoke drifting away into the air, it flowed directly from the end of the pipe into the cap perched on Rand's head. Miranda could just make out the wispy vapor circling through his head and coming out through the pipe to start the cycle again.

*:What're you doing?:*

*:Since I couldn't get ye to share yer spirits wit' me. I thought I'd take up smokin' agin. Tis a nice relaxin' 'abit. Maybe ya outa try it some time. Ya seem a wee bit upset t'is evenin':* Rand held out the pipe to Miranda who started to reach for it, then pulled her hand back.

*:I can't touch that. It's not real:*

*:Real? Might not be as real as t'is bottle is ta ye, but least I can touch me pipe:* Rand dissolved the pipe into the palm of his hand then started to swipe both hands through the brandy bottle sitting on the stump next to him. His hands kept passing through the bottle, not moving the glass, but they did dislodge fragments of red and orange murkiness that started to dance around the brandy bottle. Miranda's stomach clenched as she felt the alcohol inside her pulling her toward the bottle. An image of Susan flashed through her mind, looking at her with trust and gratitude.

It was followed by a memory of Chris's tears, after they'd had to endure a holiday visit with the abusive, alcoholic father Chris had grown up with.

Miranda took a deep breath and filled her mind with an image of Sonya's kind, accepting eyes. *I have to decide. I can't keep doing this to them.* She reached down beside her, groping along the ground. Her hand touched a broken branch, a remnant of the trees that were now long gone. Wrapping her fingers around the wood, she flung it at the brandy bottle, as though she was drowning and trying to throw herself a lifeline. The stick connected with the bottle, tipping it on its side and causing dark amber liquid to run across the stump.

Miranda stuffed her hands into her pockets to keep herself from grabbing the bottle and tipping it back upright. As the liquid flowed towards him, Rand raised himself off the wet stump and started to float in the air, one leg crossed over the other as though a chair was still supporting him. He drifted toward the next stump until he was above it, then he lowered himself onto it, wiping his hands over his pants as though cleaning off a spill. *:Careful lass, ye almost got me all covered with spirits. What would people be sayin'? Me smellin' a alcohol and at me age:* Rand shook his head, *tsk*ing several times. *:T'at's what I git fer 'angin' out wit' you solid peoples. Won't give me a drop a good spirits but ye don't think nothin' of spillin' them all over me:*

Miranda rewarded his humor with a stiff half-smile. *:Man, am I glad you showed up. I don't know how I got into this mess:* Rand leaned forward, about to speak again. *:Okay, I do know what happened. I told you I wasn't going to drink and that I could stop any time I wanted—but I didn't. I kept drinking with Sonya and then I almost got myself into a real mess:* Miranda felt completely sober, but a rational part of her mind was calculating the impossibility of all the alcohol leaving her system so quickly. So she reached for her backpack and pulled out a small bag containing a shell, matches, and some sage. She used it whenever she needed to clean her energy field and she felt especially needy at the moment. *:At least you're the only one who knows about this:*

*:Aye, and keepin' it that way—just a secret 'tween you and us spirits—will certainly make sure nothin' 'appens in the future like it almost did t'night:*

Miranda lit the sage, watching it flame briefly, reminding her of the ball of fire, then the leaves burned out and started a soothing, cleansing smoke. She placed the leaves in the shell then set the shell on the stump so she could use both hands to wash the smoke over her body. She imagined the cloud of smoke healing her energy field of all the alcohol she'd consumed.

Collecting her thoughts, she sent them telepathically to Rand. *:I suppose that's your way of hinting that I should tell someone about it. And you're right. I got into this mess by not telling Sonya I was an alcoholic, then not telling Chris I was drinking again:*

She winced remembering all the questions, and eventually accusations from Chris about how she'd "changed" since the conference, where she'd started drinking again.

Thinking back over the last months, it seemed that most of their arguments occurred after she'd snuck some alcohol. And Chris's fears about how she'd changed would've easily been explained if she'd been honest about her drinking. *I definitely need to apologize. God, eight years and I got swept back in so easily. Will Chris ever be able to forgive me? And trust! I can't even begin to expect that. I really screwed this up major.* That thought woke up her urge to drink and a desire to return to denial. *No. Whatever happens I have to be honest and deal with the consequences—not keep hiding behind alcohol.*

*:Aye lass, now t'ems good thoughts ta be 'avin'. Ya might even find yer lover is more understandin' t'en ya expect and won't even go disapperin' on ya:* With those final words, Rand vanished. Miranda was left sitting next to an empty bottle and a quiet grave. She tried to give herself more time to wash the last of the alcohol out of her system, but worries about Sonya kept intruding into her mind.

She stood up, swaying slightly. A spirit brushed against her arm, sending her strength. She turned and squinted at the tall, straight figure: no curves, just firm clear lines delineating the spirit.

It was dressed in an unadorned, amber robe that touched the ground. Miranda sensed both the familiar and unknown. Thinking carefully she asked, *:Who are you?:*

Merawl spoke from down at her ankles. *:Feel it closely. You'll recognize it:*

*:Merawl! Am I glad to see you!:* Miranda took a step and would have stumbled, but the tall, slender spirit sent her support and helped her stand up straight. She peered at it, shaking her head as she tried to sense what it was. A tendril of energy bridged between them and she felt its iron-firm power.

Staggering backwards, Miranda put up her hands, her heart clenching in fear. "You're the alcohol spirit. I thought I got rid of you."

The pillar of energy moved closer to her, emitting a strong clean force. *:I am not the alcohol spirit. I am Power. I am here for whatever you wish. I take energy when you give it. I give energy when you want it. The choice is always yours:*

Miranda's mind raced back eight years to when Merawl first helped her change her relationship with alcohol. Once she stopped drinking, she had a sense that there had been a spirit drawing energy from her whenever she drank. *:You're that spirit from before aren't you? I forgot about you, once I wasn't drinking. But that's who you are, right?:*

*:Yes, you gave me energy before. Then you no longer offered me your life essence. So I went away. Now you're giving me energy again. But you can also ask for what you want from me. I give energy. I take energy. That is what I do:*

Miranda looked down at the gray tabby, who was now perched on one of the stumps. *:Merawl? Is it safe to receive anything from this spirit? He's almost ruined my life several times, including tonight:*

Before Merawl had a chance to respond, Power answered. *:Those were your choices. I do not ruin lives. I collect energy so that I have it to give, when you or others ask for it. When some people drink alcohol they freely give me their life essence, so I collect it. You have given me much energy tonight. Do you wish any back now?:*

Miranda glanced at her cat guide, who had started grooming himself. *He certainly seems nonchalant about all this. But at least he's still here, in case I get into trouble.* She turned to the tall spirit. *:Okay, I'd like you to help me:* Miranda pursed her lips together as she tried to shift through her thoughts. *I got into this mess because of my anger at the neighbors. But I can't just leave them to harass Sonya more. I have to do something to them . . .* She pushed the last of that thought away, feeling the memory of the fire and what she almost did constricting her breathing with bands of fright.

*:If you wish to protect, I can help you make strong boundaries:*

The assurance with which Power spoke reminded Miranda of how she was never able to maneuver around his capacity to control her. Or, as he would say, his ability to take her life essence when she drank. *:You're strong, so I can imagine the solid, safe boundaries you could make. You've certainly never let me get the better of you when I was drinking. Including tonight!:*

The slender figure bowed its head at her. *:Yes, that is truth. Those who respect truth—that my power is greater than theirs—can more easily partake in my solidness. Those who ignore that truth give me their power:*

*:Can you put up a protection for Sonya so those nasty neighbors can't hurt her anymore?:*

*:Is that what she wishes?:*

*:Yeah. Well, actually, I don't know. But I'm sure she'd want it:* Miranda paused, aware that if she was going to enjoy the support of Power, everything had to be based in truth. *:I guess it's really me that wants it. I can't speak for her:*

*:Then I will help you put up a barrier for you. Use the sage to create a ring of smoke around the place your friend claims for her land. I will put my energy into it:.*

Miranda looked at the small shell with the half-burned leaves she'd used. Then she searched her pack, retrieving a bundle of sage that a man had given her for helping him connect to his spirit guides. She lit the herb then waved it in front of her until only smoke remained.

Merawl walked over and sat down in front of her. She waved the smoke over him as his form got denser and clearer. Then he leapt up, disappearing at the top of his jump. *:Good luck, Merawl. Don't run into any gremlins:* She turned and held out the sage bundle to Power.

As the smoke drifted upward the spirit began to dissolve. It melted into a mist that twisted and danced with the sage smoke. Miranda walked along the fence surrounding the Blooms' yard, carefully letting the smoke billow out ahead of her.

After twice around the property, Miranda knelt in front of the three tree stumps, allowing the smoke to drift over them, releasing the tormented energy they'd carried the last few months.

Miranda sighed as the smoke took away the sorrow and let her imagine them as gentle places to sit for her and Sonya. *:Thank you, spirit. I will try not to ignore you again. I prefer when you're helping me use energy, not taking mine from me:*

The spirit did not rematerialize but his voice came through strongly into Miranda's mind. *:I have much energy to share with you. Whenever you wish my help, ask for it:*

She rose up, brushing bark off her pants, and looked around the yard. Cat Vision showed her a reassuringly clear barrier of crimson light along the fence line. *This feels much better. Though I'm not sure I want to deal with that spirit again. Certainly not through drinking. Remembering tonight should keep me sober for at least a week.*

Feeling centered and safe, she slowly walked back to the house. As she opened the door the aroma of fresh cookies surrounded her. She walked into the kitchen to discover Sonya had arisen from her nap and the counters were full of empty mixing bowls and baking sheets displaying steaming cookies.

"What's the occasion?" Miranda asked.

"Ah, there you are. I thought maybe you were outside." Sonya smiled in welcome, then sorrow filled her face. "Sara from across the street called. I guess I'd dozed off because the phone woke me up. She was calling to check on me and asked me if I'd heard the news about the neighbors."

She nodded her head to the left to indicate the tree-hating ones on the other side of the fence. "Sara ran into the wife at the pharmacy and learned the husband has cancer."

Miranda felt a glee bounce around inside her, along with thoughts of having won. She schooled her expression to match Sonya's grave one. "That's too bad. Do you know if it's serious?"

"Sara didn't get many details, just that he has cancer and that she was picking up a lot of prescriptions and was very upset." Sonya swept her hand over the crowded counter. "So I'm making some cookies to take over to them."

Miranda stared at her as if she'd just said she was baking biscuits for gremlins. "You can't be serious? You're taking those assholes cookies? After the hell they put you through!"

"Miranda dear, if Peter were here he'd be encouraging you to find better words to express yourself."

"But they're the ones who poisoned Doogie. And they're keeping you hostage in your own home. You know they had to be the ones who called the police to get your license taken away."

"And I shouldn't have been driving anyway."

"But it wasn't their decision to make."

"And if I could have passed the test I would still be driving. They were right."

"Still, you don't need to be making them cookies! What about Doogie? You should be seething in rage toward them. They don't deserve something nice. They deserve all the rottenness they've caused you." Miranda held her breath as she felt the alcohol still swimming in her body start to feed off her fury, encouraging it. *Easy, watch it. I don't want to get trapped in that again.* A bell chimed.

"Ah, the last batch must be ready." Sonya bent down and opened the oven door.

Miranda watched her extract another steaming tray of goodness. "I just don't understand. They've lied to you, bullied you. They didn't even say they were sorry when Peter died. How can you take them cookies? You must be some manifestation of ultimate kindness."

Sonya waved a hand at her. "Don't look at me like I'm some kind of saint. I simply got tired of hating them. When you get to be my age you'll understand how heavy hate is. I'm not giving them cookies to make them feel better—I'm doing it so I can feel better. Nothing will bring Doogie back and nothing can prevent them from doing something else nasty to me. The only choices I have are to sit here in fear of what will happen next, or to bake cookies. And I decided to bake cookies."

Miranda was quiet as Sonya busied herself arranging the warm delicacies on the plate. When she'd finished she laid a hand on Miranda's arm. "What if you knew that their only daughter was killed by a drunk driver just like Sam?"

Miranda immediately felt her emotions shifting. "Oh, I didn't know. I guess that could explain some of their rudeness."

"And what if you knew that she has terrible arthritis and is in pain every day, and now he has cancer?"

"Maybe that justifies some of why she's so mean. Chronic pain is terrible. And we both know the trauma of having someone you love get cancer. Okay I guess I can feel some empathy toward them. If you're determined to go, I'll help you take these over." Miranda picked up the plate of cookies and started toward the door, while Sonya put on her coat. "How did you learn all that about them anyway? Did Sara tell you?"

Sonya started wheeling her walker behind Miranda. "No one told me. I just made it up."

Miranda spun around, staring at Sonya. "You made it up! Why?"

"Not the part about the cancer. That's true. The point is, the pain and the daughter's death could be true. Or something even worse or harder to deal with. Ever since Sam died, I've always tried to be loving in his name. He was the kindest soul. I try to do the things he never got a chance to do. And if I find I have trouble opening my heart to someone, all I have to do is imagine that they lost a child and then it's easy." She bumped the wheels of her walker gently against Miranda's shins nudging her toward the neighbors. Miranda turned and silently held the door open for her.

When they returned, Miranda headed into the kitchen to put on some water for tea, while Sonya went to the liquor cabinet and pulled out an almost empty bottle of brandy. "Do you want a little extra warmth in your tea? It was colder than I thought walking over there."

Miranda felt a twist of guilt, remembering how she'd told Rand the brandy she'd bought was for Sonya. "No thanks, I'll just have it plain tonight. Of course if they'd been nice enough to invite us in, rather than leaving us standing on the porch, we wouldn't be so cold. Shall I bring a plate of cookies for us to have with the tea?"

"That sounds lovely. I'll just rest my old bones in my chair here."

Miranda cleaned up the kitchen while the water heated, then brought in a tray with their snack.

Sonya took her cup and poured in a tiny amount of brandy, then put the bottle away.

Miranda marveled at her laissez faire attitude with the alcohol. *If I'd been drinking that brandy I would have kept it close and given myself a larger shot.*

She felt Power settle on the couch next to her.

*:The woman who is your friend is no one I know. She does not throw away her life essence when she drinks. What Rand told you is true. Spirits can absorb energy through certain humans when they're drinking, giving us the power to affect the physical realm:*

*:Yeah, you were certainly using me. You had me puppet dancing again:* It felt good to use a Susan-ism after the shock of how close she'd come to harming their relationship.

*:I do not use you. I collect energy you waste when you drink:*

*:Same difference to me:*

*:No:* the word came through strongly, making Miranda pay closer attention to what Power was saying.

*:It's your free choice to drink, take drugs, rage, or be violent. These are all your choices. Once you decided to allow the chemical essence of alcohol into your physical body, it encouraged you to continue drinking by making your body want more of the chemicals. You encouraged yourself to rage and plot violence toward the neighbors. I only responded by offering you power.*

*Then as you raged, I simply drew all the life force I could from you, taking your energy in its strongest form:*

  *:Yuck. You take my energy and then you offer it back to me, then you take it again? You make it sound like a simple business deal:*

  *:Yes, now you understand. I am Power. I am efficient at finding, storing, and giving energy:*

  *:So what was that ugly haze I saw around the bottle? I thought that was you:*

  *:The haze was the alcohol. Something powerful enough to alter your body will have an energetic form. If you look for it, you can see it:*

"Miranda?" Sonya had picked up the plate of cookies and was offering it to her. "Do you want one? Or would you prefer to wait until after you've had dinner? You can take some home for you and Chris if you want."

Miranda reached for a cookie, unable to resist the chocolate chips smiling at her from its round face. "I'll just have a few. Then I'd better be getting back home."

Sonya settled back into her easy chair. "Thank you for staying and helping me walk over there tonight. That felt nice."

Miranda looked at Sonya, squinting her eyes, trying to see what magic made her so kind in the face of such brutishness. She shook her head. "Nice? How can you mean that? They were gruff and snarly. They barely thanked you for the cookies and they didn't even invite us in."

"I wasn't referring to them. I was referring to how I felt. Ever since they built that addition to their garage there's been tension between us. I didn't want it any more. Now, I can think of them as the neighbors who've had too much heartache in their lives, and who I take cookies to."

"You're a saint, Sonya." Miranda remembered the image of Sonya offering cookies to two stiff, frowning people, wrapped in stained robes and sweats in front of a house in disarray. "I wonder what they're thinking of you now?"

"Probably nothing nice. Unfortunately they've never seemed very happy."

Miranda scanned the image of the neighbor's house in her mind, noticing the unwashed dishes, scattered papers and proliferation of empty bottles. It looked like a home that had as much sorrow as Seattle had rain. *I certainly know what it's like wrapping my life around alcohol every day.*

The spirit next to her grew taller and his voice came through clearly. *:Yes, they have been offering me their life forces for many Earth turnings:*

Miranda glanced over at Sonya, who seemed wrapped in a blanket of contemplation, so she concentrated on sending her thoughts to Power. *:I guess that could explain some of their behavior. If I could almost burn down their house while drinking, I suppose I have to understand how they could poison a dog. Not that I'm saying it's okay they did it!:* Looking over at Power, she tried to see it as evil, but it didn't feel evil. *:How can you lead people to do such terrible, evil things?:*

*:I do nothing. I offer you everything—relaxation, courage, power, the ability to do whatever you want. It is and has been your choice. I encourage you to relax and I encourage you to use power, for whatever you want:*

Miranda tried to play back the evening of drinking in her mind, to remember what Power had said, when she thought he was the genie from the bottle. It was an incoherent, unpleasant memory and she soon gave up on it and simply acknowledged to the spirit.

*:You're right. I was the one that got all 'fired' up about wanting revenge on those people. But that doesn't explain why you take all the energy you can from me and others who drink:*

*:It is how I gain the energy I then give to you and others. Were you not pleased that I had power to offer you for protecting your friend's yard?:*

Miranda used Cat Vision to check on the gentle glow that was surrounding Sonya's property. She relaxed, feeling secure within it. *:Yes, you certainly did offer me support in making Sonya safer:* She smiled and thought to herself, *And I love that you're using the neighbor's own energy to protect Sonya from their nastiness.*

*:Yes. It is efficient to use the life force that is closest to create a barrier:* Miranda jumped, realizing Power had easily heard what she believed was a very private thought. He continued, reading more of her inner thoughts. *:I know your thoughts so that I may take your energy when you are considering drinking, struggling with drinking, actually drinking alcohol, and condemning yourself after drinking. I collect all people's life force this way, which is why I am always more powerful than any one person. Those who struggle with me feed me energy:*

Miranda squirmed in her chair. *:Why are you telling me all that when you just admitted you steal my energy when I even think about drinking?:*

*:I take energy; I give energy. It is your choice:*

*:This is a lot to think about. I'm going to need some time with this:*

*:Take all the time you need. I am always with you:*

Miranda glanced at her watch, then cleared her throat to get Sonya's attention. "I'd better be getting back."

Sonya waved, indicating the kitchen. "Don't forget your cake and take some cookies for Chris too. Stop by again when you can. It's always lovely seeing you."

"I'll be back next Thursday." *If I can stay away from drinking and from doing anything really stupid.* Miranda bent down and hugged her mentor, then walked very carefully out to her car.

# Chapter 19

## *Sonya and Bear*

When Miranda arrived at the Blooms' home the next Thursday evening, she found Sonya busy in the kitchen fixing a plate of bite-size sandwiches.

She eyed the delicacies, while her stomach reminded her she had missed lunch. "Thanks for fixing these, but you didn't need to go to all this trouble for me."

"Nonsense, I did this for myself." Sonya picked up the plate, balanced it on the seat of her walker and headed for the living room. "I thought this would be healthier for both of us than cake and cookies tonight." She glanced back over her shoulder at Miranda who was following obediently behind her. "Now, why don't you get us a couple glasses of wine and we can have a nice snack while we talk."

Miranda went back into the kitchen and opened the familiar liquor cabinet. When she reached for the elegantly styled glasses she only brought out one.

She uncorked the bottle of wine and poured a small amount into the glass. Then she went to the cupboard by the sink, grabbed a plain glass and filled it with water. She returned to the living room and handed Sonya her glass of wine.

Glancing at Miranda's glass, Sonya asked, "Aren't you having wine?"

Miranda sat down next to her author idol. She bent her head, staring into her glass of water. "I um . . . I shouldn't really drink. I just . . . um . . . didn't want you thinking badly of me. But . . ."

Miranda felt Sonya's hand on her arm. "You mean you didn't want me knowing you're an alcoholic?"

Miranda's head shot up. "You knew? How did you . . .?"

"I could tell by the way you were hanging your head just now. And the fact that you can hear spirits talking. Seems to go with the trade. I used to feel like maybe there was something wrong with me because I wasn't an alcoholic."

Miranda stared mutely at Sonya, while her mentor continued. "Seems like just about every person I've known with a gift for speaking to guides or seeing into the non-physical realms is also open to alcoholism, especially the Native American mystics. I've heard some of them remark that there's a good reason why people refer to alcohol as spirits." Sonya smiled, and Miranda nodded weakly in return.

"So you didn't know anything about my drinking before now?"

"Heavens, no. You certainly gave no sign to us that you had a disease concerning alcohol. But then, by what I've been told, that's the mark of an alcoholic: to be able to be a good actor and not draw attention to your drinking."

"That's true. Hiding and denying—we're good at that. Relationships, well, we're pretty poor at them."

"Why do you say that?"

"Chris threatened to leave me eight years ago if I didn't do something about my drinking. I thought I'd taken care of it. Thought everything was fine. I was even able to convince myself when I started drinking again last fall that I could now drink socially with no problem. I'd been hiding my drinking from Chris, telling myself I was saving it for a surprise, for a special occasion to show how I could now control my drinking.

But that was all about me and drinking. All Chris wanted was honesty."

Miranda paused, looking down into her water as she slowly swirled the clear liquid. "Last week after I left here, I went home and admitted everything: how I'd started drinking again, how I'd been hiding the bottles and lying about staying after work for meetings. I was terrified that Chris would get mad and leave. But you won't believe what Chris was actually worried about!" Sonya raised her eyebrows and gave her an encouraging look. "Chris was afraid *I* was getting ready to leave, afraid I wanted a partner who was able to communicate with spirits, who could join me in working with guides. If we both talked with guides we'd have twice as many of them around to deal with. That's the last thing I need!" Miranda shook her head in disbelief. "So there we were, both of us in our own worlds, both worried about losing our relationship."

"So how'd it all work out?"

Miranda sighed. "Luckily, admitting everything helped. Together we were able to review the fights we've had this last year, to look at Chris's sadness at feeling left out, fears about my working with guides and worries that there was something else going on. And there was something else going on: my drinking. Once the alcohol piece got put back in, things started fitting together. Does any of this make sense to you?"

Sonya waved at the little sandwiches perched on Miranda's plate. "Don't forget to eat, dear." She paused, waiting while Miranda munched on a sandwich and took a sip of water. "Yes, it makes sense to someone whose life has also been complicated by spirits talking to just her and not to her partner. Add in drinking and well, enough people have told me about how . . . what's the word . . . convoluted? Yes, I think that fits. Especially when you consider the shame people feel when they have the alcohol illness and how they react to that shame. It makes things convoluted—and messy too, right?"

"Yeah, I sure made a mess out of my relationship. It's just a good thing Chris prefers honesty to perfection. I think I'd die if I'd lost Chris after all these years. But it's amazing, we're closer this week than we've been all of last year."

Sonya smiled. "Ah, I'd give anything to have a good fight with Peter again."

"You two fought? You seemed to love each other so much."

"We did. That's why we'd fight. Because we cared about each other. But it's not easy. Especially with Peter being the definitive scientist. At least your partner seems more open to the idea that guides exist. At times I felt like Peter's mission in life was to save me from my 'delusions'."

"Really? He seemed pretty open to me. He really liked talking about . . ." Miranda tensed, biting back her words.

"That's okay, dear. I'm glad he was able to open up and talk with you." Sonya turned away from Miranda and stared quietly at Peter's empty recliner.

Miranda's gut clenched. *Now I've made her feel worse. How could I be so insensitive? I just kept going on and on about Chris and my relationship. Of course she wishes she could do anything with Peter—even fight with him again. Now what do I do?*

*:Aye, everythin's ruined lass. Only t'ing ta do is ta worry 'bout 'ow you're always at da center ruinin' everythin':*

*McNally!* Miranda was horrified to see the Irish ghost sitting in Peter's recliner, casually smoking his pipe. *:Get out of Peter's chair! How can you be so disrespectful of the dead?:*

McNally stared at her, raising his eyebrows until his entire face started elongating, causing the top of his head to float several feet above his neck. Then slowly, his body started levitating off the chair, trying to catch up with his head. *:Me apologies, lass. I meant no disrespect of ta dead:*

*:How can you make jokes at a time like this? I've upset Sonya and you're clowning around:*

McNally turned and looked at Sonya. *:Seems like she's doin' fine ta me?:* Miranda followed McNally's gaze and noticed the older woman was gazing out the living room window.

"Sonya?" She asked gently as her author idol turned toward her. "What are you looking at?"

She waved out at her back yard. "At them."

Miranda looked at the tree stumps and small grave dominating her view. "Pretty rotten of the neighbors to ruin your backyard and cause you so much grief."

Sonya didn't respond and Miranda felt the silence in room growing. *Say something comforting! She needs you now.*

"Do you see them?" Sonya asked, breaking into Miranda's inner diatribe.

"What?"

"The fairies. There's an Earth fairy on top of the middle stump."

Miranda gazed out the window, amazed to see a small brown being, half-human, half-bear walking across the stump, swishing a blade of grass back and forth like a broom. *Oh my God! There's a fairy there! Why haven't I ever seen them before? And I thought Sonya was drifting into depression from my stupid comment about the neighbors. Here she was seeing fairies.* "I see it! Yes, it's cleaning the stump."

They sat in silence again, but now both women were watching fairies darting about the yard. Two fairies, with green and yellow wings, settled on top of the marker over Doogie's grave. Several were running along the fence line, fire rising from their outstretched arms, as they raced along the barrier Power had set to protect the yard and house.

*This is amazing! Sonya sees and understands so much. I bet she'd be able to help me understand what the grandmothers want me to do, since she was able to show me fairies so easily.* "How come I haven't seen the fairies before?"

"You didn't know to look for them—that's the easy answer. Our brains don't believe they exist, so they filter out anything that might hint at other worlds being possible. Our screening ability is crucial, or else we'd be overloaded with information and not be able to function, but it does make it hard on beings like fairies and guides who want to be seen by us."

Sonya paused, giving Miranda a chance to wrestle with the ideas. *If Sonya's right and she sure sounds like it, this must be what Merawl was talking about. People are creating movies and games where gremlins seem normal and that's how they got into the N-World. Why can't people choose fairies instead of gremlins to believe in? Next they'll be letting in ogres and ghouls!* Miranda pushed her thoughts aside and looked expectantly at Sonya, wanting more from her mentor.

"Seeing fairies is a matter of perception, not a matter of reality. Just because you don't see something doesn't mean it doesn't exist. There are many other worlds, and I don't just mean metaphorically or metaphysically."

Miranda shifted her gaze from the fairies to the fence separating the Blooms' yard from their neighbor's yard. *She didn't seem to mind me mentioning the neighbors before, maybe I can use them to ask her about dividing the worlds.* "Those neighbors of yours are certainly from a different world. I wish our world and their world could divide, so that their world would go away and leave our world alone, so we'd never have to see them or deal with them again."

Miranda held her breath, wondering if Sonya might respond to the implication of the worlds dividing and becoming separate. *I wish I could ask her directly about the grandmothers. But I don't want to make her feel bad. I can't let her know that there were spirits at the conference that talked to me and not to her. Maybe if Sonya didn't hear them, they don't actually exist. Don't go there! Merawl treats them as real and so does Adnarim. She even set up my being at the conference so I could meet them. But why doesn't Sonya know about them?*

"Miranda? Are you talking with your guides?"

"What?" *Oh no, did Sonya hear me? What was I thinking? Did I think anything bad about Sonya?*

"I asked if you were talking with your guides. If you were, go right ahead. I didn't mean to disturb you."

"No, I wasn't talking with my guides. That probably would've been smarter. Actually I was arguing with myself."

"What about? Can I help?"

*:How about me?:* BB arrived and sat down on the rug between Sonya and Miranda. *:Can I help too?:*

Miranda looked back and forth between the two of them. *Say something!* She scolded herself. *This is a perfect opportunity to ask Sonya about the grandmothers and their plans for dividing the world.*

*:Certainly, if you want me to:* BB stood up on her hind feet, brushed out the fur on her belly, as a person would straighten a shirt, then turned and spoke to Sonya.

*:Miranda would like to know if you are familiar with the guardian spirits who live in the cedar grove where that pharmaceutical thing thinks they own the land. She's afraid if she helps them with their plans to heal the world that it will require her to sacrifice her life:*

Miranda froze as Sonya turned toward BB and her soft, gentle voice drifted into Miranda's head. *:And who are you? Are you one of Miranda's guides?:*

BB gave her a toothy grin. *:Well, I would be—if she'd ever let herself be guided anywhere:*

*:BB!:* Miranda gulped, then spoke out loud. "Yes, that's one of my guides. She's a bear."

Sonya kept her focus on BB, but followed Miranda's lead and switched to speaking out loud. "I'm delighted to meet you. I'm Sonya, and what's your name?"

*:BB:* the bear said, doing a half-curtsy toward Sonya.

"BB? Does that stand for anything?"

Miranda gripped the edges of her chair, trying to hang on to the three way conversation.

"You heard her? Oh, I'm sorry. Of course you would hear her, you know all about speaking with spirits. I'm just not used to people hearing my guides so clearly and directly. Most of the time they might sense something and I'd help them but . . ."

Miranda let her words trail off as she watched BB turn her back to her and address Sonya. *:Thank you for asking. It's actually BeBe:* The bear swished her stubby tail at Miranda, still focusing on Sonya.

"What a lovely name!" Sonya clasped her hands together and gave the bear a little bow.

"Wait a minute. What are you two talking about? BB's just BB, right? What do you mean: what does BB stand for?"

Sonya smiled at her. "Be Be, as in: To *be* or not to *be*. Only in this case it's to Be, Be."

"Oh." *I can't believe I've known that bear for more than ten years and I never got what her name meant.*

"Now tell me about these guardians. What pharmaceutical thing is BeBe talking about? What are they asking you to do?

And why do you think you might need to sacrifice yourself for them?"

Miranda sat with her mouth open but no words came out. BeBe sighed dramatically, then turned back to Miranda and swept her paw in a grand gesture toward Sonya, indicating it was now Miranda's turn to share information with her.

"Um . . . Do you remember the first time we met? At that conference that Future Pharmaceutical sponsored?"

"Yes, dear. It was such a blessing meeting you there. It was so comforting to know who to call when I had to arrange hospice for Peter. You've been such a help for both of us through everything." Sonya reached out and patted Miranda's arm. "So there're spirits living there. I always thought that place had a nice feel to it that had nothing to do with FP having built their pharmaceutical plant there. "

As Sonya was talking, Miranda felt her shoulders relaxing slightly. "The spirits at FP spoke to me that night I met you. I don't know why they didn't speak to you. You're the expert and . . ."

"Oh, nonsense." Sonya waved away Miranda's protestations. "If all spirits only spoke to me that would make things quite impossible. That's why I wrote the book. I've always wanted there to be many people for spirits to talk to."

*Wow. That makes sense. Why was I ever worried that she'd be upset to learn the grandmothers talked to me and not to her? Now I feel stupid that I never talked with her before about them.*

"Are you talking to BeBe, dear?"

"No. Just myself. I was feeling dumb to have gotten so twisted up imagining that I'd make you feel bad if I told you the spirits at FP talked with me and not you."

"That's one reason I like talking with spirits. Much saner and better conversations than ones I have with myself. Inside my own mind I always get distracted by material, mundane worries. Talking with fairies, spirits, and guides helps me keep a larger perspective."

*:Happy to be of service:* BeBe materialized a top hat, which she then used to make a formal bow to Sonya.

"Yes, you're a wonderful guide, BeBe. Now encourage Miranda to stop arguing with herself and to tell me what these spirits want her to do."

BeBe started to turn back to Miranda, but she waved her guide off. "The grandmothers—that's what the guardian spirits call themselves there—asked for my help. There's supposed to be a healing time coming, when the planet is going to be divided into two separate worlds: one for namens, who are nature-connected humans, and a world for the greemens, who are greed-obsessed humans. Susan, my lawyer friend in California, thinks I'm going to have to sacrifice myself for the healing to occur. I'm hoping I can figure out the right side to go to so I end up in the right world when it divides. But the sides look the same from inside the cavern where the grandmothers take me and where the dividing is supposed to happen."

Sonya was silent for a moment. "Dividing the world, that's an interesting idea. And Susan thinks you'll need to die for it to happen? How old is she?"

"She's twenty-two. I've known her since she was in high school. Her father thought she was crazy to be talking with angels so he brought her to see me. Instead of telling her to stop communicating with angels, I taught her how to do it better."

"Good for you. I'm sure that was a salvation for Susan. And now I imagine she doesn't want anything to happen to you."

"Yeah, she's really worried that I'll need to sacrifice myself. But it would be worth it if the worlds could divide and we'd get all those mean, nature-killing greedy humans off of our world."

"And that's what the grandmothers told you would happen?"

"That's what I was able to figure out. Actually, talking with Peter about physics one day gave me some clues. He explained the parallel universe theory. And BB, I mean BeBe, was there helping too."

"And when is all this supposed to happen?"

"I don't know. Maybe when I can make it back to FP again."

"Hmm . . ." Sonya slowly levered herself up and started walking toward the front hall. Miranda got up and followed her. Sonya stopped at the desk by the entrance and started shuffling through papers. "I think I left it on the desk. At least I hope I did, or I might have trouble finding it."

"Finding what? What are you looking for?"

"For what you need, of course."

"I need to know how to tell the two different sides apart, so I don't end up in the wrong world. Are you saying you have the answer on your desk?"

Sonya didn't respond as she began rummaging through a second stack of papers. Miranda peered over her shoulder. There were piles of old mail that Sonya was methodically checking the return address on, shaking her head and putting the rejects into another pile.

"Sonya, what're you looking for?"

"It came last month for Peter. I remember saving it. I thought I was just being overly sentimental and not wanting to let go of anything that was Peter's. But now I'm wondering if I didn't keep it for you." Sonya was almost at the bottom of the pile when she came to a square envelope. "Here it is! I knew I'd saved it." She triumphantly handed the prize over to Miranda.

"What is it?"

"Open it!"

Miranda opened the envelope, which had a return address of Future Pharmaceutical and pulled out a bright orange pass with Peter's name on it. "But this is for Peter." Miranda looked at the accompanying papers. "It's for an invitation only event at FP. I can't use this."

"Yes you can. I often drove Peter to events there. He'd be reading something last minute and ask me to drive him. I always enjoyed wandering around or sitting on the grounds near the cedar grove, and now that you've told me about the spirits, that makes sense that it has such a good feel."

Miranda started to protest again, but Sonya waved her silent. "They've never asked for I.D. or even looked in the car. I'd just flash the pass at the security as I drove in. Once they saw the card they'd just wave us through. There's a separate entrance you use marked 'employees.' It's just past the main one. You'll be able to get in there no problem."

Miranda looked at the pass again. It was marked for September 18th, 2021 "But it's for this Saturday! I'm not prepared yet!"

"Maybe it'll just give you an opportunity to talk with the grandmothers and clarify things with them more. It doesn't mean you have to divide the worlds on Saturday."

Sonya's calm statements helped Miranda's heart slow down slightly. "Okay. I guess that'll work. Chris is at a culinary arts fair on Saturday so I do have that day free." *And I'll plan something super special for Friday night—in case it's our last one together.*

"I wish I could go with you. But maybe you can take BeBe."

*:An invitation only event. What fun!:* The bear rubbed her paws together as a pink business dress materialized on her brown body.

"Oh, yeah. She'll be a big help." BeBe wrinkled her muzzle at Miranda and disappeared. Sonya left the pass in Miranda's hands, and slowly wheeled her walker back to her chair, with Miranda trailing along behind her.

They resumed their seats and Miranda tried asking questions about Sonya's life with Peter, but her mind kept drifting to Saturday and the grandmothers. After another ten minutes Sonya offered the excuse of being tired and sent Miranda home early.

# Chapter 20

## *Dividing Worlds*

On Saturday morning, Miranda turned her car on and backed out of the garage. *I hope I get to see home again. What if I have to divide the worlds today and everything changes so much that I'm not able to recognize it? Stop it! I won't be able to contact the grandmothers if I'm all wrapped up in worries.*

Miranda activated her sound system, told it "smooth," and tried to relax as the car was filled with soothing jazz. *I can do it. Whatever the grandmothers want today—I can do it. That was so great with Chris last night. Whatever happens, we'll always have that love . . . But what if dividing the worlds somehow alters our memory of the prior world? Don't go there!*

*:Aye lass, that'd mean ya'd be fergettin' me too:* An Irishman in a black suit was now sitting in the passenger seat.

"McNally, what're you dressed like that for?"

*:Ye seemed ta be so serious and all, I t'ought we was goin' to a funeral, so I dressed fer ta occasion:*

*:Well, I hope it's a party:* BeBe said from the back seat.

Miranda glanced back and saw that the bear was wearing a tight red dress, which made her fur poke through the lace trimmings.

"BeBe, what are you doing in that thing?"

*:She's trying to be amusing. The operative word of course is trying:* Merawl materialized on the dash board. His hind legs didn't quite fit so they floated in the air above McNally's lap. *:That bear has never known the difference between serious and stupid and it doesn't look like she's going to learn it today:*

*:Just look at you—dressed in your gray fur as always. How dull:*

"All we need now is Adnarim and we'd be complete. A complete what, I don't know." Miranda tried to sound annoyed as her car filled with guides, but inside she was very grateful for their company.

Sticking the thought deep into her private consciousness, she told herself. *Sonya's right. Talking with guides is much better than riding around in my own mind, or merry-go-rounding as Susan would call it.*

She glanced at the bright orange permit lying next to Merawl on the dashboard, proclaiming that Peter Bloom was invited to Future Pharmaceutical on Saturday, September 18th, 2021. *Is this really going to work?*

*:Yes:*

Miranda smiled to herself as Adnarim's voice floated up from the back seat. "With you sitting behind me at least I don't have to worry about looking at you and having you disappear."

*:You can admire me instead. Did you notice? I changed dresses just for you:* Miranda had to brake for a stop sign, so she took the opportunity to turn and look at the right half of the back seat where BeBe was now wearing a yellow, low cut dress with a pendant of gold stars around her neck. She had on oversized matching earrings, which pulled her ears down making her look like a poor, pathetic puppy.

*:Bears, especially those with no taste, should not be allowed to wear clothing. It's fortunate that only a few humans can see you, or guides would never receive the respect we deserve:*

*:Aye, little kitty, I 'ear yer complaints. But wit' your tail in me face, yer lucky I don't go pullin' ye right off a t'at dashboard:*

Miranda laughed, then had to focus on driving as she passed through a crowded intersection. Merawl, Rand, and BeBe continued their banter, successfully keeping her mind from overflowing with worries so that by the time they all arrived at Future Pharmaceutical she was almost relaxed. They passed the entrance Miranda had used when she went to the conference, and when she drove Susan to her fake interview. The next driveway was clearly marked: "Employees Entrance." *I hope this works. Or maybe I don't hope this works.*

*:Yes. Yes:*

*:What? What do you mean, Adnarim?:* Miranda switched to telepathy as she approached the gate, afraid someone would think she was talking to herself. She slowed the car down as she joined the line of other vehicles waiting to enter FP, but her mind sped up with worries. *:Are you saying 'yes' to it's working and 'yes' to it's not working?:*

*:No:*

*:Whatever! I don't have time for riddles:* Miranda cautiously approached the guard. She held up the yellow pass with Peter's name on it for the woman to see and was quickly waved through. *First part accomplished. And Sonya said if anyone asks, just to tell them I drove someone to the conference and they won't bother me. If I can climb up to the cedar grove unnoticed I should be pretty well hidden from sight.*

*:That is possible:* A stony voice sounded in Miranda's mind.

She looked to the right and saw that in the passenger seat, instead of Rand, there was now a tall, slender human-shaped form. *:Who're you?:*

She swung the car into a parking place and turned to study the newcomer. Extending her senses to it she felt it wrap itself into her mind. She started to panic, but the spirit was not threatening; it was also not comforting. *:Power! What are you doing here? I'm definitely not going to drink now. I'm not even considering it:*

*:That is why I'm here. I have the energy you need. To fulfill the task:*

*:What task?:*

*:The task that is yours to do:* An airy voice responded.

*:Skyweb! You're here too:* Miranda mentally bit her tongue and tried to keep her thoughts to herself. *Stupid. Of course she's here. The grandmothers are here to help me make the right choice. But which guide should I be listening to now?*

*:All of us:* The calm, clear voice of Power made her feel centered so that momentarily her anxious inner voice slipped to the back of her mind.

*:Okay, so what should I do?:*

*:Climb the hill. As you thought before. I will return when the time is right and you need my energy:*

She slipped out of her car and stood staring at the hill. It looked taller and more exposed than before.

*:This isn't going to work. The guards are going to see me for sure:*

*:Not if'n ya make yerself invisible:*

Miranda's jaw clenched as she realized she'd been thinking too loudly again. Concentrating on forming her words, she asked, *:Are you just suggesting that? Or are you actually going to help me do it?:*

BeBe started twirling around the base of the hill in her yellow dress. *:I'll distract them for you. Why should they look at you when they have me to watch?:*

*:The bear isn't actually totally incorrect this time:* Merawl stated, starting to walk up what looked like a deer path, placing his paws inches above the damp earth. *:Follow me and focus on not being interesting, focus not being at all. Know the human's gaze will glance off you as though you were invisible. The guards will keep thinking they see something over there as she plays in that idiotic outfit. Their eyes will try to follow the fool, not you:*

Miranda cautiously climbed after Merawl, placing her foot on a rock here or a root there. She paused near the top, peering over her shoulder, watching for security guards. Two of them walked around the corner of the closest building and she frantically thought at them, *:Don't see anything. Don't look at me:*

*:Aye lass, t'at's ta way ta be invisible, tell 'em where not ta look:* Rand floated next to her in a bright green vest, waving down to the guards.

She hurried after Merawl, then let out a long sigh as all of them
crested the hill and entered the grove of cedar trees. The stone was
exactly in the middle of the small clearing, just as she'd seen it from
her astral body. Kneeling beside it, Miranda ran her hands over its
rough surface. Grasping the edge she flipped it over, exposing a large
opening in the earth. She sat down, swinging her legs into the hole,
dislodging several stones, which fell soundlessly down the tunnel.
Gripping the earth on either side of her, she chanted, "I can do this. I
can do this."

*:Yes. It is time. The* when *is now:* Fireweb's words illuminated
the passageway as the Eastern Grandmother placed an ephemeral
hand on Miranda's right arm and the two of them slipped into the
earth.

The journey down was wetter than before, the earth more
muddy and slippery. Miranda felt their plummet accelerating.
*:Wait, slow down. This feels too real. Am I still in my physical
body? How's this happening?:*

*:We, who are going, down to a deeper where:* Waterweb
touched her left arm and the pace increased. *:Where it is center:*

*:Center? The center of the earth?:*

*:Center of all.:* The words cascaded around her.

*:That's too deep. I can't see anything! It feels like we're going
faster:* Miranda was having trouble breathing, imagining the
tremendous weight of Earth above her and the increased pressure
she knew occurred when divers descended into the oceans.

She felt hands on her chest. *:You, who are the one. Breathe.
You, who are the one. Need not make journey harder:* Earthweb
spoke in a calm, solid voice that echoed in Miranda's mind.

She forced her chest to move slower, swallowing the bitter
saliva that had been collecting in her mouth since starting the
descent.

*:Yes. Better. You, who are the one, be:*

Their speed decreased as the chamber opened up below them.
The four of them slowly floated down into the center of the large
oval-shaped cave. As Miranda's feet touched the bottom of the
cave, the tunnel closed above them so that no opening, no escape
was perceivable.

*:We are at the where:* Waterweb's voice flowed around her.

*:Now is the time:* The cave brightened as Fireweb spoke.

*:Your task to do what is needed:* Earthweb spread her hands wide, turning slowly around as she gazed at the rock walls.

Miranda noticed the line dividing the cave was more distinct than before. She peered at it closely and realized it was actually a small crack running lengthwise through the cave, as though a giant had tried to cut the egg in two. Only she knew it was her job to separate the two sides: to divide the world. Her gaze slowly swept over the cave, searching for anything different in the two sides, but they were identical expanses of wrinkled gray rock. Finding nothing unique she turned back to the three grandmothers. *:Okay, we're here, and it's time. As long as you help me, I guess I'll try to do it:* The guardians nodded and stepped back, one to each side with Earthweb standing over the dividing line, facing her.

Bending down, she ran her hands along the crack, noticing a slight separation had already begun. Chewing on her lower lip, she sat down and continued exploring. With a little probing she was able to wedge her fingers into the opening. The cave vibrated as the two sides inched apart, and she was able to slide her entire hands into the gap. Miranda tried kneeling on one side and pushing the other side away, but she couldn't get a good enough grip to cause much movement. The best position was to squat over the center and pull on both sides equally. After moving the sides a couple hand-widths apart, she paused, breathing in the tangy rock-scent of the cave. She rubbed her fingers, surprised to find a few drops of blood from several scratches. *I didn't think astral bodies could bleed. Don't freak out! It doesn't hurt much. But something is definitely different. I'm anxious but I don't feel like my thoughts could pull me back to my body like they usually do. I'm here in a more physical way. Whatever that means, I hope I can deal with it.*

She looked down between her legs. The cave was filled with a soft amber glow, but the opening showed nothing but darkness. As she stuck her hands back in they disappeared into the abyss.

"Yikes!" her cry echoed around her, as she jerked her hands out. "Whoa, this is too weird, I'm hearing myself talk and the sound is bouncing around the cavern, just as though this was all physically real. If I can hear myself, then I can calm myself down.

It's okay, it just feels real. My body is safely at the top of the hill. I'll be ok, I just need to keep going." Slowly she inched her fingers back in, wiggling them as they entered the cleft to assure herself that they still existed.

She pushed at the sides again. A rumble radiated up her legs as the worlds began to separate. Sweat running down her back, she continued pressing firmly on both sides. They steadily moved apart until she was crouching, hands on thighs, legs barely straddling the chasm. *I'd better figure out which side is the good one. Now!* Balancing carefully over the void she raised her head to ask the grandmothers for help. But she was alone. "No! Grandmothers, where are you?"

Twisting around she searched the cave, which had grown to the size of a sports field. A hint of a presence came from her left and she pivoted quickly, hoping to see a guide or grandmother. She could see no one, but the force of her turning pushed the two sides farther apart and her feet started to slip off the edges. She threw herself toward the left side, landing hard on her chest, but leaving her lower half dangling in the void. Her legs clawed the air, frantically searching for something solid to help propel her up, but there was nothing below the ledge.

She stopped kicking and hung by her arms, elbows pressing painfully into the rock. *Think, damn it! You're supposed to be intelligent—figure a way out of this.* She moved her hands slowly around trying to find a crack to give herself leverage, but the ground was rocky and everything she grabbed broke loose. Her arms were beginning to shake and she felt spasms in her shoulders. *Why the hell didn't I go to the gym more with Chris and get some upper body strength?* Thinking of her lover brought tears to her eyes and anger to her gut. *Fuckin' greemens! They're the cause of all this. If half the world wasn't full of idiots I wouldn't be here needing to divide it.* Images of Sonya and Peter's neighbors came to mind. Miranda felt a boiling rage building in her and used it to pump energy into her arms. Rising up on her elbows she inched herself forward. Hanging half in and half out of the ravine, she flung herself forward grasping for what she hoped was a solid ridge of stone. It held for a second then broke loose in a cascade of pebbles propelling her toward the opening.

Thrashing wildly, she lost the ledge completely, falling into the void and landing in darkness. "Where am I? Grandmothers! Please help me." She was aware of her rapidly beating heart and blood drumming in her ears, but there were no other sounds. She tried moving her arms but felt nothing, not even the passage of air through her fingers.

Breathing deeply brought no hint of scents, and she couldn't determine if the space was warm or cool. She brought her hands up, touching her nose and mouth, reassuring herself she still had a face, a body. *I'm still alive—I think. Maybe I died. Maybe that was the sacrifice needed and now the worlds are dividing. I hope Chris and Susan will be okay.*

Miranda hung in the darkness thinking about the world she left, not sure of the passage of time.

*Have the worlds completely divided yet?* With that question she noticed a tiny fuzzy glow below her left foot. Focusing on it she felt herself moving toward it. It grew slowly as she approached and she realized it wasn't small, just infinitely far away.

She drifted for what could have been days or minutes, there were no reference points in her current reality. Finally the image expanded, first showing the blue-green globe of Earth, then the continent of Africa, until she was floating above a grassy plain with clumps of trees dotted across it.

She spied a small troop of men and flew towards them. They had animal skins tied around their waists and shoulders. Each carried a small bundle of short spears. They walked hunched over, below the tops of the grasses.

*Are there still tribes in Africa so untouched by civilization?* Miranda looked closer, noticing the skins were more torn than cut and the spears were sticks with sharpened points. A strong odor of animals and sweat assaulted her senses. Each man had a camouflage of olive and tan grease paintings covering his body. Most of them had strips of sinew tucked into the skin belts around their waists. *Those look like primitive sling shots. I must be back in time—somehow it feels ancient.*

She drifted down into the group, looking at the sun, which was slowly rising above the horizon. It seemed younger, brighter in the sky.

The air was alive with the buzz of insects, and Miranda was relieved to watch the large flying beetles pass through her spirit body without touching her.

*I'm either dead or journeying. Wish someone would tell me which it was!*

The men continued their travel across the savannah, with Miranda tagging along. *This must be a hunting group.*

She saw a herd of gazelle grazing to the right but the men didn't turn toward them. They came to a ridge and stopped. One of them dropped onto his hands and knees and crept upward. Miranda followed him, curious what he was searching for. Cautiously he peered over the top, spying a group of humans crouched near a stand of trees in the distance. He made a chirping sound, and the other warriors joined him, keeping low to the ground.

*They're not hunting animals. They're hunting other men!* Miranda's gut clenched at the thought. *They're too far away for those spears to hurt them. They'll just scare them off.* The leader dropped down into a dry ditch and began crawling along it toward the other humans. His band followed silently behind him, knowing the land and using it to approach the others undetected.

Miranda felt pulled along by the intensity of the leader's thoughts *:Intruders! We must destroy them. Our territory! Protect our young—kill them:* The leader stopped and carefully peered over the ditch. They were close to the other band of humans now. He removed the length of sinew from his belt and looped it around the end of one of his spears.

*That's a throwing spear!* Miranda gasped and tried to wrestle free from the hunters but she couldn't move her spirit away. The leader looked again through the grasses. She saw in his mind the other men, felt him calculate their numbers, notice their weapons, estimate their power. He nodded, satisfied, then lowered himself down, and began making complex hand gestures to the other men. They gestured back, then moved apart, each finding solid footing in the sandy stream bed. She felt the leader judging the distance, balancing the spear in the throwing strap as he readied his body.

All around her the others were doing the same: crouching low, finding their positions, one arm drawn back, a pile of spears positioned carefully at their side, easily reachable for a second or third throw. Their powerful thigh muscles were compressed like springs, waiting. She saw in the leader's mind his target: the broad bare back of the closest human. As his legs uncoiled, he raised up, releasing the spear. As it shot toward his enemy, Miranda fled.

She found herself back in the darkness of the void. Whatever body she was in was shaking. *What was that all about?* Questions bounced around her brain as she floated in nothingness. Then images of Doogie started flashing into her consciousness, followed by pictures of his grave among the tree stumps. Her hands clenched as she remembered the time she'd tried to plead with the neighbors for understanding. *What a waste of effort. Those worthless assholes! They don't deserve to . . .*

A memory of the ancient hunters erupted into Miranda's mind and for a moment she was back on the hot savannah as they readied their spears and took aim at their enemies, then all the images disappeared and she was floating in the blackness again.

*Oh my God, that was me. I wanted to kill the neighbors just like the hunters wanted to kill those intruders. I'm just like them.*

*:No. You're not. Your brain is:*

*:Adnarim. Thank God! Am I dead? What happened? Where am I?:* Miranda projected her thoughts at Adnarim, fearing what her voice might sound like if she tried speaking out loud in the void.

*:No. What was meant, happened. You are here:*

Miranda felt her body relax and even though she couldn't see Adnarim, the void no longer felt so empty. *:So where is here? And why . . . no wait, answer that first:*

*:You are here so that you can choose:*

*:Choose what?:* She sensed Adnarim gesturing around her but she saw nothing. Then she felt a furry nudge. *:Merawl, are you here too?:* The feeling left, but the thought of using Cat Vision was now in her consciousness and she quickly refocused her sight unveiling a web of millions of threads of light dancing above her.

Hanging over her were the two halves of the cave, each pulsing
with billions of miniscule dots of amber light. It was like all the
stars had clustered together into two separate spheres and were
flashing conversations among themselves. The two oblong sides
were linked by thin lines of brightness, which traveled across the
gap she had worked so hard to create. Next to her was a ribbon of
light, which pulsed along a thick bundle of cords. The ribbon
extended both far below her, and reached above her, intertwining
into the two pulsating light globes. As she watched the flashes of
brightness, she noticed the ones within and between the spheres
danced and played, making complex patterns of light and dark.
Stronger, faster pulses rushed from where she was, up the ribbon
of light and into the spheres above, overriding their dances with
intense patterns of bright vividness.

:*What am I looking at?*:

:*Your brain*:

:*What?*:

:*Your—*.:

:*I know what you said but I can't be inside my own brain. I
shouldn't be here!*: The pulses from the thick ribbon next to her
increased and grew brighter, fear gripped her as the strands around
her throbbed with energy. :*Something's wrong! What's happening?*:
The dances above stopped as urgent flashes, sent from below, tore
through the two spheres.

:*Yes. Yes. No. What is happening is happening*:

:*Quit giving me meaningless answers and tell me what I should
do!*:

:*Think*:

:*I can't think. I've got to get out of here!*:

:*Yes. Now you see. Now is the time*: She felt Adnarim's words
calming her like a relaxing massage on her spirit. :*You are where
you are meant to be. Opportunities are opening and you can
choose to stay with what was and is, or choose to change*:

The pulses around her slowed and the dancing resumed above
her. "Okay, something important just happened." Miranda spoke
out loud, using her words to slow her thoughts. "If I'm in my
brain, then those are my two hemispheres above me and I must be
in my primitive, old brainstem."

*:Exactly, you've got it! I'd give you an 'A' if it mattered any more. Now, can you explain the interaction you're witnessing? And describe to me its significance?:*

Confused by the clear tenor voice, that held a hint of humor in it, Miranda lost her Cat Vision view and found herself back in darkness. "Who . . . ?"

*:What? You didn't expect me to show up when you needed me? Once a teacher, always a teacher—body or no body:*

"Peter?"

*:Of course. And I'm still waiting for an answer to my questions:*

"Your questions?" Miranda shook her head. *First Adnarim is being too literal in her answers and now he wants me to do the answering and I still don't know what's going on.* She sighed and tried refocusing on seeing through Cat Vision. "These lines and pulses must be my nerves and impulses. Those dancing patterns above must be my thoughts." She took a breath, stilling her mind and was rewarded with seeing the lights slow and change from an intense sun-bright-white to a calm amber.

*:You're getting it. What do you know about the brainstem?:*

"It's the oldest part of the brain, the area that reacts. Like those hunters stalking the other humans."

*:Exactly and it's wired to search out 'others'—anything different that could be a threat. Think of it as the home of the three F's: flight, fight, or freeze. When it perceives a threat, real or not, it overrides the cerebral cortex: your two hemispheres above you where you have all your reasoning ability. It takes over your body and causes you to run, be aggressive, or stop completely in the hope the threat will ignore you. Think of something pleasant and safe and see what happens:*

She thought of last night with Chris and noticed a decrease of activity in her brainstem.

*:Now think of something where you perceived there was a threat:*

She brought up the memory of arriving at Future Pharmaceutical and the guards at the gate. Light flashed faster around her and she felt herself on alert, anxious. She tried a few more images then refocused on Peter. "Okay, I think I'm getting this now. What choice was Adnarim referring to?"

The images of her brain vanished and she was standing before a large ancient loom. It was crafted out of wood with four giant posts supporting a massive display of interlaced thin strings. There was a simple bench in front of it and a complex array of bars hanging above and below the strings. Piled on either side were thousands of pieces of yarn of varying thicknesses and colors. Peter was standing to the left of the loom, wearing a brown suit and looking like the middle-aged professor he once was. He gestured toward the yarn and Miranda gingerly picked up a handful, feeling the softness of the wool on her skin. As she shifted through the threads she felt a tingling in her brain. "Hey, what's this?"

*:Your chance to progress. Now that you've seen how your brain is wired, want to try something new and different?:*

"No!" Miranda stared at the loom in horror. "What if I make a mistake?"

*:Good, let's start with that concept:*

"It's not a concept. I don't know how to weave. I could really mess up here."

Peter ignored her protests and stretched out his arm. A pointer appeared in his hand and he used it to wave at the loom, which tilted so that it was now upright. Another swish of his wand and a weaving appeared on the loom. *:Wish I'd had this kind of multimedia support in my classrooms. Let's see . . . we don't need the loom right now:* Another wave of his arm and the loom obligingly vanished, leaving only a tapestry of soft grays hanging in the air in front of them. *:Let's look at that fear you mentioned, in relation to how our ancestors' brains were programmed:* Huge scarlet letters appeared in the center of the tapestry forming the word: SURVIVAL and below it, in bright firehouse-red, were the words: THREAT, OTHERS, MISTAKES, and OSTRACISM. Circling all of those words in a wreath of red flame were hundreds of tiny flashing signs declaring: DEATH.

Miranda stared at the picture, feeling on-edge and exposed. "See? Mistakes are serious. Right?"

*:Let's look at this closer:* They both bent forward to read smaller words that were woven in among the larger ones. *:Can you read to me what you see here?:*

Miranda swallowed her thoughts about this being the weirdest class she'd ever been in and answered. "There's attack, scarcity, drought, famine, floods, and fire. There are some others but I can't quite make out what they say." She waited but Peter didn't say anything. "This all seems pretty real to me. You make a mistake, you might not survive. Back in the time of those hunters you needed to be part of a tribe for protection, shelter, and food. Being ostracized by the tribe could certainly mean death."

*:Do you think you can manage to explain to me what ostracism means in our time?:* Peter crossed his arms over his chest and scowled at her.

She tried remembering times it had happened to her. "Um . . . I think first there's rejection, then shame, feeling really bad about yourself, humiliation. I don't know . . . I guess it means being unpopular?"

*:Unpopular! Now that sounds pretty dangerous:* Peter smirked as he wagged his pointer at her.

"Oh yeah! You try being the strange one in school with Mr. Popular for an older brother." She held back her other thoughts. *Damn you, why are you doing this to me? It's not fair. Why are you going off on this. It has nothing to do with dividing the worlds.*

*:Feeling threatened?:* Peter's usual calm, kind voice cut through her inner turmoil.

"What?"

*:I asked if you were feeling agitated, annoyed, wanting to get this over with. Have me stop lecturing you?:*

"Actually, yes, I was feeling that way." *How did he know that?*

*:I could tell because I was watching your neural activity:*

She spun around and saw the light display of her brain behind her. The urgent pulses from the brainstem were overwhelming the thinner lines of activity in the two hemispheres.

*:Try being curious:*

"Actually, I am." As she let her puzzlement and wonder increase the light show in the front part of her cortex became more complex and the torrent of impulses from her old brain began to quiet.

"So, I think you're trying to show me how my fear of making mistakes, or being criticized and rejected, is still wired into an overpowering survival urge, even though I'm not in danger of dying like my ancestors were." Peter nodded encouragingly so she continued. "I may be safer in my life. But it's not true of others. There're still wars, prejudice, illness, slavery, especially economic slavery. It's not like we live in a paradise here."

*:And why not have a paradise here?:*

"You've sure changed now that you're a ghost. You're the one that told me there was no hope for humankind."

*:And I didn't see any when I was locked in a body and a brain like yours. Let me demonstrate with the concept of resources:* His wand turned into a laser pointer that he flashed on the display of her brainstem. *:Concentrate here on material possessions. What do you feel?:*

"The need to protect, preserve, horde them. The idea of losing anything, or something being taken away feels threatening."

*:Okay, let's shift that concept higher:* He moved the point of light up her brainstem, through the mid brain and eventually placed it in the frontal lobes. *:Now what are you aware of?:*

Miranda smiled to herself, no longer threatened by Peter or his lessons. "There're lots of possibilities, it's simple. If we all share and work together we can make the resources include everyone. So am I ready for the final exam yet? Or are there more twists you want to take me on?"

*:No, I think you're ready:* He turned back to the loom, which was again displaying a bare array of strings, awaiting the piles of yarn stacked on either side.

"Even with all your fancy lecturing, I still don't know how to weave."

Peter tilted his head at her. *:But doesn't it make a nice metaphor? Here, why don't you use this?:* He handed her his pointer. *:Just aim it at the loom and tell it what you want woven in:*

She balanced the wand in her hand, turning it over several times. "Well, I think in place of survival I'd like HEALTH. And instead of all my energy going toward searching for threats, how about focusing on CONNECTION?"

She waved her wand and on the loom was a tapestry of soft gray colors with the new words embroidered in gold and black velvet, along with other concepts like SHARING, LOVE, RESPECT, FUN, and HAPPINESS. "I suppose I do need some kind of an alarm system though. Unless you're proposing that all the plants are going to shed their thorns, and no one will mistakenly harm me again."

*:Yes, of course you need that part of your brain. But the alarm system can notify and give information, and when necessary help your body move quickly—quicker than you can think. But it shouldn't set the patterns for the rest of your thoughts and reactions:*

Miranda waved at the loom again and below the central words in soft pink pastels were the words: PHYSICAL HARM, PAIN, and GRIEF. Stitched around them was a blue-green circle that said: SUPPORT, UNDERSTANDING, PERMISSION TO FEEL, ENCOURAGEMENT TO ASK FOR HELP, and around all those words were woven thousands of tiny messages of HEALING, and HOPE.

She stepped back from the loom and used the wand to raise it up as Peter had done, then let the wooden supports disappear so that the tapestry hung in the air by itself. The threads that wove the letters began to shift and blend creating an array of moving colors and patterns.

A flash of rainbow silks appeared to her right, covering a tall figure. *:Are you ready to choose now?:*

"I thought I had."

*:No:*

"After all this, I still get word games from my troublesome twin. Okay, what else do I need to do?"

*:You have created it. Now choose it:*

"How? I don't have the energy, nor ability to change something like this.

*:I have your energy. I have been storing it—yours and others who give me their life force. I have control here:* The words were strong, spoken with conviction as Power appeared next to her. He was wearing a long amber robe, with tiny gold stars dancing through it. *I have access to your automatic actions and reactions.*

*You have the choice. I understand your brain and your neural patterns. That is how I have so easily taken your life force when you have offered it to me:*

Taking a deep breath, she opened her arms to the tapestry. It moved toward her, and for a moment she felt fear and panic rising in her, then the weaving reached her, melting into her skin. The threads, now microscopic, wove into her nervous system replacing and refining old patterns. Her head tingled, then quieted. Being in her brain was like standing in an empty stadium after players had been competing with vivid fierceness and thousands had been yelling and cheering for their favorite teams. Now all that was left was a silent echo and an empty amphitheater.

*:Yes. You have chosen:*

Miranda turned to her right, seeing an exact image of herself. "Adnarim."

*:Yes:* Her formerly elusive guide, held out her hands. The two selves stood facing each other hands clasp together. *:Now that you have done it for yourself. It is time to do it for all others:*

"Show me how."

Adnarim pointed up. Hanging above them were the two, star-patterned hemispheres. Next to them was the busy brainstem, maintaining breath, heartbeat, and health.

Miranda felt herself infinitely small next to her neural network. Like one drop of water in a river. Then she began to expand, becoming as big as a twig floating down the river, then as large as a boat.

She reached out her arms, feeling as though she was stretching beyond the cave to touch the edges of the earth. And still she kept growing, until the universe of stars was now inside her own brain, only they were no longer stars, but individual consciousnesses, each a human being.

She reached out to them and felt them tense, test for danger. *:No threat:* She thought at them.

*:What?:* millions of programmed brains asked her.

*:No threat. You have survived. You are alive. No threat:*

From the collective consciousness of all the brains she touched came the response, *:We have been waiting. For twenty centuries we have been waiting for those words:*

As though that was the key to unlock the patterns, they opened to her. Each star of consciousness taking HEALTH and CONNECTION as its guiding principles and weaving around them a pattern that was uniquely its own.


She was immense, floating, holding the universe inside her. Testing her brain, she found it calm and curious. She expanded beyond her skull, feeling her face, the air between her lips, cool on the inhale, warming her tongue on the exhale. As her tongue woke up it swam around her mouth, testing the back of her teeth, her gums. She swallowed, then moved her jaw. *I never realized it could sway so easily side to side. I must have been clenching it all the time.* Her shoulders flexed and flowed, sending rivers of movement down her arms. Her fingers were cool, wet. She moved them, identifying a weaving of grass matted under her hand. *I'm back. I'm in my body again.* Gently stroking the blades she encouraged them upward. She massaged her thighs and ankles, slightly sore from sitting cross legged on the ground. Raising her hands to her face she inhaled the aroma of plants and earth. Opening her eyes she looked into the dark depths of Earthweb's gaze. To her right was Fireweb and to her left was Waterweb.

*:And I must be Skyweb. Which is why I was never able to see or find her, only hear her voice in my head:* Her words whispered in her mind in the same familiar ethereal alto voice that she heard when she first came to the conference a year ago.

Earthweb spoke in her solid, slow voice. *:No, not precisely. All beings have many parts. You, who are a part of Skyweb. And Skyweb, who is a part of you:*

*:So, I was waiting for part of myself?:*

Earthweb nodded. *:We have all been waiting to complete ourselves. Waiting for* who *we are. As many sun turnings as a tree has leaves, we have been waiting:*

*:And now the time has happened:* Fireweb's voice was like a candle being lit, illuminating their circle.

*:The task has been done:* Earthweb added her definite acknowledgement

*:We are in a new place:* Waterweb's voice flowed around them.

:*And we are new beings:* Miranda and Skyweb finished the circle of thought. Then the grandmothers began fading from her view, but fixing themselves firmly and forever into her being.

She rose from the circle and stretched her legs, testing her weight from one side to the other. Bowing to the grove of cedar trees she backed out and turned to descend the hill. As she walked down she saw a security guard strolling below her and waved to him. The guard looked up, at first startled, then waved back and continued walking toward a brown building. Miranda paused and looked around the complex of structures that was Future Pharmaceutical. "You have no clue," she told the giant drug company. "You think you're changing brain chemistry. You have no idea what it means to really change it."

She continued down the hill, got into her electric car and drove home.

# Chapter 21

## *Being One*

Miranda brought a visitor with her to Sonya's the next Saturday. As they walked up to the house she watched the clouds playing with the sun and stars against a silver-blue backdrop. The familiar constellations were forming bright dots in the mid-morning sky.

The door opened just as she was about to knock, so she flowed directly into a loving bear hug with her friend.

Miranda stepped back to do introductions. "Sonya, this is Susan: the crazy law student from California I've told you about."

Susan stuck her tongue out at her friend. "Thanks a lot. I admire you too." She gave Sonya a hug, saying, "It's an honor to meet you. Yours was the first book she," Susan flipped her head toward Miranda, "gave me to read when I was trying to decipher this Angel spirit thing."

Their hostess backed up her walker and motioned for both of them to enter. "Well, I'm glad to meet you. Come in."

Sonya turned her walker and they followed her down the hallway. "Miranda didn't tell me you were going to be visiting. What brings you back up here?"

"The California Assembly decided they wanted to try something new and set aside time to get to know each other as people, rather than as members of opposing parties. They all gave their staff a week's vacation and they're off connecting together. So I bought a seat on one of the new ecological planes and flew up here to check out firsthand what Miranda's mystical messings with our world looks like."

They arrived at the kitchen where a tray with a plate of scones, a pot of tea, and two cups was waiting for them. Miranda went to the cupboard to get down another mug. "So how's my mess looking so far?"

"Well, you might be causing me to lose my job. After all I'm paid to deal with the strife of politics. If the assemblymen and women start getting along I could be out of work."

Sonya motioned them toward the food and drinks. "What would you do then, dear?"

"I was thinking of starting up ESE for real this time."

"What? I'm afraid I don't know what that is."

Miranda put the extra tea cup down on the tray. "You have to excuse Susan, she likes making up her own language. She's referring to the Extinct Species Express."

"Hey, don't mock me! I've had some good success with it already. I'm thinking of making GB my partner and maybe Thomas too. Now that he's dating a woman from our office it's easier to hang around him."

"Don't try to understand her, Sonya. GB is actually a grizzly bear, so we really don't want to know more about that. And Thomas is a friend of hers." Miranda rolled her eyes at Susan and picked up the tray. "It's one of those nice warm fall days today. Do we want to eat inside or out?"

"I put the tablecloth on outside, with the hope we could eat out there. Grab an extra spoon and a napkin and let's see how it is."

Once they were settled outside, Sonya turned to Susan.

"You're not the first surprise visitor I've had this week.

Alice came by yesterday with some barley stew. She'd made more than she and Fred could eat and thought I might enjoy it. We had a very nice chat. Though she did seem kind of disoriented, but I could certainly understand that."

*Alice?* Miranda scanned her memory. *That name feels very significant, but I can't remember which of Sonya's friends she is. Oh, well.* "Who's Alice?"

"I'm not surprised you don't recognize her name. We've always just referred to them as 'the neighbors.'"

Susan sat up straight and stared at Sonya. "The neighbors? You mean those mean ones Miranda told me about?"

"Shush, dear. Don't talk so loud, she might hear you. And yes, those neighbors."

Miranda shook her head. "Well, that's another indication I did something that actually changed the world."

Susan leaned toward her friend. "Oh? What other indications are there?"

Miranda looked up at the lone tree, its branches swaying above them. It was the one Sam used to swing on. It rose up between two stumps and a small grave. The leaves of the liquid amber tree were fully displaying the fall rainbow. The sun shone on the leaves and the stars winked through its branches. *Funny, neither of them seem to think it's odd that the one tree is here, nor that there are stars in the daytime. Should I tell them or not?*

*:I don't think it's the time for a physics lesson right now:*

Miranda closed her eyes, enjoying the familiar feel of her teacher friend and remembering their last time together. She heard Susan tell Sonya that they might as well ignore her since she was blissing in and tuning them out. *:So Peter, can you at least explain all this to me? How in the world:*—Miranda smiled at her own pun—*:did what we do to the human mind change the stars and replant a tree?*

*:In terms of the stars they've always been there. Pretty amazing how the human tendency to divide and polarize could literally change how we believe the world looks. We've literally been seeing only in black and white—or day and night. Makes me wish I was back teaching physics. I'd love to see what the young minds could create in terms of unifying theories now:*

:So what about the tree?:

:You'll have to ask your friend about that. Maybe she'll create EPE: Extinct Plant Express, too:

:Okay then, how about the planes flying without fuel? Can you enlighten me on that one?:

Peter's voice came through softly. :I'll explain it all later:

Miranda looked over at Sonya, whose eyes were closed as a gentle smile spread across her face. :No worries. It's nice to feel you two together: She motioned to Susan and the two of them went over by Doogie's grave, giving her widowed friend privacy.

Susan nudged her in the ribs and gave her a sly grin. "So Alice is the neighbor you told me those terrible stories about. She sounds nice to me. Are you sure it wasn't all your imagination?"

"You can't bait me like that anymore. I've advanced beyond those kinds of reactions."

"Darn, I'm not sure this new world is going to be as much fun if I can't get a rise out of you anymore."

"It's better—no doubt of that—and I'm glad to be free of so many doubts. It was definitely time to evolve beyond evolution."

"Good thing Peter isn't around to hear you say that. You told me he was devoted to evolution."

Miranda smiled and looked back at Sonya. She could see a soft black cloud of love surrounding her. "I don't think Peter would mind. As a species we've survived a lot of threats, but now we need to move beyond survival to continue as a species."

:It's about time too: A gray tabby jumped on the nearest stump. :You humans were way too attached to this survival of the meanest:

Miranda grinned, thinking back to one of her visits with Peter when she'd spotted a book called *Spiritual Evolution: Theory or Reality?* Peter had emphatically explained that the book was Sonya's, not his. "Not everyone agreed with the scientific view. There were plenty of people who objected and rejected the theory of evolution. They believed we were cutting God out of the world. And maybe we were—forgetting our ability to create and resigning ourselves to a random pattern of mutations for growth.

We weren't taking evolution seriously enough and putting ourselves into the equation so that we could decide to evolve and start to thrive instead of just survive."

Merawl purred his words into Miranda's and Susan's minds. *:I won't have to worry about traveling around your N-World anymore. It was that misguided survival instinct you humans had that invited the gremlins in. You weren't getting enough real threats anymore—and with your system still geared toward identifying and destroying enemies, you had to create them somehow. So in came gremlins and out went spirit cats:*

Merawl launched himself off the stump, sailing through the air and over the fence, then disappearing from their sight.

Susan smiled, watching the cat's aerial display. "Angel prefers this new world too. But you both have it wrong. What you did, Miranda, was change evolution of the strongest to *love-olution*. Now the ones who can love the most will live the longest."

Miranda sat down on a stump, running her hand over the rough surface. "Now that we're loving and connecting no one is going to feel the urge to kill off another's offspring to ensure that their genes are the ones that procreate. Now all children are our children. And we are every child's parent."

"Makes me glad I'm already an adult. I don't want to imagine what it would be like growing up with fifty parents smothering me. Two was enough for me! In fact it was too much for me."

"What are you two talking about?" Sonya called from the patio.

"Susan is just being her usual weird self." Miranda wrapped an arm around the younger woman's shoulder and hugged her sideways.

They stayed that way, leaning into each other, then Susan pulled a tissue out of her pocket and rubbed her eyes and blew her nose. "I'm just glad you didn't need to sacrifice yourself for all of this to happen."

"I sure got that wrong. It wasn't about dividing. It was about healing the divide: between people, between the N-World and the spirit world, between our thinking minds and our reacting brains.

The opening the guardians kept talking about wasn't to open the space between the worlds but to open to possibilities. Only thing I don't understand is why early on they mentioned Don and the world that was born from the energy of his body being cremated. I thought for sure that referred to my needing to help make a new world—for the 'good' people to go to." *Funny, saying 'good' now feels bad.*

"I guess you haven't figured everything out yet. But it's obvious now the grandmothers wanted you to *convide*—not to divide—the worlds." Susan grinned through her remaining tears. "You know—convide: to get rid of the view that says we're divided so that we can be connected."

Sonya motioned them back to the table and pushed the plate of scones in their direction. "That reminds me of when Peter and I used to make up terms. Like *surlove*, which referred to how we felt we couldn't survive without the other's love. I'm not saying ours was the perfect relationship. He was *very* annoying at times. But I could no more think of intentionally hurting him, than I could cut off my hand—we were connected."

"You know, I think there was something in a science course I took at Berkeley about that idea. Something about not only are we connected to those we love, but to everything. I can't remember the name they used. Hang on, let me check."

Susan pulled her computer out of her pocket and unfolded it so that it was large enough for the three of them to see the screen. "I think it might be under neural connections or maybe universal mapping." Susan hunched over the screen and began typing.

Sonya poured them more tea, ignoring the electronic display. "You don't need to look it up. It's called Entanglement theory, dear."

"What?" Susan pushed aside the computer and looked at Sonya.

"It simply means we are all connected. Entanglement theory was one of the things that Peter and I could both agree on. It has enough science for him and enough mystical for me. It's a fancy way of saying we're all one."

"Here's to being *one*." Miranda raised her cup and the three of them clinked mugs.

Susan put her tea down and rubbed her hands together. "Now that we've got this new connection consciousness, we gotta get focused. We got a mess of a planet to clean up. Species to bring back. Green governments to grow. New namens to nurture . . ."

As Susan continued to plan out the new N-World, Miranda leaned back in her chair. She smiled as she noticed a translucent form floating above the lone tree in Sonya's yard.

Skyweb soared above the three women. The air felt lighter to her, as though there were already less toxins in it. Peering down, the women were clearly visible, their bodies covered in soft rainbow patterns. She let out a long sigh, like a gentle rain over the desert. Then she began to expand. Her form enlarged as it merged with the cosmos, until she touched every star, and was part of the web of all the guiding lights in the sky.

# Glossary

## Key Terms and Susan-isms

**Awaring:** An active process of expanding one's consciousness by becoming aware.

**Be-ness**: Adding -*ness* to make a person or thing larger and more inclusive. *Miranda-ness* refers to the state or quality of being Miranda.

**BFI**: Book and Folder Incident or Big F-ing Irritation. When guides give vague hints instead of specific directions, which makes it harder to understand and follow their advice.

**Blissing in:** Finding peace and bliss inside one's self.

**Calling a mountain a molehill:** Grossly understating something.

**Cat Vision:** Extrasensory technique that Merawl taught Miranda to see the energy web that connects all beings. Also, what cats and dogs use to know when family members are getting close to home.

**Co-knowing:** When the one who knows and the known are interrelated. Based on the idea of how light changes from wave to particle depending on the viewer. The type of relational knowing that is dependent on both sides knowing the other.

**Convide:** To change from seeing things and people as being divided into opposite extremes to viewing them as all connected.

**Earth turnings and Earth cycles:** Years.

**Evappening:** An Event happening. Refers to the feeling when you are swept up in a mystical Event and everything feels just right. These are the moments that happen when you feel one with everything.

**Event:** A very special mystical experience that is life altering.

**Gath:** The state of feeling guided on one's *path* or following God's *path*. The concept of everything being connected and everyone having a unique path to walk in their life. It is both a noun and a verb and is useful when referring to an action that *feels* like the right thing to do, when there are no rational reasons substantiating the decision.

**Go-flow:** The kind of adventure when you have to just go-with-the-flow and see what happens.

**Greemens:** (gree-mens) Greedy humans who are focused on accumulating power, as contrasted with namens who are nature based humans.

**Journey over:** To understand a concept from another's point of view.

**Life essence:** The electromagnetic energy field around people, animals, and all things. The more one is alive in the present moment the more life essence one has.

**Love-olution:** The concept that those who can love the most, survive the longest.

**Merry-go-rounding**: Going around and around in your mind with worries.

**Namens:** (naw-mens) Natural humans who are aware of their connections to all life. They will often have an emotional or physical sense of unease when exposed to ways humans are out of balance with nature (i.e. pollution, species extinction, clear cutting forests).

**N-World:** The "normal" physical world, as different from the mystical world of guides.

**Puppet dancing:** When a person or substance (such as drugs or alcohol), has control over someone's life.

**See where the river flows:** Go along with something to discover an answer or to understand a view point.

**Send me a boat. I am not on your island:** Not understanding and wanting clarification.

**Spirit-essence:** The non physical part of a person that can travel outside the body. Spirit–essence refers more to a matter of attention and focus than to a form, like an astral body.

**Surlove:** Realization that everyone needs love to survive

**TMSC:** Susan's nickname for Thomas because he says, "<u>T</u>his <u>M</u>ight <u>S</u>ound <u>C</u>razy . . ." so often.

# Mystical Friends

**Adnarim:** (Miranda spelled backwards) Miranda's troublesome "twin". She is the part of Miranda's spirit-essence that did not enter the N-World when Miranda was born. Adnarim is unfamiliar with N-World customs but is able to see through a broader perspective since she is a spirit connected to Miranda.

**BB** or **BeBe:** A spirit that enjoys showing up in bear form and wearing outlandish costumes.

**Earthweb:** Northern Grandmother – knows the **How** of the healing transformation.

**Fireweb:** Eastern Grandmother – knows the **When** of the healing transformation.

**GB:** Both a spirit and a grizzly bear who is friends with Susan.

**Guardians:** Four spirit beings, calling themselves the grandmothers, who guard the sacred site where Future Pharmaceutical built their manufacturing plant.

**Merawl:** A spirit cat who was once in physical form, when Miranda was in high school. After he died, he continued to help her as a spirit guide.

**Power:** A spirit who collects the life essence (energy) from people using substances or doing violent acts that waste their life essence. It also offers the energy it collects to people who want to use it. But if the person asking for energy from Power then abuses it, Power will take all the wasted life essence back from that person.

**Rand McNally:** An Irish ghost.

**Skyweb:** Southern Grandmother – knows the **Who** of the healing transformation.

**Waterweb:** Western Grandmother – knows the **Where** of the healing transformation.

My hope in writing this book is to help facilitate a global consciousness shift where the guiding principle is health, not survival. Or as Susan would say, to change evolution to *love-olution*. We already have the knowledge and skills to individually reweave our patterns of automatic responses, like Miranda did for herself in the cave. Now is the time to expand so that all people have the freedom to follow their gaths and together we can create a new N-World.

Please visit my website, www.JanOgren.net, to learn more.

For more information about current advances in the study of consciousness, visit *Institute of Noetic Sciences* at www.Noetic.org.